PUFFIN BOOKS

The Adventures of Milly-Molly-Mandy

Joyce Lankester Brisley wrote and drew books from an early age; she had her first fairy story published in a children's paper at the age of thirteen. She studied at art school and, when she was twenty, had pictures hung in the Royal Academy. However, she enjoyed writing and illustrating stories best, and her immortal creation, the *Milly-Molly-Mandy* series, set a seal on her success. Miss Brisley died in 1978 aged eighty-two.

JOYCE LANKESTER BRISLEY

The Adventures of Milly-Molly-Mandy

PUFFIN BOOKS

PUFFIN BOOKS

Published by the Penguin Group
Penguin Books Ltd, 80 Strand, London WC2R 0RL, England
Penguin Putnam Inc., 375 Hudson Street, New York, New York 10014, USA
Penguin Books Australia Ltd, 250 Camberwell Road, Camberwell, Victoria 3124, Australia
Penguin Books Canada Ltd, 10 Alcorn Avenue, Toronto, Ontario, Canada M4V 3B2
Penguin Books India (P) Ltd, 11 Community Centre, Panchsheel Park, New Delhi – 110 017, India
Penguin Books (NZ) Ltd, Cnr Rosedale and Airborne Roads, Albany, Auckland, New Zealand
Penguin Books (South Africa) (Pty) Ltd, 24 Sturdee Avenue, Rosebank 2196, South Africa

Penguin Books Ltd, Registered Offices: 80 Strand, London WC2R 0RL, England

www.penguin.com

Milly-Molly-Mandy Stories (1928), *More of Milly-Molly-Mandy* (1929), *Further Doings of Milly-Molly-Mandy* (1932) and *Milly-Molly-Mandy Again* (1948) first published by George G. Harrap
Published in one volume in Puffin Books 1992

24

Copyright © Joyce Lankester Brisley, 1928, 1929, 1932, 1948, 1992
All rights reserved

Set in Monotype Baskerville

Made and printed in England by Clays Ltd, St Ives plc

The stories and most of the illustrations in the *Milly-Molly-Mandy Stories, More of Milly-Molly-Mandy* and *Further Doings of Milly-Molly-Mandy* first appeared in the Children's Page of the *Christian Science Monitor,* and are here printed by permission

British Library Cataloguing in Publication Data
A CIP catalogue record for this book is available from
the British Library

ISBN 0–140–34865–4

CONTENTS

Milly-Molly-Mandy Stories

Contents

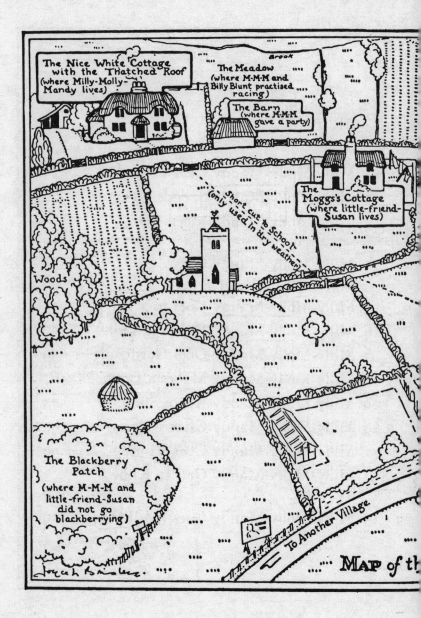

The Nice White Cottage with the Thatched Roof (where Milly-Molly-Mandy lives)

The Meadow (where M-M-M and Billy Blunt practised racing)

Brook

The Barn (where M-M-M gave a party)

The Moggs's Cottage (where little-friend-Susan lives)

Short cut to School (only used in dry weather)

Woods

The Blackberry Patch

(where M-M-M and little-friend-Susan did not go blackberrying)

Joseph Bradley.

To Another Village

MAP of th

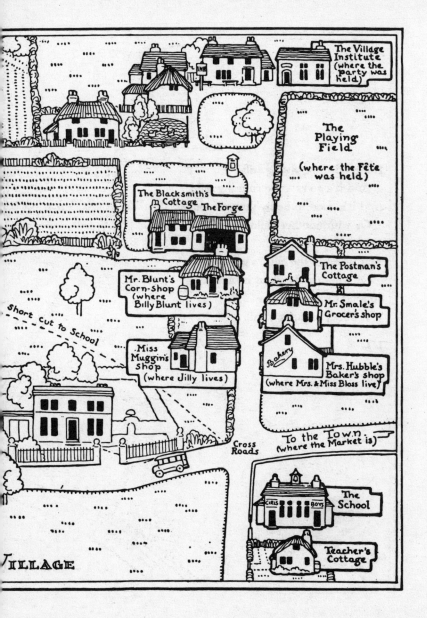

The Village Institute (where the party was held)

The Playing Field (where the Fête was held)

The Blacksmith's Cottage The Forge

Short cut to School

Mr. Blunt's Corn-Shop (where Billy Blunt lives)

The Postman's Cottage

Mr. Smale's Grocer's shop

Miss Muggin's shop (where Jilly lives)

Bakery

Mrs. Hubble's Baker's shop (where Mrs. & Miss Bloss live)

Cross Roads

To the Town (where the Market is)

GIRLS BOYS

The School

VILLAGE

Teacher's Cottage

It's good to be sitting still,
  And it's good to be running wild,
And it's good to be by yourself alone
  Or with another child.

And whether the child's grown up,
  Or whether the child is small,
So long as it really is a Child
  It doesn't matter at all.

J. L. B.

1. Milly-Molly-Mandy Goes Errands

Once upon a time there was a little girl.

She had a Father, and a Mother, and a Grandpa, and a Grandma, and an Uncle, and an Aunty; and they all lived together in a nice white cottage with a thatched roof.

This little girl had short hair, and short legs, and short frocks (pink-and-white-striped cotton in summer, and red serge in winter). But her name wasn't short at all. It was Millicent Margaret Amanda. But Father and Mother and Grandpa and Grandma and Uncle and Aunty couldn't very well call out 'Millicent Margaret Amanda!' every time they wanted her, so they shortened it to 'Milly-Molly-Mandy,' which is quite easy to say.

Now everybody in the nice white cottage with the thatched roof had some particular job to do – even Milly-Molly-Mandy.

Father grew vegetables in the big garden by the cottage. Mother cooked the dinners and did the washing. Grandpa took the vegetables to market in his little pony-cart. Grandma knitted socks and mittens and nice warm woollies for them all. Uncle kept cows (to give them milk) and chickens (to give them eggs). Aunty sewed frocks and shirts for them, and did the sweeping and dusting.

And Milly-Molly-Mandy, what did she do?

Well, Milly-Molly-Mandy's legs were short, as I've told you, but they were very lively, just right for running errands. So Milly-Molly-Mandy was quite busy, fetching and carrying things, and taking messages.

One fine day Milly-Molly-Mandy was in the garden playing with Toby the dog, when Father poked his head out from the other side of a big row of beans, and said:

'Milly-Molly-Mandy, run down to Mr Moggs' cottage and ask for the trowel he borrowed of me!'

So Milly-Molly-Mandy said 'Yes, Farver!' and ran in to get her hat.

At the kitchen door was Mother, with a basket of eggs in her hand. And when she saw Milly-Molly-Mandy she said:

'Milly-Molly-Mandy, run down to Mrs Moggs and give her these eggs. She's got visitors.'

So Milly-Molly-Mandy said 'Yes, Muvver!' and took the basket. 'Trowel for Farver, eggs for Muvver,' she thought to herself.

Then Grandpa came up and said:

'Milly-Molly-Mandy, please get me a ball of string from Miss Muggins' shop – here's the penny.'

So Milly-Molly-Mandy said 'Yes, Grandpa!' and took the penny, thinking to herself, 'Trowel for Farver, eggs for Muvver, string for Grandpa.'

As she passed through the kitchen Grandma, who was sitting in her armchair knitting, said:

'Milly-Molly-Mandy, will you get me a skein of red wool? Here's a sixpence.'

So Milly-Molly-Mandy said 'Yes, Grandma!' and took the sixpence. 'Trowel for Farver, eggs for Muvver, string for Grandpa, red wool for Grandma,' she whispered over to herself.

As she went into the passage Uncle came striding up in a hurry.

'Oh, Milly-Molly-Mandy,' said Uncle, 'run like

a good girl to Mr Blunt's shop, and tell him I'm waiting for the chicken-feed he promised to send!'

So Milly-Molly-Mandy said 'Yes, Uncle!' and thought to herself, 'Trowel for Farver, eggs for Muvver, string for Grandpa, red wool for Grandma, chicken-feed for Uncle.'

As she got her hat off the peg Aunty called from the parlour where she was dusting:

'Is that Milly-Molly-Mandy? Will you get me a packet of needles, dear? Here's a penny!'

So Milly-Molly-Mandy said 'Yes, Aunty!' and took the penny, thinking to herself, 'Trowel for Farver, eggs for Muvver, string for Grandpa, red wool for Grandma, chicken-feed for Uncle, needles for Aunty, and I do hope there won't be anything more!'

But there was nothing else, so Milly-Molly-Mandy started out down the path. When she came to the gate Toby the dog capered up, looking very excited at the thought of a walk. But Milly-Molly Mandy eyed him solemnly, and said:

'Trowel for Farver, eggs for Muvver, string for Grandpa, red wool for Grandma, chicken-feed for Uncle, needles for Aunty. No, Toby, you musn't come now, I've too much to think about. But I promise to take you for a walk when I come back!'

GRANDPA · GRANDMA · FATHER · MOTHER · UNCLE · AUNTY · MILLY-MOLLY-MANDY.

So she left Toby the other side of the gate, and set off down the road, with the basket and the pennies and the sixpence.

Presently she met a little friend, and the little friend said:

'Hello, Milly-Molly-Mandy! I've got a new see-saw! Do come on it with me!'

But Milly-Molly-Mandy looked at her solemnly and said:

'Trowel for Farver, eggs for Muvver, string for Grandpa, red wool for Grandma, chicken-feed for Uncle, needles for Aunty. No, Susan, I can't come now, I'm busy. But I'd like to come when I get back – after I've taken Toby for a walk.'

So Milly-Molly-Mandy went on her way with the basket and the pennies and the sixpence.

Soon she came to the Moggs' cottage.

'Please, Mrs Moggs, can I have the trowel for Farver? – and here are some eggs from Muvver!' she said.

Mrs Moggs was very much obliged indeed for the eggs, and fetched the trowel and a piece of seed-cake for Milly-Molly-Mandy's own self. And Milly-Molly-Mandy went on her way with the empty basket.

Next she came to Miss Muggins' little shop.

'Please, Miss Muggins, can I have a ball of

string for Grandpa and a skein of red wool for Grandma?'

So Miss Muggins put the string and the wool into Milly-Molly-Mandy's basket, and took a penny and a sixpence in exchange. So that left Milly-Molly-Mandy with one penny. And Milly-Molly-Mandy couldn't remember what that penny was for.

'Sweeties, perhaps?' said Miss Muggins, glancing at the row of glass bottles on the shelf.

But Milly-Molly-Mandy shook her head.

'No,' she said, 'and it can't be chicken-feed for Uncle, because that would be more than a penny, only I haven't got to pay for it.'

'It must be sweeties!' said Miss Muggins.

'No,' said Milly-Molly-Mandy, 'but I'll remember soon. Good morning, Miss Muggins!'

So Milly-Molly-Mandy went on to Mr Blunt's, and gave him Uncle's message, and then she sat down on the doorstep and thought what that penny could be for.

And she couldn't remember.

But she remembered one thing: 'It's for Aunty,' she thought, 'and I love Aunty.' And she thought for just a little while longer. Then suddenly she sprang up and went back to Miss Muggins's shop.

'I've remembered!' she said. 'It's needles for Aunty!'

So Miss Muggins put the packet of needles into the basket, and took the penny, and Milly-Molly-Mandy set off for home.

'That's a good little messenger to remember all those things!' said Mother, when she got there. They were just going to begin dinner. 'I thought you were only going with my eggs!'

'She went for my trowel!' said Father.

'And my string!' said Grandpa.

'And my wool!' said Grandma.

'And my chicken-feed!' said Uncle.

'And my needles!' said Aunty.

Then they all laughed; and Grandpa, feeling in his pocket, said:

'Well, here's another errand for you – go and get yourself some sweeties!'

So after dinner Toby had a nice walk and his mistress got her sweets. And then Milly-Molly-Mandy and little-friend-Susan had a lovely time on the see-saw, chatting and eating raspberry-drops, and feeling very happy and contented indeed.

2. Milly-Molly-Mandy Spends a Penny

Once upon a time Milly-Molly-Mandy found a penny in the pocket of an old coat.

Milly-Molly-Mandy felt very rich indeed.

She thought of all the things she could buy with it, and there were so many that she did not know which to choose. (That is the worst of a penny). So Milly-Molly-Mandy asked everybody with whom she lived, in the nice white cottage with the thatched roof, what they would do with it if they were her.

'Put it in the bank,' said Grandpa promptly. He was making up accounts. Milly-Molly-Mandy thought that a wise idea.

'Buy a skein of rainbow wool and learn to knit,' said Grandma, who was knitting by the kitchen door. Milly-Molly-Mandy thought that a good idea.

'Buy some seeds and grow mustard-and-cress,' said Father, who was gardening. Milly-Molly-Mandy thought that quite a good idea.

'Buy a little patty-pan and make a cake in it,' said Mother, who was cooking. Milly-Molly-Mandy thought that a very good idea.

'Save it up until you get three, and I'll let you buy a baby duckling with them,' said Uncle, who was scooping out corn for his chickens. Milly-Molly-Mandy thought that an excellent idea.

'Get some sweets,' said Aunty, who was very busy sewing, and did not want to be interrupted. Milly-Molly-Mandy thought that a very pleasant idea.

Then she went to her own little corner of the garden for a 'think', for she still could not make up her mind which of all those nice things to do. She thought and thought for a long time.

And then – what do you think she bought?

Some mustard-and-cress seeds, which she planted in a shallow box of earth and stood in a nice warm place by the tool-shed.

She watered it every day, and shaded it if the sun were too hot; and at last the little seeds grew into a lovely clump of fresh green mustard-and-cress, that made you quite long for some bread-and-butter to eat it with.

When it was ready to cut Milly-Molly-Mandy went to Mrs Moggs, their neighbour down the road, who sometimes had summer visitors.

'Mrs Moggs,' said Milly-Molly-Mandy, 'if you should want some mustard-and-cress for your visitors' tea I have some to sell. It's very good, and quite cheap.'

'Why Milly-Molly-Mandy,' said Mrs Moggs, 'that's exactly what I am wanting! Is it ready for cutting now?'

So Milly-Molly-Mandy ran home and borrowed a pair of scissors and a little basket, and she snipped that lovely clump of fresh green mustard-and-cress (all but a tiny bit for her own tea) and carried it to Mrs Moggs.

And Mrs Moggs gave her twopence for it.

So Milly-Molly-Mandy had done one of the nice things and spent her penny, and now she had twopence!

Then Milly-Molly-Mandy took one of the pennies to the little village shop, and bought a skein of beautiful rainbow wool.

'Grandma,' she said, when she got home, 'please will you teach me to knit a kettle-holder?'

So Grandma found some knitting-needles and

showed Milly-Molly-Mandy how to knit. And though it had to be undone several times at first, Milly-Molly-Mandy really did knit quite a nice kettle-holder, and there was just enough wool for it.

When she had put a loop in one corner to hang it up by she went to Mother, who was just putting the potatoes on to boil.

'Mother,' said Milly-Molly-Mandy, 'would you think this kettle-holder worth a penny?'

'Why, Milly-Molly-Mandy,' said Mother, 'that is exactly what I am wanting, for my old one is all worn out! But the penny only pays for the wool, so you are making me a present of all your trouble.' And Mother gave Milly-Molly-Mandy a penny and a kiss, and Milly-Molly-Mandy felt well paid.

So Milly-Molly-Mandy had done another of the nice things, had spent her penny, and learnt to knit, and still she had her penny!

Then Milly-Molly-Mandy took her penny down to the little village shop and bought a shiny tin patty-pan. And next baking-day Mother let her make a little cake in the patty-pan and put it in the oven. And it was such a beautiful little cake, and so nicely browned, that it seemed almost too good to eat.

Milly-Molly-Mandy put it outside on the window-sill to cool.

Milly-Molly-Mandy finds a penny

Presently along came a lady cyclist, and as it was a very hot day she stopped at the nice white cottage with the thatched roof, and asked Milly-Molly-Mandy's Mother if she could have a glass of milk. And while she was drinking it she saw the little cake on the window-sill, and the little cake looked so good that the lady cyclist felt hungry and asked if she could have that too.

Milly-Molly-Mandy's Mother looked at Milly-Molly-Mandy, and Milly-Molly-Mandy gave a little gulp, and said 'Yes.' And the lady cyclist ate up the little patty-cake. And she did enjoy it!

When she had gone Milly-Molly-Mandy's Mother took up the pennies the lady cyclist had put on the table for the milk and the cake, and she gave one to Milly-Molly-Mandy because it was her cake.

So Milly-Molly-Mandy had done yet another of the nice things and spent her penny, but still she had her penny.

Then Milly-Molly-Mandy took her penny down to little village shop and bought some sweets, lovely big aniseed-balls, that changed colour as you sucked them.

She would not eat one until she got home, and then gave one to Grandpa and one to Grandma and one to Father and one to Mother and one to

Uncle and one to Aunty. And then she found there were six for herself, so she ate them, and they were very nice.

So Milly-Molly-Mandy had done another of the nice things and spent her penny. But she still had one penny from the mustard-and-cress.

Then she went to Grandpa, and asked him please to put it in the bank for her.

And then she went to Uncle.

'Uncle,' said Milly-Molly-Mandy, 'I've done everything with my penny that everybody said, but you. And though I can't buy a little baby duckling yet, I've got a penny saved towards it, in the bank.'

And it was not very long before Milly-Molly-Mandy had saved up to threepence; and then Uncle let her have a little yellow baby duckling all for her own.

3. Milly-Molly-Mandy Meets her Great-Aunt

Once upon a time, one fine evening, Milly-Molly-Mandy and her Father and Mother and Grandpa and Grandma and Uncle and Aunty were all sitting at supper (there was bread-and-butter and cheese for the grown-ups, and bread-and-milk for Milly-Molly-Mandy, and baked apples and cocoa for them all), when suddenly there came a loud *Bang-bang!* on the knocker.

'Run, Milly-Molly-Mandy,' said Mother. 'That sounds like the postman!'

So Milly-Molly-Mandy jumped down from her chair in a great hurry, and fetched the letter, which was for Mother. Then she climbed on her chair again, and every one looked interested while Mother opened it.

It was from someone who called Milly-Molly-Mandy's Mother 'Dear Polly', and was to ask if that someone might spend a few days with them, and it finished up, 'Your affectionate Aunt Margaret.'

Father and Mother and Grandpa and Grandma and Uncle and Aunty were quite pleased, and Milly-Molly-Mandy was pleased too, although she did not know who it was until Grandma said to her,

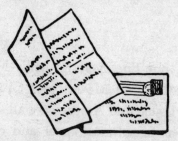

'It is my sister Margaret, your great-aunty, who is coming.' Then Milly-Molly-Mandy was very interested indeed.

'Is she my great-aunty and your sister too?' she asked Grandma.

'Yes, and she's my sister-in-law,' said Grandpa.

'And my aunty,' said Mother.

'And my aunty-in-law,' said Father.

'And my aunty-in-law too,' said Aunty.

'And my aunty,' said Uncle.

'Fancy!' said Milly-Molly-Mandy. 'She's all that, and she's a great-aunty too! I would like to see her!'

The next day Milly-Molly-Mandy helped Mother make up the spare-room bed.

'I could wish the spare room were a little bigger,'

'That sounds like the postman!'

said Mother, and Milly-Molly-Mandy looked around gravely, and thought it really was rather small for a great-aunty. But she went and fetched some marigolds from her own little garden, and put them in a vase on the chest of drawers, for she knew there was lots of room for love, even if there was not much for great-aunties.

Then Milly-Molly-Mandy helped Father bring the big armchair out of the best parlour into the room where they always sat. Milly-Molly-Mandy was glad it was such a big chair – it really looked quite large enough even for a great-aunty.

Then Mother cooked some big fruit-cakes and some little seed-cakes and some sponge-cakes and a whole lot of other things, and Milly-Molly-Mandy (who helped to clean up the cooking-bowls and spoons) supposed a great-aunty must take quite a lot of feeding.

As soon as ever the last bowl was scraped Milly-Molly-Mandy ran down the road to tell little-friend-Susan the news.

Little-friend-Susan was walking on the wall, but she jumped down as soon as she saw Milly-Molly-Mandy.

'Oh, Susan!' said Milly-Molly-Mandy, 'you know my Aunty?'

'Yes,' said little-friend-Susan.

'Well,' said Milly-Molly-Mandy, 'she's just a usual aunty, but I've got a great-aunty coming to stay with us!'

Little-friend-Susan, being a best friend, was just as interested as Milly-Molly-Mandy, and it was soon settled that next morning she should come and play in Milly-Molly-Mandy's garden, so that she might see Great-Aunty Margaret for herself.

Then Milly-Molly-Mandy ran back home to dinner.

After dinner Mother and Grandma and Aunty and Milly-Molly-Mandy hurried through the washing-up, and tidied the cottage, while Father put the pony in the trap. And then they changed their dresses, while Father drove to the station.

And then Milly-Molly-Mandy, in her clean frock, kept running to the gate to see if the pony-trap were in sight yet.

And at last it was – and Milly-Molly-Mandy was so excited that she raced into the cottage and jumped up and down, and then she ran out to the gate again, and opened it wide.

The pony trotted up to the gate and stopped, and Father got down first. And then he took down Great-Aunty Margaret's great basket. And then he helped down Great-Aunty Margaret her own self!

And what do you think Great-Aunty Margaret was like?

She was a little, little, white-haired lady, in a black bonnet and dress spotted with little mauve flowers, and she had a kind little face with pink cheeks.

Milly-Molly-Mandy was so surprised, it was all she could do to mind her manners and not stare.

Great-Aunty Margaret was soon seated in the great armchair, and instead of filling it, as Milly-

Molly-Mandy had expected, why – there was heaps of room for Milly-Molly-Mandy there too! And instead of eating up all the big fruit-cakes and the little seed-cakes and the sponge-cakes and other things, there was lots for everybody in the family, including Milly-Molly-Mandy.

And as for the spare room being too small, it looked almost big, because Great-Aunty Margaret was such a little lady.

When Great-Aunty Margaret saw the flowers on her chest of drawers she said gently:

'Why, Millicent Margaret Amanda, I believe that is your doing! Thank you, my dearie!'

'Oh, Great-Aunty Margaret!' said Milly-Molly-Mandy, reaching to kiss her again. 'I do like you! Would you mind if I showed you to Susan this evening, instead of making her wait till tomorrow?'

4. *Milly-Molly-Mandy Goes Blackberrying*

Once upon a time Milly-Molly-Mandy found some big ripe blackberries on her way home from school. There were six great beauties and one little hard one, so Milly-Molly-Mandy put the little hard one in her mouth and carried the others home on a leaf.

She gave one to Father, and Father said, 'Ah! that makes me think the time for blackberry puddings has come!'

Then she gave one to Mother, and asked what it made her think of. And Mother said, 'A whole row of pots of blackberry jam that I ought to have in my store-board!'

Then she gave one to Grandpa, and Grandpa said it made him think 'Blackberry tart!'

And Grandma said, 'Blackberry jelly!'

And Uncle said, 'Stewed blackberry-and-apple!'

And Aunty said, 'A plate of fresh blackberries with sugar and cream!'

'My!' thought Milly-Molly-Mandy, as she threw away the empty leaf, 'I must get a big, big basket and go blackberrying the very next Saturday, so

that there can be lots of puddings and jam and tarts and jelly and stewed blackberry-and-apple and fresh blackberries, for Farver and Muvver and Grandpa and Grandma and Uncle and Aunty – and me! I'll ask Susan to come too.'

So the very next Saturday Milly-Molly-Mandy and little-friend-Susan set out with big baskets (to hold the blackberries) and hooked sticks (to pull the brambles nearer) and stout boots (to keep the prickles off) and old frocks (lest the thorns should catch). And they walked and they walked, till they came to a place where they knew there was always a lot of blackberries – at the proper time of year, of course.

But when they came to the place – oh, dear! – they saw a notice-board stuck up just inside a gap in the fence. And the notice-board said, as plain as anything:

TRESPASSERS
WILL BE
PROSECUTED

Milly-Molly-Mandy and little-friend-Susan knew that meant 'You mustn't come here, because the owner doesn't want you, and it's his land.'

Milly-Molly-Mandy and little-friend-Susan looked at each other very solemnly indeed. Then Milly-Molly-Mandy said, 'I don't s'pose anyone would see if we went in.'

And little-friend-Susan said, 'I don't s'pose they'd miss any of the blackberries.'

And Milly-Molly-Mandy said, 'But it wouldn't be right.'

And little-friend-Susan shook her head very firmly.

So they took up their baskets and sticks and moved away, trying not to feel hurt about it, although they had come a long way to that place.

They didn't know quite what to do with themselves after that, for there seemed to be no blackberries anywhere else, so they amused themselves by walking in a dry ditch close by the fence, shuffling along in the leaves with their stout little boots that were to have kept the prickles off.

And suddenly – what do you think they saw? A little ball of brown fur, just ahead of them among the grasses in the ditch.

'Is it a rabbit?' whispered little-friend-Susan. They crept closer.

Milly-Molly-Mandy and little-friend-Susan set out

'It is a rabbit!' whispered Milly-Molly-Mandy.

'Why doesn't it run away?' said little-friend-Susan, and she stroked it. The little ball of fur wriggled. Then Milly-Molly-Mandy stroked it, and it wriggled again.

Then Milly-Molly-Mandy exclaimed, 'I believe it's got its head stuck in a hole in the bank!'

And they looked, and that was just what had happened. Some earth had fallen down as bunny was burrowing, and it couldn't get its head out again.

So Milly-Molly-Mandy and little-friend-Susan carefully dug with their fingers, and loosened the earth round about, and as soon as bunny's head was free he shook his ears and stared at them.

Milly-Molly-Mandy and little-friend-Susan sat very still, and only smiled and nodded gently to show him he needn't be afraid, because they loved him.

And then little bunny turned his head and ran skitter-scutter along the ditch and up the bank, into the wood and was gone.

'Oh!' said Milly-Molly-Mandy, 'we always wanted a rabbit, and now we've got one, Susan!'

'Only we'd rather ours played in the fields with his brothers and sisters instead of stopping in a poky hutch,' said little-friend-Susan.

'And if we'd gone trespassing we should never have come here and found him,' said Milly-Molly-Mandy. 'I'd much rather have a little rabbit than a whole lot of blackberries.'

And when they got back to the nice white cottage with the thatched roof, where Milly-Molly-Mandy lived, Father and Mother and Grandpa and Grandma and Uncle and Aunty all said they would much rather have a little rabbit running about in the woods than all the finest blackberries in the world.

However, the next Saturday Milly-Molly-Mandy and little-friend-Susan came upon a splendid place for blackberrying, without any notice-board; and Milly-Molly-Mandy gathered such a big basketful that there was enough to make blackberry puddings and jam and tarts and jelly and stewed blackberry-and-apple and fresh blackberries for Father and

41

Mother and Grandpa and Grandma and Uncle and Aunty – and Milly-Molly-Mandy too.

And all the time a little rabbit skipped about in the woods and thought what a lovely world it was.

(And that's a true story!)

5. Milly-Molly-Mandy Goes to a Party

Once upon a time something very nice happened in the village where Milly-Molly-Mandy and her Father and Mother and Grandpa and Grandma and Uncle and Aunty lived. Some ladies clubbed together to give a party to all the children in the village, and of course Milly-Molly-Mandy was invited.

Little-friend-Susan had an invitation too, and Billy Blunt (whose father kept the corn-shop where Milly-Molly-Mandy's Uncle got his chicken-feed), and Jilly, the little niece of Miss Muggins (who kept the shop where Milly-Molly-Mandy's Grandma bought her knitting-wool), and lots of others whom Milly-Molly-Mandy knew.

It was exciting.

Milly-Molly-Mandy had not been to a real party for a long time, so she was very pleased and interested when Mother said, 'Well, Milly-Molly-Mandy, you must have a proper new dress for a party like this. We must think what we can do.'

So Mother and Grandma and Aunty thought

together for a bit, and then Mother went to the big
wardrobe and rummaged in her bottom drawer
until she found a most beautiful white silk scarf,
which she had worn when she was married to
Father, and it was just wide enough to be made into
a party frock for Milly-Molly-Mandy.

Then Grandma brought out of her best handker-
chief-box a most beautiful lace handkerchief, which
would just cut into a little collar for the neck of the
party frock.

And Aunty brought out of her small top drawer
some most beautiful pink ribbon, all smelling of
lavender – just enough to make into a sash for the
party frock.

And then Mother and Aunty set to work to cut
and stitch at the party frock, while Milly-Molly-
Mandy jumped up and down and handed pins
when they were wanted.

The next day Father came in with a paper parcel for Milly-Molly-Mandy bulging in his coat-pocket, and when Milly-Molly-Mandy unwrapped it she found the most beautiful little pair of red shoes inside!

And then Grandpa came in and held out his closed hand to Milly-Molly-Mandy, and when Milly-Molly-Mandy got his fingers open she found the most beautiful little coral necklace inside!

And then Uncle came in, and he said to Milly-Molly-Mandy, 'What have I done with my hand-kerchief?' And he felt in all his pockets. 'Oh, here it is!' And he pulled out the most beautiful little handkerchief with a pink border, which of course Milly-Molly-Mandy just knew was meant for her, and she wouldn't let Uncle wipe his nose on it, which he pretended he was going to do!

Milly-Molly-Mandy was so pleased she hugged everybody in turn – Father, Mother, Grandpa, Grandma, Uncle, and Aunty.

At last the great day arrived, and little-friend-Susan, in her best spotted dress and silver bangle, called for Milly-Molly-Mandy, and they went to-gether to the village institute, where the party was to be.

There was a lady outside who welcomed them in, and there were more ladies inside who helped them to take their things off. And everywhere looked so pretty, with garlands of coloured paper looped from the ceiling, and everybody in their best clothes.

Most of the boys and girls were looking at a row of toys on the mantelpiece, and a lady explained that they were all prizes, to be won by the children who got the most marks in the games they were going to have. There was a lovely fairy doll and a big Teddy Bear and a picture-book and all sorts of things.

And at the end of the row was a funny little white cotton-wool rabbit with a pointed paper hat on his head. And directly Milly-Molly-Mandy saw him she wanted him dreadfully badly, more than any of the other things.

Little-friend-Susan wanted the picture-book, and Miss Muggins' niece, Jilly, wanted the fairy doll. But the black, beady eyes of the little cotton-wool rabbit gazed so wistfully at Milly-Molly-Mandy that she determined to try ever so hard in all the games and see if she could win him.

Then the games began, and they were fun! They had a spoon-and-potato race, and musical chairs, and putting the tail on the donkey blindfold, and all sorts of guessing-games.

And then they had supper – bread-and-butter with coloured hundreds-and-thousands sprinkled on,

At last the great day arrived

and red jellies and yellow jellies, and cakes with icing and cakes with cherries, and lemonade in red glasses.

It was quite a proper party.

And at the end the names of prize-winners were called out, and the children had to go up and receive their prizes.

And what do you think Milly-Molly-Mandy got?

Why, she had tried so hard to win the little cotton-wool rabbit that she won first prize instead, and got the lovely fairy doll!

And Miss Muggins' niece Jilly, who hadn't won any of the games, got the little cotton-wool rabbit with the sad, beady eyes – for do you know, the cotton-wool rabbit was only the booby prize, after all!

It was a lovely fairy doll, but Milly-Molly-Mandy was sure Miss Muggins' Jilly wasn't loving the booby rabbit as it ought to be loved, for its beady eyes did look so sad, and when she got near Miss Muggins' Jilly she stroked the booby rabbit, and Miss Muggins' Jilly stroked the fairy doll's hair.

Then Milly-Molly-Mandy said, 'Do you love the fairy doll more than the booby rabbit?'

And Miss Muggins' Jilly said, 'I should think so!'

So Milly-Molly-Mandy ran up to the lady who had given the prizes, and asked if she and Miss Muggins' Jilly might exchange prizes, and the lady said, 'Yes, of course.'

So Milly-Molly-Mandy and the booby rabbit went home together to the nice white cottage with the thatched roof, and Father and Mother and Grandpa and Grandma and Uncle and Aunty all liked the booby rabbit very much indeed.

And do you know, one day one of his little bead eyes dropped off, and when Mother had stuck it on again with a dab of glue, his eyes didn't look a bit sad any more, but almost as happy as Milly-Molly-Mandy's own!

6. Milly-Molly-Mandy Enjoys a Visit

Once upon a time Milly-Molly-Mandy was invited to go for a little visit to an old friend of Mother's who lived in a near-by town. Uncle was to take her in the pony-trap on Saturday morning on his way to market, and fetch her on Sunday evening, so that she should be ready for school next day. So Milly-Molly-Mandy would spend a whole night away from home, which was very exciting to think of. But just a day or two before she was to go Mother received a letter from her friend to say she was so sorry, but she couldn't have Milly-Molly-Mandy after all, as a married son and his wife had come unexpectedly to pay her a visit.

Milly-Molly-Mandy had to try very hard not to feel dreadfully disappointed, for she had never been away from home by herself before, and she had been looking forward to it so much.

'Never mind, Milly-Molly-Mandy,' said Mother, when Saturday morning arrived and Milly-Molly-Mandy came down to breakfast looking rather solemn, 'there are nice things happening all the time, if you keep your eyes open to see them.'

Milly-Molly-Mandy said, 'Yes, Muvver,' in a small voice, as she took her seat, though it didn't seem just then as if anything could possibly happen as nice as going away to stay.

But while Father and Mother and Grandpa and Grandma and Uncle and Aunty and Milly-Molly-Mandy were at breakfast Mrs Moggs, who was little-friend-Susan's mother, came round in a great hurry without a hat. And Mrs Moggs told them how some friends, who had to go to the town on business, had offered her a seat in their gig. And as Mrs Moggs' mother lived there Mrs Moggs thought it was a nice opportunity to go and see her, only she didn't like leaving Susan alone all day, Mr Moggs being out at work.

So Milly-Molly-Mandy's mother said, 'Let her come round here, Mrs Moggs. Milly-Molly-Mandy would like to have her. And I don't suppose you'll be back till late, so she'd better spend the night here too.'

Milly-Molly-Mandy was pleased, and Mrs Moggs thanked them very much indeed, and they all wished Mrs Moggs a nice trip, and then Mrs Moggs ran back home to get ready.

'Where will Susan sleep? – in the spare room?'

asked Milly-Molly-Mandy, making haste to finish her breakfast.

'Yes, said Mother, 'and you had better sleep there too, to keep her company.'

Milly-Molly-Mandy was very much pleased at that, for she had never slept in the spare room – her cot-bed was in one corner of Father's and Mother's room.

'Why, Muvver!' she said, 'I can't have a visit of my own, but I'll just be able to enjoy Susan's instead, shan't I? P'r'aps it'll be almost quite as nice!'

She helped to wash up the breakfast things, and to make the spare-room bed, and to dust.

And then she was just looking out of the window, thinking how nice it would be for Susan to wake up in the morning with a new view outside, when what did she see but little-friend-Susan herself, trudging along up the road with a basket on one arm and her coat on the other. So she ran down to the gate to welcome her in.

And though Milly-Molly-Mandy and little-friend-Susan met almost every day, and very often spent the whole day together, somehow it felt so different to think little-friend-Susan was going to stay the night with Milly-Molly-Mandy that they couldn't help giving an extra skip or two after they had kissed each other.

Unpacking little-friend-Susan's basket

Milly-Molly-Mandy took her to see Mother, and then they went up to the spare room to unpack little-friend-Susan's basket.

They put her nightgown and brush and comb and toothbrush and slippers in their proper places, and decided which sides of the bed they were going to

sleep – and they found each wanted the side that the other one didn't, which was nice – though of course Milly-Molly-Mandy would have given little-friend-Susan first choice, anyway.

Then Milly-Molly-Mandy showed little-friend-Susan round the room, and let her admire the fat silk pin-cushion on the dressing-table, and the hair-tidy that Aunty had painted, and the ornaments on the chest of drawers – the china dogs with the rough-feeling coats, and the little girl with the china lace skirt.

And while they were looking at the fretwork bracket which Father had made for Mother before they were married, Aunty came running up to say Uncle was just going to drive to market, and they might go with him if they were quick.

So they scrambled into their coats and hats, and Milly-Molly-Mandy ran to ask Mother in a whisper if she might take a penny from her money-box to spend in town. And soon they were sitting up close together beside Uncle in the high pony-trap, while the little brown pony (whose name was Twinkle-toes) trotted briskly along the white road.

Little-friend-Susan hadn't been for many drives. Milly-Molly-Mandy often went, but she enjoyed this one much more than usual, because little-friend-Susan was so interested and pleased with every-thing.

Billy Blunt was whipping a top outside his father's corn-shop as they drove through the village. They waved to him, and he waved back. And a little far-ther on Miss Muggins' niece, Jilly, was wheeling her doll's pram along the pavement, and called out, 'Hello, Milly-Molly-Mandy! Hello, Susan!'

And then they drove along a road through corn-fields, where the little green blades of wheat were busy growing up to make big loaves of bread – which is why you must never interrupt them by walking in the corn, even if you see a poppy.

When they came to the town there were crowds of people everywhere, shouting about the things they had to sell. And Milly-Molly-Mandy and little-friend-Susan followed Uncle about the market-place, looking at all the stalls of fruit and sweets and books and fish and clothes and a hundred other things.

Milly-Molly-Mandy spent her penny on a big yellow sugar-stick for little-friend-Susan, who broke it carefully in two, and gave her half.

When Uncle had done his business he took them to have dinner at a place where all the tables had marble tops, which made such a sharp clatter unless you put your glass down very gently. There were crowds of people eating at other tables round about, and a lot of talking and clattering of cups and plates. It was very exciting. Little-friend-Susan was having a splendid holiday.

When they had finished Uncle paid the bill and led the way back to where Twinkletoes was waiting patiently, munching in his nosebag. And off they drove again, clippety-cloppety, with Uncle's parcels stowed under the seat.

And when they got near home it did seem queer

for Milly-Molly-Mandy and little-friend-Susan to go straight past the Moggs' cottage and not have to stop and say good-bye to each other. They squeezed each other's hand all the rest of the way home to the nice white cottage with the thatched roof, because they felt so pleased.

When bedtime drew near they had their baths together, just as if they were sisters. And then Milly-Molly-Mandy in her red dressing-gown, and little-friend-Susan in Grandma's red shawl, sat in front of the fire on little stools (with Toby the dog on one side, and Topsy the cat on the other), while Mother made them each a lid-potato for their suppers.

First Mother took two well-baked potatoes out of the oven. Then she nearly cut the tops off them – but not quite. Then she scooped all the potato out of the skins and mashed it up with a little salt and a little pepper and a lot of butter. And then she

57

pushed it back into the two potato-skins, and shut the tops like little lids.

Then Milly-Molly-Mandy and little-friend-Susan were given a mug of milk and a plate of bread-and-butter, and one of the nice warm lid-potatoes. And they opened the potato-lids and ate out of them with little spoons.

They did enjoy their suppers.

And when the last bit was gone Mother said, 'Now, you two, I've set the candle in your room, and I'll be up to fetch it in ten minutes.'

So Milly-Molly-Mandy and little-friend-Susan kissed good-night to Father and Mother and Grandpa and Grandma and Uncle and Aunty, and stroked Toby the dog and Topsy the cat. And then they went upstairs to bed, hopping and skipping all the way, because they were so pleased they were going to sleep together in the spare room.

And next day, when Mrs Moggs came round to tell how she had enjoyed her trip, and to fetch Susan, Milly-Molly-Mandy said, 'Thank you very much indeed, Mrs Moggs, for Susan's visit. I have enjoyed it!'

7. Milly-Molly-Mandy Goes Gardening

Once upon a time, one Saturday morning, Milly-Molly-Mandy went down to the village. She had to go to Mr Blunt's corn-shop to order a list of things for Uncle – and would Mr Blunt please send them on Monday without fail?

Mr Blunt said, 'Surely, surely! Tell your uncle he shall have them first thing in the morning.'

And then Milly-Molly-Mandy, who loved the smell of the corn-shop, peeped into the great bins, and dug her hands down into the maize and bran and oats and let them sift through her fingers. And then she said good-bye and came out.

As she passed the Blunts' little garden at the side of the shop she saw Billy Blunt's back, bending down just the other side of the palings. It looked very busy.

Billy Blunt was a little bigger than Milly-Molly-Mandy, and she did not know him very well, but they always said 'Hullo!' when they met.

So Milly-Molly-Mandy peeped through the palings and said, 'Hullo, Billy!'

'What's the matter?' Milly-Molly-Mandy asked

Billy Blunt looked round for a moment and said, 'Hullo!' And then he turned back to his work.

But he didn't say, 'Hullo, Milly-Molly-Mandy!' and he didn't smile. So Milly-Molly-Mandy stuck her toes in the fence and hung on and looked over the top.

'What's the matter?' Milly-Molly-Mandy asked.

Billy Blunt looked round again. 'Nothing's the matter,' he said gloomily. 'Only I've got to weed these old flower-beds right up to the house.'

'I don't mind weeding,' said Milly-Molly-Mandy.

'Huh! You try it here, and see how you like it!' said Billy Blunt. 'The earth's as hard as nails, and the weeds have got roots pretty near a mile long.'

Milly-Molly-Mandy wasn't quite sure whether he meant it as an invitation, but anyhow she accepted it as one, and pushed open the little white gate and came into the Blunts' garden.

It was a nice garden, smelling of wallflowers.

Billy Blunt said, 'There's a garden-fork.' So Milly-Molly-Mandy took it up and started work on the other side of the flower-bed which bordered the little brick path up to the house. And they dug away together.

Presently Milly-Molly-Mandy said, 'Doesn't the earth smell nice when you turn it up?'

And Billy Blunt said, 'Does it? Yes, it does rather.' And they went on weeding.

Presently Milly-Molly-Mandy, pulling tufts of grass out of the pansies, asked, 'What do you do this for, if you don't like it?'

And Billy Blunt, tugging at a dandelion root, grunted and said, 'Father says I ought to be making myself useful.'

'That's our sort of fruit,' said Milly-Molly-Mandy.

My Muvver says we'd be like apple-trees which didn't grow apples if we didn't be useful.'

'Huh!' said Billy Blunt. 'Funny idea, us growing fruit! Never thought of it like that.' And they went on weeding.

Presently Milly-Molly-Mandy asked, 'Why're there all those little holes in the lawn?'

'Dad's been digging out dandelions,' said Billy Blunt. 'He wants to make the garden nice.'

Then Milly-Molly-Mandy said, 'There's lots of grass here, only it oughtn't to be. We might plant it in the holes.'

'Umm!' said Billy Blunt, 'and then we'll be making the lawn look as tidy as the beds. Let's!'

So they dug, and they turned the earth, and they pulled out what didn't belong there. And all the weeds they threw into a heap to be burned, and all the tufts of grass they carefully planted in the lawn. And after a time the flower-beds began to look most beautifully neat, and you could see hardly any bald places on the lawn.

Presently Mr Blunt came out of the shop on to the pavement. He had a can of green paint and a brush in his hand, and he reached over the palings and set them down among the daisies on the lawn.

'Hullo, Milly-Molly-Mandy!' said Mr Blunt. 'Thought you'd gone home. Well, you two have been doing good work on those beds there. Billy, I'm going to paint the water-butt and the handle of the roller some time. Perhaps you'd like to do it for me? You'll have to clean off the rust first with sand-paper.'

Billy Blunt and Milly-Molly-Mandy looked quite eager.

Billy Blunt said, 'Rather, Dad!' And Milly-Molly-Mandy looked with great interest at the

green can and the garden-roller. But she knew she
ought to be starting back to dinner at the nice white
cottage with the thatched roof, or Father and
Mother and Grandpa and Grandma and Uncle and
Aunty would be wondering what had become of her.
So she handed her garden-fork back to Billy Blunt
and walked slowly to the gate

But Billy Blunt said, 'Couldn't you come again
after dinner? I'll save you some of the painting.'

So Milly-Molly-Mandy gave a little skip and said
'I'd like to, if Muvver doesn't want me.'

So after dinner, when she had helped with the
washing-up, Milly-Molly-Mandy ran hoppity-skip
all the way down to the village again. And there in
the Blunts' garden was Billy Blunt, busy rubbing the
iron bands on the water-butt with a sheet of sand-
paper.

'Hullo, Billy!' said Milly-Molly-Mandy.

'Hullo, Milly-Molly-Mandy!' said Billy Blunt.
He looked very hot and dirty, but he smiled quite
broadly. And then he said, 'I've saved the garden-
roller for you to paint – it's all sandpapered ready.'

Milly-Molly-Mandy thought that was nice of
Billy Blunt, for the sandpapering was the nasty,
dirty part of the work.

Billy Blunt got the lid off the can, and stirred up
the beautiful green paint with a stick. Then all by

himself he thought of fetching a piece of newspaper to pin over her frock to keep her clean. And then he went back to rubbing the water-butt, while Milly-Molly-Mandy dipped the brush carefully into the lovely full can of green paint, and started work on the lawn mower.

The handle had a pattern in wriggly bits of iron, and it was great fun getting the paint into all the cracks. And you can't imagine how beautiful and new that roller looked when the paint was on it.

Billy Blunt had to keep leaving his water-butt to see how it was going on, because the wriggly bits looked so nice when they were green, and he hadn't any wriggly bits on his water-butt.

By the end of the afternoon you ought to have seen how nice the garden looked! The flower-beds were clean and trim, the lawn tidied up, the water-butt

65

stood glistening green by the side of the house, and the roller lay glistening green on the grass.

And when Mr Blunt came out and saw it all he was pleased!

He called Mrs Blunt, and Mrs Blunt was pleased too. She gave them each a banana, and they ate them sitting on one of the corn-bins in the shop.

And afterwards Billy Blunt buried Milly-Molly-Mandy in the corn, right up to the neck. And when he helped her out again she was all bits of corn, down her neck, and in her socks, and on her hair. But Milly-Molly-Mandy didn't mind a scrap. She liked it.

8. Milly-Molly-Mandy Makes a Cosy

Once upon a time Milly-Molly-Mandy went out visiting, in her best hat and new shoes and white cotton gloves. Milly-Molly-Mandy felt very proper indeed. She walked down the road, past the Moggs' cottage, past Mr Blunt's corn-shop, till she came to Miss Muggins' small shop. For Milly-Molly-Mandy was going to tea with Miss Muggins and her little niece, Jilly.

Miss Muggins' shop and the passage behind smelt so interesting – like calico and flannelette and brown paper, with faint whiffs of peppermint and rasp-berry-drops. (For Miss Muggins sold a few sweets too, from bottles on a shelf in her window.)

But the little sitting-room at the back of the shop smelt mostly of warm buttered scones and sugary cakes, for the table was all laid ready, and Miss Muggins and Jilly were waiting for her. And over the teapot in front of Miss Muggins was a most beautiful cosy, all made of odd-shaped pieces of bright-coloured silks and velvets, with loops of coloured cord on top. Milly-Molly-Mandy did like it!

After Milly-Molly-Mandy had eaten two buttered scones she couldn't help saying, 'Isn't that a beautiful cosy!'

And Jilly said, 'Aunty made it!'

Milly-Molly-Mandy thought how nice it would be to have such a beautiful cosy on the table at home.

When she had eaten a pink sugary cake she said, 'Wasn't that cosy very difficult to make?'

And Miss Muggins (who had just come back from serving a lady with a card of linen buttons and some black elastic) said, 'Oh, no, it was quite easy! You ought to get your aunty to teach you feather-stitching, Milly-Molly-Mandy, so that you could make one!'

Milly-Molly-Mandy thought how nice it would be to make Mother such a beautiful cosy, but she didn't know how she could get the stuffs.

After the meal she played with Jilly and her dolls' house, and when it was time to go Miss Muggins came out of the shop with a small piece of bright red satin, to start Milly-Molly-Mandy making a cosy. Milly-Molly-Mandy was pleased!

Then she thanked Miss Muggins very much for having her, and ran home to the nice white cottage with the thatched roof.

She hid the red satin in her doll's cradle, and

She couldn't help saying, 'Isn't that a beautiful cosy!'

wondered a great deal how she could get enough pieces of stuff to make a cosy.

And then, one morning, Mother turned out of her piece-bag some scraps of green ribbon, and said Milly-Molly-Mandy might have them. Milly-Molly-Mandy *was* pleased!

But as she didn't like the thought of Mother giving anything for her own secret present she looked round for something she could do in exchange for it. And she saw, behind the kitchen door, a muddy pair of Mother's shoes waiting to be cleaned. So Milly-Molly-Mandy quietly got out the boot-box and cleaned them.

So now Milly-Molly-Mandy had some red pieces and some green pieces.

And then, one afternoon, Father gave her a penny to buy some sweets. And Milly-Molly-Mandy said, 'Would you mind, Farver, if I bought something else instead, for a great secret!'

And Father didn't mind, so Milly-Molly-Mandy went to Miss Muggins' shop and bought a skein of black silk to do the feather-stitching with.

So now Milly-Molly-Mandy had some red pieces and some green pieces and a skein of black silk.

And then, one day, Grandma altered her best dress, which was of velvet, and the part she cut off she gave to Milly-Molly-Mandy to play with.

So now Milly-Molly-Mandy had some red pieces and some green pieces and a skein of black silk and some black pieces.

And then, one morning, Grandpa let her come with him in the pony-trap to the town. And while they were there he looked at the shop windows and asked Milly-Molly-Mandy what she would like for a little present. And Milly-Molly-Mandy said, 'Oh, Grandpa, could I have some coloured cord for a great secret?' So Grandpa bought her some coloured cord without asking any questions.

So now Milly-Molly-Mandy had some red pieces and some green pieces and a skein of black silk and some black pieces and some coloured cord.

And then, one afternoon, Aunty was retrimming a hat, and when she took off the old lavender ribbon it had on it she said Milly-Molly-Mandy could have it. And Milly-Molly-Mandy found some parts of it were quite good.

So now Milly-Molly-Mandy had some red pieces and some green pieces and a skein of black silk and some black pieces and some coloured cord and some lavender pieces.

And then, one day, Uncle was turning over the neckties in his drawer, and there was one blue one with yellow spots which Uncle didn't like, and he threw it to Milly-Molly-Mandy, saying, 'Here,

Milly-Molly-Mandy, this'll do for a doll's sash, or something.'

So now Milly-Molly-Mandy had some red pieces and some green pieces and a skein of black silk and some black pieces and some coloured cord and some lavender pieces and some blue pieces with yellow spots.

And Milly-Molly-Mandy thought she really had enough now to begin the cosy!

She went to Aunty and asked if she would kindly teach her to do feather-stitching for a great secret. So

Aunty showed her how to cut up the pieces and feather-stitch them together.

And then, for weeks, Milly-Molly-Mandy spent nearly all her spare time in the attic or in the barn, sewing and sewing, and never showed anyone but Aunty what she was doing.

One evening Father said, 'Whatever is Milly-Molly-Mandy up to these days?'

And Mother said, 'I can't think.'

And Grandpa said, 'I haven't seen her properly for days.'

And Grandma said, 'I think she's got some kind of a secret on.'

And Uncle said, 'I shouldn't be surprised.'

But Aunty said nothing at all, and only put the tablecloth straight.

And then, just when Mother had finished laying the supper, Milly-Molly-Mandy came in with a very pink face and her hands behind her back.

Mother went to the oven to bring out a plate of hot potato-cakes. And when she turned round again, there, at her end of the table, was the most beautiful patchwork cosy keeping the cocoa-jug hot!

'Milly-Molly-Mandy!' said Mother.

She hurried to her place, while Milly-Molly-Mandy jumped up and down, and Father and

Grandpa and Grandma and Uncle and Aunty all looked on admiringly.

'Oh, Milly-Molly-Mandy!' said Mother, 'what – a – *beautiful* – cosy!'

And Mother was so pleased, and Milly-Molly-Mandy was so glad she was pleased, that they just had to hug and kiss each other very hard indeed.

And the potato-cakes got almost cold, but the cocoa was just as hot as hot!

9. Milly-Molly-Mandy Keeps Shop

Once upon a time Milly-Molly-Mandy was walking home from school with some little friends – Billy Blunt, Miss Muggins's niece Jilly, and, of course, little-friend-Susan. And they were all talking about what they would like to do when they were big.

Billy Blunt said he would have a motor-bus and drive people to the station and pull their boxes about. Miss Muggins' Jilly said she would curl her hair and be a lady who acts for the pictures. Little-friend-Susan wanted to be a nurse with long white streamers, and push a pram with two babies in it.

Milly-Molly-Mandy wanted a shop like Miss Muggins, where she could sell sweets, and cut pretty coloured stuff for people's dresses with a big pair of scissors. And 'Oh, dear!' said Milly-Molly-Mandy, 'I wish we didn't have to wait till we had growed up!'

Then they came to Miss Muggins's shop, and Jilly said 'Good-bye,' and went in.

And then they came to Mr Blunt's corn-shop, which was only a few steps farther on, and Billy Blunt said 'Good-bye,' and went in.

And then Milly-Molly-Mandy and little-friend-Susan, with their arms round each other, walked up the white road with the fields each side till they came to the Moggs' cottage, and little-friend-Susan said 'Good-bye' and went in.

And Milly-Molly-Mandy went hoppity-skipping on alone till she came to the nice white cottage with the thatched roof, where Mother was at the gate to meet her.

Next day was Saturday, and Milly-Molly-Mandy went down to the village on an errand for Mother. And when she had done it she saw Miss Muggins standing at her shop door, looking rather worried.

And when Miss Muggins saw Milly-Molly-Mandy she said, 'Oh, Milly-Molly-Mandy, would you mind running to ask Mrs Jakes if she could come and mind my shop for an hour? Tell her I've got to go to see someone on very important business, and I don't know what to do, and Jilly's gone picnicking.'

So Milly-Molly-Mandy ran to ask Mrs Jakes. But Mrs Jakes said, 'Tell Miss Muggins I'm very sorry, but I've just got the cakes in the oven, and I can't leave them.'

So Milly-Molly-Mandy ran back and told Miss Muggins, and Miss Muggins said, 'I wonder if Mrs Blunt would come.'

So Milly-Molly-Mandy ran to ask Mrs Blunt. But Mrs Blunt said, 'I'm sorry, but I'm simply up to my eyes in house-cleaning, and I can't leave just now.'

So Milly-Molly-Mandy ran back and told Miss Muggins, and Miss Muggins said she didn't know of anyone else she could ask.

Then Milly-Molly-Mandy said, 'Oh, Miss Muggins, couldn't I look after the shop for you? I'll tell people you'll be back in an hour, and if they only want a sugar-stick or something I could give it them – I know how much it is!'

Miss Muggins looked at Milly-Molly-Mandy, and then she said. 'Well, you aren't very big, but I know you're careful, Milly-Molly-Mandy.'

So she gave her lots of instructions about asking people if they would come back in an hour, and not selling things unless she was quite sure of the price, and so on. And then Miss Muggins put on her hat and feather boa and hurried off.

And Milly-Molly-Mandy was left alone in charge of the shop!

Milly-Molly-Mandy felt very solemn and careful indeed. She dusted the counter with a duster which she saw hanging on a nail; and then she peeped into the window at all the handkerchiefs and socks and bottles of sweets – and she could see Mrs Hubble arranging the loaves and cakes in her shop-window opposite, and Mr Smale (who had the grocer's shop with a little counter at the back where you posted parcels and bought stamps and letter-paper) standing at his door enjoying the sunshine. And Milly-Molly-Mandy felt so pleased that she had a shop as well as they.

And then, suddenly, the door-handle rattled, and the little bell over the door jangle-jangled up and down, and who should come in but little-friend-Susan! – And how little-friend-Susan did stare when she saw Milly-Molly-Mandy behind the counter!

'Miss Muggins has gone out on 'portant business, but she'll be back in an hour. What do you want?' said Milly-Molly-Mandy.

'A packet of safety-pins for Mother. What are you doing here?' said little-friend-Susan.

'I'm looking after the shop,' said Milly-Molly-Mandy. 'And I know where the safety-pins are, because I had to buy some yesterday.'

So Milly-Molly-Mandy wrapped up the safety-pins in a piece of thin brown paper, and twisted the end just as Miss Muggins did. And she handed the packet to little-friend-Susan, and little-friend-Susan handed her a penny.

And then little-friend-Susan wanted to stay and play 'shops' with Milly-Molly-Mandy.

But Milly-Molly-Mandy shook her head solemnly and said, 'No, this isn't play; it's business. I've got to be very, very careful. You'd better go, Susan.'

And just then the bell jangled again, and a lady came in, so little-friend-Susan went out. (She peered through the window for a time to see how Milly-Molly-Mandy got on, but Milly-Molly-Mandy wouldn't look at her.)

The lady was Miss Bloss, who lived opposite, over the baker's shop, with Mrs Bloss. She wanted a quarter of a yard of pink flannelette, because she was making a wrapper for her mother, and she hadn't bought quite enough for the collar. She said she didn't like to waste a whole hour till Miss Muggins returned.

Milly-Molly-Mandy stood on one leg and

wondered what to do, and Miss Bloss tapped with one finger and wondered what to do.

And then Miss Bloss said, 'That's the roll my flannelette came off. I'm quite sure Miss Muggins wouldn't mind my taking some.'

So between them they measured off the pink flannelette, and Milly-Molly-Mandy fetched Miss Muggins' big scissors, and Miss Bloss made a crease exactly where the quarter-yard came; and Milly-Molly-Mandy breathed very hard and cut slowly and carefully right along the crease to the end.

And then she wrapped the piece up and gave it to Miss Bloss, and Miss Bloss handed her half a crown, saying, 'Ask Miss Muggins to send me the change when she gets back.'

And then Miss Bloss went out.

And then for a time nobody came in, and Milly-Molly-Mandy amused herself by trying to find the rolls of stuff that different people's dresses had come off. There was her own pink-and-white-striped cotton (looking so lovely and new) and Mother's blue-checked apron stuff and Mrs Jakes' Sunday gown. . .

Then rattle went the handle and jangle went the bell, and who should come in but Billy Blunt!

'I'm Miss Muggins,' said Milly-Molly-Mandy. 'What do you want to buy?'

'I'm Miss Muggins. What do you want to buy?'

'Where's Miss Muggins?' said Billy Blunt.

So Milly-Molly-Mandy had to explain again. And then Billy Blunt said he had wanted a penny-worth of aniseed-balls. So Milly-Molly-Mandy stood on a box and reached down the glass jar from the shelf.

They were twelve a penny she knew, for she had often bought them. So she counted them out, and then Billy Blunt counted them.

And Billy Blunt said, 'You've got one too many here.'

So Milly-Molly-Mandy counted again, and she found one too many too. So they dropped one back in the jar, and Milly-Molly-Mandy put the others into a little bag and swung it over by the corners, just as Miss Muggins did, and gave it to Billy Blunt. And Billy Blunt gave her his penny.

And then Billy Blunt grinned, and said, 'Good morning, ma'am.'

And Milly-Molly-Mandy said, 'Good morning, sir,' and Billy Blunt went out.

After that an hour began to seem rather a long time, with the sun shining so outside. But at last the little bell gave a lively jangle again, and Miss Muggins had returned!

And though Milly-Molly-Mandy had enjoyed herself very much, she thought perhaps, after all, she would rather wait until she was grown up before she kept a shop for herself.

10. Milly-Molly-Mandy Gives a Party

Once upon a time Milly-Molly-Mandy had a plan.
And when she had thought over the plan for a while
she went to look in her money-box. And in the
money-box were four pennies and a ha'penny,
which Milly-Molly-Mandy did not think would be
enough for her plan. So Milly-Molly-Mandy went off
to talk it over with little-friend-Susan down the road.

'Susan,' said Milly-Molly-Mandy, 'I've got a
plan (only it's a great secret). I want to give a party
in our barn to Farver and Muvver and Grandpa
and Grandma and Uncle and Aunty. And I want to
buy refreshments. And you and I will be waitresses.
And if there's anything over we can eat it up afterwards.'

Little-friend-Susan thought it a very good plan
indeed.

'Will we wear caps?' she asked.

'Yes,' said Milly-Molly-Mandy, 'and aprons.
Only I haven't got enough money for the refreshments, so I don't think there'll be any over. We
must think.'

So Milly-Molly-Mandy and little-friend-Susan sat down and thought hard.

'We must work and earn some,' said Milly-Molly-Mandy.

'But how?' said little-friend-Susan.

'We might sell something,' said Milly-Molly-Mandy.

'But what?' said little-friend-Susan. So they had to think some more.

Presently Milly-Molly-Mandy said, 'I've got pansies and marigolds in my garden.'

And little-friend-Susan said, 'I've got nasturtiums in mine.'

'We could run errands for people,' said Milly-Molly-Mandy.

'And clean brass,' said little-friend-Susan.

That was a lovely idea, so Milly-Molly-Mandy fetched a pencil and paper and wrote out very carefully:

Millicent Margaret Amanda & Susan & Co. have bunches of flowers for sale and clean brass very cheap (we do not spill the polish) and run errands very cheap.

'What's "and Co."?' said little-friend-Susan.

'It's just business,' said Milly-Molly-Mandy, 'but perhaps we might ask Billy Blunt to be it. And he could be a waiter.'

Then they hung the notice on the front gate, and waited just the other side of the hedge.

Several people passed, but nobody seemed to want anything. Then at last a motor-car came along with a lady and gentleman in it; and when they saw the nice white cottage with the thatched roof they stopped at the gate to ask if they could get some cream there.

Milly-Molly-Mandy said, 'I'll go and ask Muvver,' and took the little pot they held out. And when she came back with it full of cream the lady and gentleman had read the notice and were asking little-friend-Susan questions. As the lady paid for the cream she said they must certainly have some flowers. So they each bought a bunch. And then the gentleman said the round brass thing in front of his car needed cleaning very badly – could the firm do it straight away?

So Milly-Molly-Mandy said, 'Yes, sir,' and raced back to the cottage to give Mother the cream-money and to borrow the brass-polishing box. And then she cleaned the round brass thing in front of the car with one piece of cloth and little-friend-Susan rubbed it bright with another piece of cloth, and the lady and gentleman looked on and seemed very satisfied.

Then the gentleman asked 'How much?' and paid them twopence for the flowers and a penny for the polishing. Milly-Molly-Mandy wanted to do some more polishing for the money, but the gentleman said they couldn't stop. And then they said good-bye and went off, and the lady turned and waved, and Milly-Molly-Mandy and little-friend-Susan waved back until they were gone.

Milly-Molly-Mandy and little-friend-Susan felt very happy and pleased.

And now they had sevenpence-ha'penny for the refreshments. Father and Mother and Grandpa and Grandma and Uncle and Aunty and Mrs Moggs, little-friend-Susan's mother, made seven.

Then who should look over the hedge but Mr Jakes, the Postman, on his way home from collecting letters from the letter-boxes. He had seen the notice on the gate.

'What's this? You trying to make a fortune?' said the Postman.

'Yes,' said Milly-Molly-Mandy, 'we've earned threepence!'

'My! And what do you plan to do with it?' said the Postman.

'We've got a secret!' said Milly-Molly-Mandy, with a little skip.

'Ah!' said the Postman, 'I guess it's a nice one, too!'

Milly-Molly-Mandy looked at little-friend-Susan,

and then she looked at the Postman. He was a nice Postman. 'You won't tell if we tell you?' she asked.

'Try me!' said the Postman promptly. So Milly-Molly-Mandy told him they were planning to give a party to Father and Mother and Grandpa and Grandma and Uncle and Aunty and Mrs Moggs.

'They're in luck, they are!' said the Postman. 'Nobody asks me to parties.'

Milly-Molly-Mandy looked at little-friend-Susan again, and then she looked at the Postman. He was a very nice Postman. Then she said, 'Supposing you were invited, would you come?'

'You try me!' said the Postman promptly again. And then he hitched up his letter-bag and went on.

'Farver and Muvver and Grandpa and Grandma and Uncle and Aunty and Mrs Moggs and the Postman. We've got to earn some more,' said Milly-Molly-Mandy. 'Let's go down to the village and ask Billy Blunt to be "and Co.," and p'r'aps he'll have an idea.'

Billy Blunt was in the road outside the corn-shop, mending the handles of his box on wheels. He had made it nearly all himself, and it was a very nice one, painted green like the water-butt and the lawn-roller. He thought 'and Co.' was rather a funny name, but said he would be it all right, and offered to make them a box with a slit in it, where they could keep their earnings. And he put in four farthings out of his collection. (Billy Blunt was collecting farthings – he had nineteen in an empty bird-seed bag.)

So now they had eightpence-ha'penny for the refreshments.

On Monday morning, on their way home to dinner, Milly-Molly-Mandy and little-friend-Susan passed Mrs Jakes, the Postman's wife, at her door, getting a breath of fresh air before dishing up her dinner. And Mrs Jakes said, 'Good morning! How's the firm of Millicent Margaret Amanda, Susan, and Co. getting on?'

Milly-Molly-Mandy said, 'Very well, thank you!'

'My husband's told me about your brass-cleaning,' said Mrs Jakes. 'I've got a whole mantel-shelf full that wants doing!'

Milly-Molly-Mandy and little-friend-Susan were very pleased, and arranged to come in directly school was over in the afternoon and clean it.

And they cleaned a mug and three candlesticks and two lamps – one big and one little – and a tray and a warming-pan, and they didn't spill or waste any of the polish. Mrs Jakes seemed very satisfied, and gave them each a penny and a piece of cake.

So now they had tenpence-ha'penny for refreshments.

But when they got outside Milly-Molly-Mandy said, 'Farver and Muvver and Grandpa and Grandma and Uncle and Aunty and Mrs Moggs and the Postman and Mrs Postman – I wonder if we've earned enough, Susan!'

As they turned home they passed the forge, and of course they had to stop a moment at the doorway, as usual, to watch the fire roaring, and Mr Rudge the Blacksmith banging with his hammer on the anvil.

Little-friend-Susan was just a bit nervous of the Blacksmith – he was so big, and his face was so dirty it made his teeth look very white and his eyes very twinkly when he smiled at them. But Milly-Molly-Mandy knew he was nice and clean under the dirt, which he couldn't help while he worked. So she smiled back.

And the Blacksmith said, 'Hullo!'

And Milly-Molly-Mandy said, 'Hullo!'

Then the Blacksmith beckoned with his finger and said, 'Come here!'

Milly-Molly-Mandy gave a little jump, and little-friend-Susan pulled at her hand, but Milly-Molly-Mandy knew he was really just a nice man under the dirt, so she went up to him.

And the Blacksmith said, 'Look what I've got here!' And he showed them a tiny little horseshoe, just like a proper one, only smaller, which he had made for them to keep. Milly-Molly-Mandy and little-friend-Susan were pleased!

Milly-Molly-Mandy thanked him very much. And then she looked at the Blacksmith and said, 'If you were invited to a party, would you come?'

And the Blacksmith looked at Milly-Molly-Mandy with twinkly eyes and said he'd come quite fast – so long as it wasn't before five o'clock on Saturday, when he was playing cricket with his team in the meadow.

When they got outside again Milly-Molly-Mandy said, 'Farver and Muvver and Grandpa and Grandma and Uncle and Aunty and Mrs Moggs and the Postman and Mrs Postman and the Blacksmith. We'll ask them for half-past five, and we ought to earn some more money, Susan!'

Just then they met Billy Blunt coming along, pulling his box on wheels with a bundle in it. And Billy Blunt grinned and said, 'I'm fetching Mrs

Bloss's washing, for the firm!' Milly-Molly-Mandy and little-friend-Susan were pleased!

When Saturday morning came all the invitations had been given out, and the firm of Millicent Margaret Amanda, Susan, and Co. was very busy putting things tidy in the barn, and covering up things which couldn't be moved with lots of green branches which Grandpa was trimming from the hedges.

And when half-past five came Milly-Molly-Mandy and little-friend-Susan, with clean hands and paper caps and aprons, waited by the barn door to welcome the guests. And each gentleman received a marigold buttonhole, and each lady a pansy.

Everybody arrived in good time, except the Blacksmith, who was just a bit late – he looked so clean and pink in his white cricket-flannels, Milly-Molly-Mandy hardly knew him – and Billy Blunt. But Billy Blunt came lugging a gramophone and two records which he had borrowed from a bigger boy at school. (He never told, but he had given the boy all the rest of his collection of farthings – fifteen of them, which makes three-pence-three-farthings – in exchange.)

Then Billy Blunt, who didn't want to dance, looked after the gramophone, while Father and

Mother and Grandpa and Grandma and Uncle and Aunty and Mrs Moggs and the Postman and Mrs Postman and the Blacksmith and Milly-Molly-Mandy and little-friend-Susan danced together in the old barn till the dust flew. And Milly-Molly-Mandy danced a lot with the Blacksmith as well as with everybody else, and so did little-friend-Susan.

They did enjoy themselves!

And then there were refreshments – raspberry-drops and aniseed-balls on saucers trimmed with little flowers; and late blackberries on leaf plates; and sherbet drinks, which Billy Blunt prepared while Milly-Molly-Mandy and little-friend-Susan stood by to tell people just the very moment to drink, when it was fizzing properly. (It was exciting!) And a jelly which Milly-Molly-Mandy and little-friend-Susan had made themselves from a packet, only it had to be eaten rather like soup, as it wouldn't stand up properly.

But Father and Mother and Grandpa and Grandma and Uncle and Aunty and Mrs Moggs and the Postman and Mrs Postman and the Blacksmith all said they had never enjoyed a jelly so much. And the Blacksmith, in a big voice, proposed a vote of thanks to the firm for the delightful party and refreshments, and everybody else said 'Hear! hear!' and clapped. And Milly-Molly-Mandy and little-

And then there were refreshments

friend-Susan joined in the clapping too, which wasn't quite proper, but they were so happy they couldn't help it!

And then all the guests went home.

And when the firm came to clear up the refreshments they found there was only one aniseed-ball left. But placed among the empty saucers and glasses on the bench were a small basket of pears and a bag of mixed sweets with a ticket 'For the Waiter and Waitresses' on it!

11. Milly-Molly-Mandy Goes Visiting

Once upon a time Milly-Molly-Mandy had a letter. It was from Mrs Hooker, who had been a friend of Mother's ever since she was a little girl. And it said how sorry Mrs Hooker was to have to put Milly-Molly-Mandy off last time she had invited her – that time Milly-Molly-Mandy had enjoyed little-friend-Susan's visit instead of her own. But now Mrs Hooker's son and his wife had gone abroad to live, and Mrs Hooker would be very pleased if Mother would let Milly-Molly-Mandy come and spend a week-end with her, as promised.

Milly-Molly-Mandy was very pleased, and Father and Mother and Grandpa and Grandma and Uncle and Aunty were very pleased for her. They talked of Milly-Molly-Mandy going away nearly all supper-time, and Aunty promised to put a new ribbon round her best hat, and Mother said she must make her a very nice 'going-away' nightdress in a case, and Uncle said he would feel very honoured if she were to borrow his small leather bag to take it in, and Father gave her sixpence to put in her purse.

Milly-Molly-Mandy felt so excited!

When Saturday morning came Grandpa got the pony-trap ready to go to market as usual, and Milly-Molly-Mandy came skipping down the path,

ready to go with him and meet Mrs Hooker as arranged. Her hat looked just like new, and she had on a pair of nice warm woolly gloves that Grandma had knitted for her, and Aunty's best nice warm woolly scarf, lent for the occasion.

Mother gave her a bunch of late chrysanthemums and a cream cheese for Mrs Hooker, with her love. And then Grandpa got up in the trap and took the reins, and Milly-Molly-Mandy was lifted up beside him. Then off trotted Twinkletoes, and Father and Mother and Grandma and Uncle and Aunty called, 'Good-bye, Milly-Molly-Mandy! Have a nice time!' and waved, and Milly-Molly-Mandy waved back till she couldn't see them any longer. And she was really off for her visit!

They didn't see little-friend-Susan or Billy Blunt as they drove through the village, but Milly-Molly-Mandy waved at their houses, in case they might see her. And then they were out in the open country, and Milly-Molly-Mandy was glad of Aunty's nice warm woolly scarf and her own nice warm woolly gloves.

They came to the town, and got down by the big clock in the market-place, and Mrs Hooker came hurrying up, looking quite different, somehow (for Milly-Molly-Mandy had seen her only once before, and had nearly forgotten what she looked like).

And then Grandpa kissed Milly-Molly-Mandy good-bye, and went off to do his business in the market. And Milly-Molly-Mandy took Mrs Hooker's hand in its grey kid glove, and went off with her.

Milly-Molly-Mandy had never been away from home to stay before without either Father or Mother or Grandpa or Grandma or Uncle or Aunty, and it felt so strange and exciting.

'Well, Milly-Molly-Mandy,' said Mrs Hooker, 'I just want to buy some crochet-cotton, and then we will be getting home.'

So they went into a big draper's shop, heaps of times bigger than Miss Muggins' shop at home, and Mrs Hooker asked for crochet-cotton. And while

'Good-bye, Milly-Molly-Mandy! Have a nice time!'

she was buying it Milly-Molly-Mandy looked about and felt the purse in her pocket. Presently she saw some pretty little guards to put over the points of knitting-needles, which she thought would be so useful to Grandma.

And suddenly Milly-Molly-Mandy had an idea: What fun it would be to take presents home for everybody! She had five pennies of her own as well as the sixpence Father had given her.

She wondered what everybody would like, and remembered Mother once saying, 'Handkerchiefs always make an acceptable present.' So when she had bought the guards for Grandma she asked the lady behind the counter if she had some handkerchiefs that weren't at all expensive, and the lady behind the counter brought out a boxful, each one marked with a letter in one corner. So Milly-Molly-Mandy looked at them all, and chose one for Mother with 'M' in the corner, and one for Aunty with 'A' in the corner. And then she had only two pennies left. She wondered whatever she could get for Father and Grandpa and Uncle with twopence.

Presently Mrs Hooker finished her purchases, and they went out into the street to go to Mrs Hooker's house. There were such a lot of people, all over the pavement and road, for it was market-day, and there seemed so much to look at that Milly-Molly-

Mandy wished she had a dozen pairs of eyes. But still, with only two, she managed to keep one on the shop-windows as they passed, hoping to see something which Father and Grandpa and Uncle might like. And suddenly she saw a tray of pink sugar mice in a sweet-shop, labelled 'Two a penny.'

'Oh, Mrs Hooker!' said Milly-Molly-Mandy, 'would you mind waiting a moment while I get a sugar mouse to take home to Farver and Grandpa and Uncle?'

So Mrs Hooker held the leather bag and chrysanthemums and cream cheese until Milly-Molly-Mandy came out with a bag of sugar mice in her hand (she had bought four, and one was to be a good-bye present for Mrs Hooker). She wished she could get presents for little-friend-Susan and Billy Blunt, but that didn't seem possible, for she had used up all her money.

When they got to Mrs Hooker's house they put the chrysanthemums in a vase on the table, and the cream cheese in a dish on the sideboard. (Mrs Hooker was very pleased with them.) And then there was just time before dinner for Milly-Molly-Mandy to unpack her small leather bag in the little room she was to sleep in all by herself. And she found Mother had popped in Booby Rabbit, the toy she had won at a party once, and had slept with ever since. She was so glad to see him, and hid him in her nightdress-case so that he shouldn't be seen, because he hadn't been invited. (It was such fun for Booby Rabbit!)

The plates at dinner were so pretty – quite different from the ones they had at home – and so were the wall-paper and the carpet. Altogether, there seemed so much to think about that there wasn't time to say much more than 'Yes, please,' and 'No, thank you.' But she enjoyed her dinner very much.

After dinner Mrs Hooker said, 'I have asked Milly next door to come and spend the afternoon with you, and you can play with my old toys.'

Milly-Molly-Mandy was very interested. And then she said, 'Will Milly-next-door put her hat and coat on to come here?' – for their nearest neighbours at home were little-friend-Susan and the Moggs's, and they lived five minutes' walk down the road (but only three minutes if you ran).

Mrs Hooker said she really couldn't say. And presently the next-door gate squeaked, and then Mrs Hooker's gate squeaked, and then the door-bell rang, and Milly-next-door came in (with a coat on and no hat).

Mrs Hooker told Milly-Molly-Mandy to take Milly-next-door upstairs to her little room, to take her coat off. So Milly-Molly-Mandy played hostess, and let Milly-next-door use her comb, and asked her if her name was really Millicent Margaret Amanda, like Milly-Molly-Mandy's own. And Milly-next-door said no, it was Mildred.

Then Milly-next-door admired the new nightdress-case lying on the bed, and when Milly-Molly-Mandy showed her the new nightdress inside (which was pink) Milly-next-door admired that too. (She didn't see Booby Rabbit.) But when Milly-Molly-Mandy showed her the handkerchiefs marked 'M' for Mother and 'A' for Aunty Milly-next-door was quite surprised.

'Oh,' said Milly-next-door, 'my mother never has her handkerchiefs marked "M"! She has them marked "R", because her other name's Rose. What's your mother's other name?'

'It's Polly,' said Milly-Molly-Mandy, in a sad little voice.

'Oh, well,' said Milly-next-door comfortingly, 'I expect they can use them, even if they aren't quite proper.'

But Milly-Molly-Mandy didn't feel very comforted, for she had so wanted to give Mother and Aunty proper presents.

Then they went downstairs and played all the afternoon with Mrs Hooker's funny old-fashioned toys. And when the lamps were lit Mrs Hooker brought out a beautiful paint-box and a fashion-paper full of little girls, and Milly-Molly-Mandy and Milly-next-door each painted a little girl very carefully, and cut it out with Mrs Hooker's scissors, and gave it to each other for a keepsake.

And during tea Milly-Molly-Mandy had another good idea: she would paint and cut out some paper dolls, very, very nicely, and take them home to little-friend-Susan for a present! Milly-Molly-Mandy didn't think Billy Blunt would care for paper dolls; she didn't know what she could give him. She wished she had another ha'penny for a sugar mouse.

And now it was time for Milly-next-door to put on her coat again and go home. Milly-Molly-Mandy and she said good-bye, and promised to write to each other and exchange paper dolls.

Milly-Molly-Mandy had never slept all alone before, and when bedtime came she felt quite pleased and excited. Mrs Hooker came and tucked her in, and she admired her new nightdress. Booby Rabbit was under the bedclothes, but he couldn't resist coming up for a peep at Mrs Hooker, and Mrs Hooker saw him and stroked his ears, and said she would certainly have invited him if she had thought he cared to come. And then she kissed Milly-Molly-Mandy good night, and Milly-Molly-Mandy lay in the dark and enjoyed going to sleep in a different bed.

Sunday was a nice day. They went to church in the morning, and in the afternoon Milly-Molly-Mandy painted paper dolls for little-friend-Susan.

And then came Monday, and Milly-Molly-Mandy's visit was over. It was in the afternoon that Grandpa and Twinkletoes came with the trap to fetch her home.

She was all ready but for slipping the sugar mouse on to the mantelshelf with a note, 'With Love from M. M. M.', where Mrs Hooker would see it when she came in from seeing Milly-Molly-Mandy off; and then Milly-Molly-Mandy was perched in her seat beside Grandpa.

And just as they drove off Mrs Hooker put a little packet of chocolate in Milly-Molly-Mandy's lap, to eat on the way home, and they cried 'Good-bye!' to each other, and waved, and soon Twinkletoes' twinkling feet had carried them right out of sight.

Presently Milly-Molly-Mandy, sitting in the trap, had yet another good idea; she could give the little packet of chocolate to Billy Blunt for a present!

So she said, 'Grandpa, would you be very disappointed if we didn't eat this chocolate?' adding in a whisper, 'I've got something in my bag for you!'

And Grandpa said, 'Milly-Molly-Mandy, I'm just feeling too excited to eat any chocolate now!'

So when they got home to the nice white cottage with the thatched roof, and Milly-Molly-Mandy had hugged Father and Mother and Grandpa and Grandma and Uncle and Aunty, she opened the leather bag, and gave:

Father a sugar mouse – and Father was pleased!

And Mother a handkerchief, marked 'M' for Mother. But when Mother saw it she said, 'Oh, how nice to have it all ready marked "M" for Mary!' And Milly-Molly-Mandy suddenly remembered Mother's real name was Mary, and she was only called Polly 'for short'! Milly-Molly-Mandy was so relieved that she had to jump up and down several times.

And then she gave Grandpa a sugar mouse – and Grandpa was pleased!

And Grandma the guards for her knitting-needles – and Grandma was pleased!

And Uncle a sugar mouse – and Uncle was pleased!

And Aunty a handkerchief marked 'A' for Aunty. But when Aunty saw it she said, 'How nice! mine is marked too – "A" for Alice!' And Milly-Molly-Mandy suddenly remembered that Aunty and Alice both began with the same letter, and she was so very relieved that she had to jump up and down a great many times.

Next morning she ran down to the road to little-friend-Susan's and gave her the painted paper dolls, and little-friend-Susan was pleased!

And later in the day she saw Billy Blunt, and gave him the little packet of chocolate – and Billy Blunt was very surprised, and pleased too, and he made her eat half, and it was the bigger half.

And then Milly-Molly-Mandy wrote a little letter to say 'thank you' to Mrs Hooker.

Milly-Molly-Mandy just does enjoy going away visiting!

12. Milly-Molly-Mandy Gets to Know Teacher

Once upon a time there were changes at Milly-Molly-Mandy's school. Miss Sheppard, the head-mistress, was going away, and Miss Edwards, the second teacher, was to be head-mistress in her place, and live in the teacher's cottage just by the school, instead of coming in by the bus from the town each day.

Miss Edwards was very strict, and taught arithmetic and history and geography, and wore high collars.

Milly-Molly-Mandy wasn't particularly interested in the change, though she liked both Miss Sheppard and Miss Edwards quite well. But one afternoon Miss Edwards gave her a note to give to her Mother, and the note was to ask if Milly-Molly-Mandy's Mother would be so very good as to let Miss Edwards have a bed at the nice white cottage with the thatched roof for a night or two until Miss Edwards got her new little house straight.

Father and Mother and Grandpa and Grandma and Uncle and Aunty talked it over during supper, and they thought they might manage it for a few nights.

Milly-Molly-Mandy was very interested, and tried to think what it would be like to have Teacher sitting at supper with them, and going to sleep in the spare room, as well as teaching in school all day. And she couldn't help feeling just a little bit glad that it was only to be for a night or two.

Next day she took a note to school for Teacher from Mother, to say, yes, they would be pleased to have her. And after school Milly-Molly-Mandy told little-friend-Susan and Billy Blunt about it.

And little-friend-Susan said, 'Oooh! Won't you have to behave properly! I'm glad she's not coming to us!'

And Billy Blunt said, 'Huh! – hard lines!'

Milly-Molly-Mandy was quite glad Teacher was only coming to stay for a few nights.

Miss Edwards arrived at the nice white cottage with the thatched roof just before supper-time the following evening.

Milly-Molly-Mandy was looking out for her, and directly she heard the gate click she called Mother and ran and opened the front door wide, so that the hall lamp could shine down the path. And Teacher came in out of the dark, just as Mother hurried from the kitchen to welcome her.

Teacher thanked Mother very much for having her, and said she felt so dusty and untidy because she had been putting up shelves in her new little cottage ever since school was over.

So Mother said, 'Come right up to your room, Miss Edwards, and Milly-Molly-Mandy will bring you a jug of hot water. And then I expect you'll be glad of some supper straight away!'

So Milly-Molly-Mandy ran along to the kitchen for a jug of hot water, thinking how funny it was to hear Teacher's familiar voice away from school. She tapped very politely at the half-open door of the spare room (she could see Teacher tidying her hair in front of the dressing-table, by the candlelight), and Teacher smiled at her as she took the steaming jug, and said:

'That's kind of you, Milly-Molly-Mandy! This is just what I want most. What a lovely smell of hot cakes!'

Milly-Molly-Mandy smiled back, though she was quite a bit surprised that Teacher should speak in that pleased, hungry sort of way – it was more the kind of way she, or little-friend-Susan, or Father or Mother or Grandpa or Grandma or Uncle or Aunty, might have spoken.

When Teacher came downstairs to the kitchen they all sat down to supper. Teacher's place was just opposite Milly-Molly-Mandy's, and every time she caught Milly-Molly-Mandy's eye she smiled across at her. And Milly-Molly-Mandy smiled back, and tried to remember to sit up, for she kept on almost expecting Teacher to say, 'Head up, Milly-Molly-Mandy! Keep your elbows off the desk!' – but she never did!

They were all a little bit shy of Teacher, just at first; but soon Father and Mother and Grandpa and Grandma and Uncle and Aunty were talking away, and Teacher was talking too, and laughing. And she looked so different when she was laughing that Milly-Molly-Mandy found it quite difficult to get on with her bread-and-milk before it got cold. Teacher enjoyed the hot cakes, and wanted to know just how Mother made them. She asked a lot of questions, and Mother said she would teach Teacher how to do it, so that she could make them in her own new little kitchen.

Milly-Molly-Mandy thought how funny it would be for Teacher to start having lessons.

After supper Teacher asked Milly-Molly-Mandy if she could make little sailor-girls, and when Milly-Molly-Mandy said no, Teacher drew a little sailor-girl, with a sailor-collar and sailor-hat and pleated skirt, on a folded piece of paper, and then she cut it out with Aunty's scissors. And when she unfolded the paper there was a whole row of little sailor-girls all holding hands.

Milly-Molly-Mandy did like it. She thought how funny it was that she should have known Teacher all that time and never known she could draw little sailor-girls.

Then Mother said, 'Now, Milly-Molly-Mandy, it is bedtime.' So Milly-Molly-Mandy kissed Father and Mother and Grandpa and Grandma and Uncle and Aunty, and went to shake hands with Teacher. But Teacher said she wanted a kiss too. So they kissed each other in quite a nice friendly way.

But still Milly-Molly-Mandy felt when she went upstairs she must get into bed extra quickly and quietly, because Teacher was in the house.

Next morning Milly-Molly-Mandy and Teacher went to school together. And as soon as they got there Teacher was just her usual self again, and told Milly-Molly-Mandy to sit up, or to get on with her work, as if she had never laughed at supper, or cut out little sailor-girls, or kissed anyone good night.

After school Milly-Molly-Mandy showed little-friend-Susan and Billy Blunt the row of little sailor-girls.

And little-friend-Susan opened her eyes and said, 'Just fancy Teacher doing that!'

And Billy Blunt folded them up carefully in the

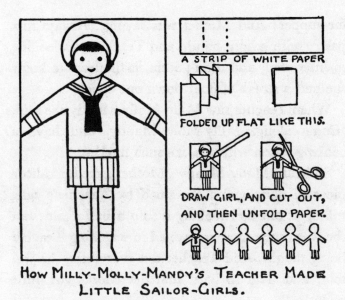

HOW MILLY-MOLLY-MANDY'S TEACHER MADE
LITTLE SAILOR-GIRLS.

creases so that he could see how they were made, and
then he grinned and gave them back.

And little-friend-Susan and Billy Blunt didn't
feel so very sorry for Milly-Molly-Mandy having
Teacher to stay, then.

That evening Teacher came up to the nice white
cottage with the thatched roof earlier than she did
the day before. And when Milly-Molly-Mandy
came into the kitchen from taking a nice meal out
to Toby the dog, and giving him a good bedtime
romp round the yard, what did she see but Teacher,
with one of Mother's big aprons on and her sleeves
tucked up, learning how to make apple turn-overs

113

for supper! And Mother was saying, 'Always mix pastry with a light hand,' and Teacher was looking so interested, and didn't seem in the least to know she had a streak of flour down one cheek.

When Teacher saw Milly-Molly-Mandy she said, 'Come along, Milly-Molly-Mandy, and have a cooking-lesson with me, it's such fun!'

So Milly-Molly-Mandy's Mother gave her a little piece of dough, and she stood by Teacher's side, rolling it out and making it into a ball again; but she was much more interested in watching Teacher being taught. And Teacher did everything she was told, and tried so hard that her cheeks got quite pink.

When the turn-overs were all made there was a small piece of dough left on the board, so Teacher shaped it into the most beautiful little bird; and the bird and the turn-overs were all popped into the oven, together with Milly-Molly-Mandy's piece (which had been a pig and a cat and a teapot, but ended up a little grey loaf).

When Father and Mother and Grandpa and Grandma and Uncle and Aunty and Teacher and Milly-Molly-Mandy sat down to supper, Teacher put her finger on her lips to Milly-Molly-Mandy when the apple turn-overs came on, so that Milly-Molly-Mandy shouldn't tell who made them until

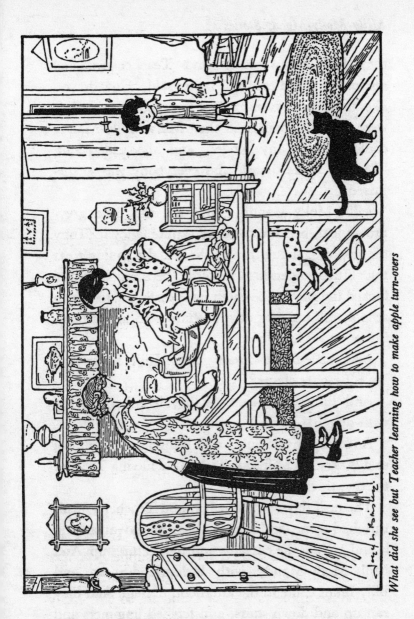

What did she see but Teacher learning how to make apple turn-overs

they had been tasted. And Teacher watched anxiously, and presently Mother said, 'How do you like these turn-overs?' And everybody said they were most delicious, and then Milly-Molly-Mandy couldn't wait any longer, and she called out, 'Teacher made them!' and everybody was so surprised.

Milly-Molly-Mandy didn't eat the little grey-brown loaf, because she didn't quite fancy it (Toby the dog did, though), and she felt she couldn't eat the little golden-brown bird, because it really looked too good to be eaten just yet. So she took it to school with her next day, to share with little-friend-Susan and Billy Blunt.

And little-friend-Susan said, 'Isn't it pretty? Isn't Teacher clever?'

And Billy Blunt said, 'Fancy Teacher playing with dough!'

And little-friend-Susan and Billy Blunt didn't feel at all sorry for Milly-Molly-Mandy having Teacher to stay, then.

The next day was Saturday, and Teacher's furniture had come, and she was busy all day arranging it and getting the curtains and the pictures up. And Milly-Molly-Mandy with little-friend-Susan and Billy Blunt came in the afternoon to help. And they ran up and down stairs, and fetched hammers and nails, and held things, and made themselves very useful indeed.

And at four o'clock Teacher sent Billy Blunt out to get some cakes from Mrs Hubble's shop, while the others laid the table in the pretty little sitting-

room. And they had a nice kind of picnic, with Milly-Molly-Mandy and little-friend-Susan sharing a cup, and Billy Blunt having a saucer for a plate, because everything wasn't unpacked yet. And they all laughed and talked, and were as happy as anything.

And when Teacher said it was time to send them all off home Milly-Molly-Mandy was so sorry to think Teacher wasn't coming to sleep in the spare room any more that she wanted to kiss Teacher without being asked. And she actually did it, too. And little-friend-Susan and Billy Blunt didn't look a bit surprised, either.

And after that, somehow, it didn't seem to matter that Teacher was strict in school, for they knew that she was really just a very nice, usual sort of person inside all the time!

13. Milly-Molly-Mandy Goes to a Fête

Once upon a time, while Milly-Molly-Mandy was shopping in the village for Mother, she saw a poster on a board outside Mr Blunt's corn-shop. So she stopped to read it, and she found that there was to be a *fête* held in the playing-field, with sports and competitions for children, and other things for grown-ups. And while she was reading Billy Blunt looked out of the shop door.

Milly-Molly-Mandy said, 'Hullo, Billy!'

And Billy Blunt grinned and said, 'Hullo, Milly-Molly-Mandy!' and he came and looked at the poster too.

'When's the *fête* to be?' said Milly-Molly-Mandy, and Billy Blunt pointed with his toe to the date. And then he pointed to the words, 'Hundred-yard races, three-legged races etc.,' and said, 'I'm going in for them.'

'Are you?' said Milly-Molly-Mandy, and began to be interested. She thought a *fête* would be quite fun, and decided to ask Mother when she got home if she might go to it too.

A day or two later, as Milly-Molly-Mandy was swinging on the meadow-gate after school, she saw someone running along in the middle of the road in a very steady, businesslike fashion. And who should it be but Billy Blunt?

'Hullo, Billy! Where're you going?' said Milly-Molly-Mandy.

Billy Blunt slowed up and wiped his forehead, panting. 'I'm getting into training,' said Billy Blunt, 'for the races.'

Milly-Molly-Mandy thought that was a very good idea.

'I'm going to do some running every day,' said Billy Blunt, 'till the *fête*.'

Milly-Molly-Mandy was sure Billy Blunt would win.

And then Billy Blunt asked if Milly-Molly-Mandy could count minutes, because it would be nice to have someone to time his running sometimes. Milly-Molly-Mandy couldn't, because she had never tried. But after that she practised counting minutes with the kitchen clock, till she got to know just about how fast to count sixty so that it was almost exactly a minute.

And the next day Billy Blunt stood right at one end of the meadow, by the nice white cottage with the thatched roof where Milly-Molly-Mandy lived, and Milly-Molly-Mandy stood at the other end. And when Billy Blunt shouted 'Go!' and began running, Milly-Molly-Mandy shut her eyes tight so that she wouldn't think of anything else, and began counting steadily. And Billy Blunt reached her side in just over a minute and a half. They did it several times, but Billy Blunt couldn't manage to do it in less time.

After that they tied their ankles together – Billy Blunt's left and Milly-Molly-Mandy's right – with Billy Blunt's scarf, and practised running with three legs across the field. It was such fun, and Milly-Molly-Mandy shouted with laughter sometimes because they just couldn't help falling over. But Billy Blunt was rather solemn, and very keen to do it properly – though even he couldn't keep from letting out a laugh now and then, when they got very entangled.

By the time of the *fête* Billy Blunt was able to get across the meadow in a little over a minute, and their three-legged running was really quite good, so they were full of hopes for winning some prizes in the sports.

The day of the *fête* was nice and fine, even if not very warm. But, as Billy Blunt said, it was just as well to have it a bit cool for the sports. As it was Bank Holiday nearly everybody in the village turned

Off they all started

up, paying their sixpences at the gate, and admiring the flags, and saying 'Hullo!' or 'How do you do?' to each other.

Milly-Molly-Mandy went with her Father and Mother and Grandpa and Grandma and Uncle and Aunty. And little-friend-Susan was there with her mother, who was also looking after Miss Muggins's niece Jilly, as Miss Muggins didn't care much for *fêtes*. And Mr Jakes, the Postman, was there with his wife; and Mr Rudge, the Blacksmith, in his Sunday suit.

There were coconut-shies (Uncle won a coconut); and throwing little hoops (three throws a penny) over things spread out on a table (Mother got a pocket-comb, but she tried to get an alarm-clock), and lots of other fun.

And then the Children's Sports began. Milly-Molly-Mandy paid a penny for a try at walking along a very narrow board to reach a red balloon at the other end, but she toppled off before she got it, and everybody laughed. (Miss Muggins's Jilly got a balloon.)

Then they entered for the three-legged race – little-friend-Susan and Miss Muggins's Jilly together, and Milly-Molly-Mandy and Billy Blunt (because they had practised), and a whole row of other boys and girls.

A man tied their ankles, and shouted 'Go!' and off they all started, and everybody laughed, and couples kept stumbling and tumbling round, but Milly-Molly-Mandy and Billy Blunt careered steadily along till they reached the winning-post!

Then everybody laughed and clapped like anything, and Billy Blunt pulled the string from round their ankles in a great hurry and cleared off, and Milly-Molly-Mandy had to take his box of chocolates for him, as well as her own.

Then there was the hundred yards race for boys. There was one rather shabbily dressed boy who had stood looking on at all the games, so Father asked him if he didn't want to join in, and he said he hadn't any money. So Father paid for him to join in the race, and he looked so pleased!

A man shouted 'Go!' and off went all the boys in a mass – and how they did run! Milly-Molly-Mandy was so excited that she had to keep jumping up and down. But Billy Blunt presently got a little bit ahead of the others. (Milly-Molly-Mandy held herself tight.) And then he got a little bit farther – and so did the shabby boy – only not so far as Billy Blunt. And then Billy Blunt saw him out of the corner of his eye as he ran, and then the race was over, and somehow the shabby boy had won. And he got a striped tin of toffee.

And Billy Blunt grinned at the shabby boy, who looked so happy hugging his tin of toffee, and asked him his name, and where he lived, and would he come and practise racing with him in the meadow next Saturday.

The next day, as Milly-Molly-Mandy and Billy Blunt and one or two others were coming home from school, they saw a big man with a suitcase waiting at the crossroads for the bus, which went every hour into the town. And just as the bus came in sight the man's hat blew off away down the road, ever such a distance. The man looked for a moment as if he didn't know what to do; and then he caught sight of them and shouted:

'Hi! – can any of you youngsters run?'

Milly-Molly-Mandy said, 'Billy Blunt, can!' And

instantly off went Billy Blunt down the road in his best racing style. And just as the bus pulled up at the stopping-place, he picked up the hat and came tearing back with it.

'I should just say you can run!' said the man. 'You've saved me an hour's wait for the next bus, and a whole lot of business besides.'

'What a good thing you were in training!' said Milly-Molly-Mandy to Billy Blunt, as the bus went off.

'Huh! more sense, that, than just racing,' said Billy Blunt, putting his hair straight.

More of
Milly-Molly-Mandy

Contents

The Nice White Cottage
with the Thatched Roof
(where Milly-Molly-
Mandy lives)

The Brook
(where M-M-M
did not wash her face)

The Tree
where
M-M-M
has a nest)

The Oth

(where t
the mu

The Barn

The
Moggs' Cottage
(where little-friend-Susan
and Baby Moggs live)

Short cut to School

Woods

(whe
Mrs Gree
the little
Jessam
live)

Blackberry
Patch

To the Next Village
(where the Picture Show was)

MAP of t

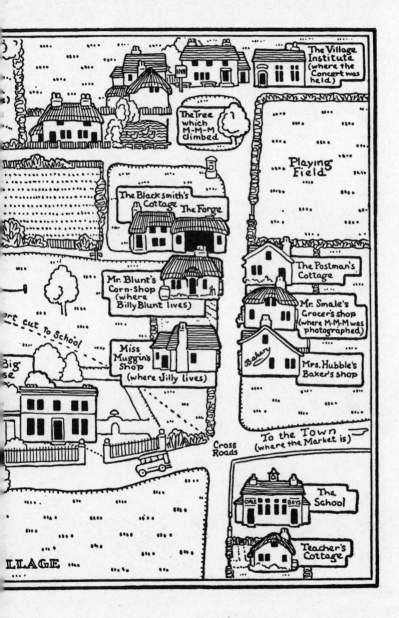

1. Milly-Molly-Mandy Gets Up Early

Once upon a time, one beautiful summer morning, Milly-Molly-Mandy woke up very early.

She knew it was very early, because Father and Mother were not moving (Milly-Molly-Mandy's cot-bed was in one corner of Father's and Mother's room). And she knew it was a beautiful summer morning, because the cracks around the window-blinds were so bright she could hardly look at them.

Milly-Molly-Mandy (whose full name was really Millicent Margaret Amanda) knelt up on the foot of her cot-bed and softly lifted one corner of the blind, and peeped out.

And it was the most beautiful, quiet summer morning that ever was.

The doves in the dove-cote were saying '*Coo-roo-o-o!*' to each other, in a soft, lazy sort of way; and the hens round the hen-house in the field were saying '*Ker-ruk-ruk!*' to each other, in a soft, busy sort of way; and Old Marmaduke the cock was yelling '*Doodle-doo!*' to everybody, at the top of his voice,

133

only it sounded soft because he was right the other side of the barn.

'Well!' said Milly-Molly-Mandy to herself. 'It's much too beautiful a morning to stay in bed till breakfast-time. I think I'll get up very, very quietly, so's not to wake Father and Mother.'

So Milly-Molly-Mandy slid out of bed very, very quietly, and she slid into her socks, and into her clothes as far as her petticoat.

And then she crept to the wash-stand, but she didn't think she could manage the big water-jug without waking Father and Mother. So she took up her shoes and her pink-striped cotton frock, and she creepy-crept to the door and opened it, only making just one tiny little click.

And then she creepy-crept down the stairs, without disturbing Grandpa or Grandma or Uncle or Aunty, into the kitchen.

It looked funny and dark in the kitchen, for the curtains were still drawn. Topsy the cat jumped off Grandma's chair and came yawning and stretching to meet her, and Milly-Molly-Mandy had to stoop down and let Topsy the cat dab her little cold nose very, very lightly against her warm cheek, for 'Good morning'.

And then Milly-Molly-Mandy went into the scullery to wash.

But when she turned on the tap she suddenly thought of the brook at the bottom of the meadow. So she just washed her hands and neck and saved her face to wash in the brook. And then she put on her frock and shoes and softly unlocked the back door, and slipped outside.

It really was a most beautiful fresh morning, full of little bird-voices; and Toby the dog was making little thumping noises in his kennel, because he had heard her and was excited to think somebody was up.

So Milly-Molly-Mandy ran and let him off the chain, but she held his collar and whispered, 'Hush, Toby! Hush, Toby!' very sternly, until they got as far as the meadow.

Then she let him go, and Toby the dog barked and capered, and Milly-Molly-Mandy, with the breeze in her hair, ran hoppity-skip down to the brook through the long grass and dewdrops that sparkled all colours in the sun.

The water looked so lovely and clear and cold, rippling over the stones, that Milly-Molly-Mandy couldn't decide all at once which was the nicest spot to wash her face in. So she was walking along beside it a little way, when suddenly whom should she see in the next field but little-friend-Susan, up early too.

'Su-san!' called Milly-Molly-Mandy.

'Milly-Molly-Mandy!' called little-friend-Susan, 'There're mushrooms in this field!'

So Milly-Molly-Mandy and Toby the dog ran and clambered through the railings into the next field. And there *were* mushrooms in that field, for Milly-Molly-Mandy nearly trod on one straight away. Only she just didn't – she picked it and ran to show it to little-friend-Susan and say, 'Fancy you being up so early, Susan!' And little-friend-Susan ran to show Milly-Molly-Mandy her three mushrooms and say, 'Fancy you being up so early, Milly-Molly-Mandy!'

Then they searched all over the field together, but they didn't find any more mushrooms. And then

they came to another field, and suddenly whom should they see in the middle of the other field but Billy Blunt, up early too.

'Bil-ly' called Milly-Molly-Mandy.

'Mushrooms!' called Billy Blunt.

So Milly-Molly-Mandy and little-friend-Susan and Toby the dog ran and clambered over the stile into the other field, and went to show Billy Blunt their mushrooms and say, 'Fancy you being up so early, Billy!' And Billy Blunt came to show them his two mushrooms and say, 'Fancy anybody stopping in bed!'

And then they found quite a lot of mushrooms growing together in one patch, and they all gave a gasp and a shout and set to work picking in great excitement.

When they had finished gathering whom should they see coming into the field with a basket over his arm but a shabby boy who had run in a race with Billy Blunt at a fête last Bank Holiday (and beaten him!).

He seemed to be looking for mushrooms too; and as he came near Milly-Molly-Mandy smiled at him a bit, and he smiled a bit back. And little-friend-Susan said, 'Hullo!' and he said, 'Hullo!' And Billy Blunt said, 'Plenty of mushrooms here.' And the boy said, 'Are there?'

Then Milly-Molly-Mandy said, 'Look what we've got!' And the boy looked.

And then little-friend-Susan said, 'How many've you got?' And the boy showed his basket, but there weren't many in it.

And then Billy Blunt said, 'What are you going to do with them?'

And the boy said, 'Sell them to Mr Smale the Grocer, if I can get enough. If not, we eat them, my grandad and I. Only we'd rather have the money.'

Then Milly-Molly-Mandy said, 'Let's help to get the basket full!'

So they spread about over the field and looked everywhere for mushrooms, and they really got quite a lot; but the basket wasn't full. Then Billy Blunt and Milly-Molly-Mandy and little-friend-Susan looked questioningly at each other and at their own heap of mushrooms, and then they nodded to each other and piled them all into the basket.

'My word!' said the boy, with a beaming face. 'Won't Grandad be pleased today!' Then he thanked them all very much and said good-bye and went off home.

Milly-Molly-Mandy and little-friend-Susan and Billy Blunt felt very satisfied with their morning's work. They had enjoyed it so much that they made plans to get up early another morning and go mushrooming together, with baskets – for themselves, this time.

And then they all said 'Good-bye' till they should meet again for school, and Milly-Molly-Mandy called Toby the dog, and they went off home to their breakfast.

And it wasn't until she got in that Milly-Molly-Mandy remembered she had never washed her face in the brook after all, and she had to go up and do it in a basin in the ordinary way!

2. Milly-Molly-Mandy Has a Surprise

Once upon a time Milly-Molly-Mandy was helping Mother to fetch some pots of jam down from the little storeroom.

Father and Mother and Grandpa and Grandma and Uncle and Aunty and Milly-Molly-Mandy between them ate quite a lot of jam, so Mother (who made all the jam) had to keep the pots upstairs because the kitchen cupboard wouldn't hold them all.

The little storeroom was up under the thatched roof, and it had a little square window very near to the floor, and the ceiling sloped away on each side so that Father or Mother or Grandpa or Grandma or Uncle or Aunty could stand upright only in the very middle of the room. (But Milly-Molly-Mandy could stand upright anywhere in it.)

When Mother and Milly-Molly-Mandy had found the jams they wanted (strawberry jam and blackberry jam and ginger jam), Mother looked round the little storeroom and said,

'It is a pity I haven't got somewhere else to keep my jam-pots!'

And Milly-Molly-Mandy said, 'Why, Mother, I think this is a very nice place for jam-pots to live in!'

And Mother said, 'Do you?'

But a few days later Father and Mother went up to the little storeroom together and took out all the jam-pots and all the shelves that held the jam-pots, and Father stood them down in the new shed he was making outside the back door, while Mother started cleaning out the little storeroom.

Milly-Molly-Mandy helped by washing the little square window – 'So that my jam-pots can see out!' Mother said.

The next day Milly-Molly-Mandy came upon

Father in the barn, mixing colour-wash in a bucket. It was a pretty colour, just like a pale new primrose, and Milly-Molly-Mandy dabbled in it with a bit of stick for a while, and then she asked what it was for.

And Father said, 'I'm going to do over the walls and ceiling of the little storeroom with it.' And then he added, 'Don't you think it will make the jam-pots feel nice and cheerful?'

And Milly-Molly-Mandy said she was sure the jam-pots would just love it! (It was such fun!)

A little while afterwards Mother sent Milly-Molly-Mandy to the village to buy a packet of green dye at Mr Smale the Grocer's shop. And then Mother dyed some old casement curtains a bright green for the little storeroom window. 'Because,' said Mother, 'the window looks so bare from outside.'

And while she was about it she said she might as well dye the coverlet on Milly-Molly-Mandy's little cot-bed (which stood in one corner of Father's and Mother's room), as the pattern had washed nearly white. So Milly-Molly-Mandy had a nice new bedspread, instead of a faded old one.

The next Saturday, when Grandpa came home from market, he brought with him in the back of the pony-trap a little chest of drawers, which he said he had 'picked up cheap'. He thought it might come in useful for keeping things in, in the little storeroom.

And Mother said, yes, it would come in very useful indeed. So (as it was rather shabby) Uncle, who had been painting the door of the new shed with apple-green paint, painted the little chest of drawers green too, so that it was a very pretty little chest of drawers indeed.

'Well,' said Uncle, 'that ought to make any jam-pot taste sweet!'

Milly-Molly-Mandy began to think the little storeroom would be almost too good just for jam-pots.

Then Aunty decided she and Uncle wanted a new mirror in their room, and she asked Mother if their little old one couldn't be stored up in the little storeroom. And when Mother said it could, Uncle said he might as well use up the last of the green paint, so that he could throw away the tin. So he painted the frame of the mirror green, and it looked a very pretty little mirror indeed.

'Jam-pots don't want to look at themselves,' said Milly-Molly-Mandy. She thought the mirror looked much too pretty for the little storeroom.

'Oh well – a mirror helps to make the room lighter,' said Mother.

Then Milly-Molly-Mandy came upon Grandma

embroidering a pretty little wool bird on either end of a strip of coarse linen. It was a robin, with a brown back and a scarlet front. Milly-Molly-Mandy thought it *was* a pretty cloth: and she wanted to know what it was for.

And Grandma said, 'I just thought it would look nice on the little chest of drawers in the little store-room.' And then she added, 'It might amuse the jam-pots!'

And Milly-Molly-Mandy laughed, and begged Grandma to tell her what the pretty cloth really was for. But Grandma would only chuckle and say it was to amuse the jam-pots.

The next day, when Milly-Molly-Mandy came home from school, Mother said, 'Milly-Molly-Mandy, we've got the little storeroom in order again. Now, would you please run up and fetch me a pot of jam?'

Milly-Molly-Mandy said, 'Yes, Mother. What sort?'

And Father said, 'Blackberry.'

And Grandpa said, 'Marrow-ginger.'

And Grandma said, 'Red-currant.'

And Uncle said, 'Strawberry.'

And Aunty said, 'Raspberry.'

But Mother said, 'Any sort you like, Milly-Molly-Mandy!'

Milly-Molly-Mandy thought something funny must be going to happen, for Father and Mother and Grandpa and Grandma and Uncle and Aunty all looked as if they had got a laugh down inside them. But she ran upstairs to the little storeroom.

And when she opened the door – she saw –

Her own little cot-bed with the green coverlet on, just inside. And the little square window with the green curtains blowing in the wind. And a yellow pot of nasturtiums on the sill. And the little green chest of drawers with the robin cloth on it. And the little green mirror hanging on the primrose wall, with Milly-Molly-Mandy's own face reflected in it.

And then Milly-Molly-Mandy knew that the little storeroom was to be her very own little bed-

She said 'O-h-h-h!' in a very hushed voice

room, and she said 'O-h-h-h!' in a very hushed voice, as she looked all round her room.

Then suddenly she tore downstairs back into the kitchen, and just hugged Father and Mother and Grandpa and Grandma and Uncle and Aunty; and they all said she was their favourite jam-pot and pretended to eat her up!

And Milly-Molly-Mandy didn't know how to wait till bedtime, because she was so eager to go to sleep in the little room that was her Very Own!

3. *Milly-Molly-Mandy Gets Up a Tree*

Once upon a time Milly-Molly-Mandy saw a ladder leaning against the branch of a tree just past the duck-pond at the corner of the village.

It was a nice long ladder and a nice big branch and a nice green spreading tree, and Milly-Molly-Mandy thought how nice to climb the ladder and sit on the branch in the spreading tree and see how much she could see up there!

So she climbed the ladder very carefully, and then she sat on the branch, with the green leaves tickling her legs and flipping up and down on her hat.

It was such a nice place – she could see right down the village street as far as the crossroads (where the red bus was just passing). And she could see right up the white road, with the hedges each side, as far as the nice white cottage with the thatched roof (where she lived with Father and Mother and Grandpa and Grandma and Uncle and Aunty). And she could see at one glance the whole of the duck-pond (where three ducks were waggling their tails and making gabbly sounds in the water with their beaks).

Milly-Molly-Mandy wished she could stay up there all day, only she thought perhaps she had better be getting down now. But she just waited until a cart had passed, and then she just waited until the Grocer's boy had gone out of sight with his basket of groceries. And then she turned carefully to climb down the ladder again.

But Milly-Molly-Mandy had never noticed that the man who left the ladder there had come and fetched it while the cart was rattling past (not dreaming there was anyone up in the tree).

She only saw that the ladder was ab-so-lute-ly gone!

Milly-Molly-Mandy sat and held on and thought. It had felt so nice being up in the tree while she thought she could get down from it any minute; it was very funny, but it didn't feel a little bit nice directly she found she couldn't.

'If I shouted as loud as ever I can, somebody might hear,' thought Milly-Molly-Mandy, 'only

The ladder was ab-so-lute-ly gone!

I'd have to scream so loud they might think I was in trouble, and I'm not really. I only want to get down.'

So Milly-Molly-Mandy held on and thought some more. 'Somebody's sure to go by soon,' thought Milly-Molly-Mandy, 'and then I'll ask them please to help me down.'

So Milly-Molly-Mandy sat and tried to remember how nice the tree was before she found she couldn't get out of it. And while she was thinking that she saw a nest on a branch with a little bird peeping out of it.

'It's all right, Mrs Bird,' said Milly-Molly-Mandy. 'I won't frighten you. I'm *glad* you're here to keep me company.'

And then she saw a little red lady-bird on a leaf. 'Hullo, Mrs Lady-bird!' said Milly-Molly-Mandy. 'You don't mind being up in a tree, do you? I expect you like it quite a lot.' And somehow the tree seemed nicer again.

Presently a horse came slowly clip-clopping along from the crossroads, led by a man, and they walked down the village street; and Milly-Molly-Mandy got all ready to call out politely as soon as they came near enough. But the man turned off by the forge, and the horse clip-clopped after him, to have some new shoes put on.

Next Milly-Molly-Mandy saw Mrs Jakes, the Postman's wife, come out into her back garden and hang up a towel. Milly-Molly-Mandy waved, but Mrs Jakes didn't see her, and went in and shut the door.

Presently Milly-Molly-Mandy saw old Mr Hubble step out of the Baker's shop, and come walking along with his stick. Old Mr Hubble always walked about all day saying, 'Fine morning!' to everybody he met. But when he met Milly-Molly-Mandy he always pretended to give her a little poke with his stick, and it made Milly-Molly-Mandy feel rather shy, as she didn't know quite what to answer to that – she just used to smile a bit and run as hard as she could on her way.

So Milly-Molly-Mandy watched old Mr Hubble and his stick coming along towards her down the street, and wondered if he would see her. And when he didn't, she suddenly felt shy, thinking of his stick, and didn't want to call out as he went past (though a moment afterwards she wished she had, for she didn't *really* think he would poke her with his stick up there).

'Oh dear!' thought Milly-Molly-Mandy. 'I *must* shout out to the next person who comes by.'

The next person who came in sight was a little girl in a white muslin frock, who went into Miss

Muggins's shop. Milly-Molly-Mandy had seen her before – she had just come to live at the Big House with the iron railings, past the crossroads. Presently the little girl came out again with a little paper

bag (Milly-Molly-Mandy wondered if it held raspberry-drops or aniseed-balls). She was rather a long way off, but Milly-Molly-Mandy thought she must try to shout loud enough to make her hear.

But then she couldn't think what to shout! The little girl didn't look quite the sort of little girl you'd suddenly shout 'Hi!' to, and Milly-Molly-Mandy didn't want to call out 'Help!' as if she were falling, and she didn't know the little girl's name. It was really quite awkward.

And then the little girl popped something from

the paper bag into her mouth and wandered down to look at the ducks. And when she got near she suddenly saw Milly-Molly-Mandy up in the tree!

The little girl stopped and looked at Milly-Molly-Mandy, and Milly-Molly-Mandy held on and looked at the little girl. And then the little girl said, 'Can't you get down?'

And Milly-Molly-Mandy said, 'Oh, *please* will you help to get me down? I've been up here such a *long* time!'

So the little girl looked around, and then she ran back to Mr Blunt's garden and beckoned someone to the palings. And then Billy Blunt's head looked over. And then the little girl explained what was the matter. And then Billy Blunt ran out of the garden into the corn-shop. And then Mr Blunt came out of the corn-shop with a long ladder. And then he set the ladder under the tree and climbed up. And then he hoisted Milly-Molly-Mandy off the branch on to his shoulder, and brought her safely down. (And it was good to be on the ground once more!)

Milly-Molly-Mandy said, 'Thank you very much!' to Mr Blunt and Billy Blunt, and then the little girl gave her a raspberry-drop, and they talked. And then they had another raspberry-drop, and the little girl said she had a summer-house in her garden, and asked if Milly-Molly-Mandy would come and play in it with her that afternoon.

So, as soon as Milly-Molly-Mandy had finished dinner, Mother put a clean pink-and-white cotton frock on her, and she ran hoppity-skip all the way down to the village.

And Milly-Molly-Mandy felt very glad indeed that she hadn't called out sooner, or she might never have been invited to play with the little girl at the Big House with the iron railings!

4. Milly-Molly-Mandy Goes to a Concert

Once upon a time Milly-Molly-Mandy was going to a grown-up concert with Father and Mother and Grandpa and Grandma and Uncle and Aunty. (They had all got their tickets.)

It was to be held in the Village Institute at seven o'clock, and it wouldn't be over until quite nine o'clock, which was lovely and late for Milly-Molly-Mandy. But you see this wasn't like an ordinary concert, where people you didn't know sang and did things.

It was a quite extra specially important concert, for Aunty was going to play on the piano on the platform, and the young lady who helped Mrs Hubble in her Baker's shop was going to sing, and some other people whom Milly-Molly-Mandy had heard spoken of were going to do things too. So it was very exciting indeed.

Aunty had a new mauve silk scarf for her neck, and a newly trimmed hat, and her handkerchief was sprinkled with the lavender-water that Milly-Molly-Mandy had given her last Christmas.

Milly-Molly-Mandy felt so proud that it was being used for such a special occasion. (Aunty put a drop on Milly-Molly-Mandy's own handkerchief too.)

When they had all got into their best clothes and shoes, they said good-bye to Toby the dog and Topsy the cat, and started off for the village – Father and Mother and Grandpa and Grandma and Uncle and Aunty and Milly-Molly-Mandy. And they as nearly as possible forgot to take the tickets with them off the mantelpiece! But Mother remembered just in time.

There were several people already in their seats when Father and Mother and Grandpa and Grandma and Uncle and Aunty and Milly-Molly-Mandy got to the Institute. Mr and Mrs Hubble and the young lady who helped them were just in front, and Mr and Mrs Blunt and Mr and Mrs Moggs (little-friend-Susan's father and mother) were just behind (Billy Blunt and little-friend-Susan weren't there, but then they hadn't got an aunty who was going to play on the platform, so it wasn't so important for them to be up late).

The platform looked very nice, with plants in crinkly green paper. And the piano was standing there, all ready for Aunty. People were coming in very fast, and it wasn't long before the hall was full, everybody was talking and rustling programmes. Then people started clapping, and Milly-Molly-Mandy saw that some ladies and gentlemen with violins and things were going up steps on to the platform, with very solemn faces. A lady hit one or two notes on the piano, and the people with violins played a lot of funny noises without taking any notice of each other (Mother said they were 'tuning up'). And then they all started off playing properly, and the concert had begun.

Milly-Molly-Mandy did enjoy it. She clapped as hard as ever she could, and so did everybody else, when the music stopped. After that people sang one at a time, or a lot at a time, or played the piano, and one man sang a funny song (which made Milly-Molly-Mandy laugh and everybody else too).

But Milly-Molly-Mandy was longing for the time to come for Aunty to play.

She was just asking Mother in a whisper when Aunty was going to play, when she heard a queer little sound, just like a dog walking on the wooden floor. And she looked round and saw people at the back of the hall glancing down here and there, smiling and pointing.

And presently what should she feel but a cold, wet nose on her leg, and what should she see but a white, furry object coming out from under her chair.

And there was Toby the dog (without a ticket), looking just as pleased with himself as he could be for having found them!

Milly-Molly-Mandy was very shocked at him, and so was Mother. She said, 'Naughty Toby!' in a whisper, and Father pushed him under the seat and made him lie down. They couldn't disturb the concert by taking him out just then.

So there Toby the dog stayed and heard the concert without a ticket; and now and then Milly-Molly-Mandy put down her hand and Toby the dog licked it and half got up to wag his tail. But Father said, 'Ssh!' so Milly-Molly-Mandy put her hand back in her lap, and Toby the dog settled down again. But they liked being near each other.

Then the time came for the young lady who helped Mrs Hubble to sing, and Aunty to play for her. So the young lady got up and dropped her handbag, and Aunty got up and dropped her music (it made Toby the dog jump!). But they were picked up again, and then Aunty and the young lady went up on to the platform.

And who *do* you think went up with them?

Why, Toby the dog! Looking just as if he thought Aunty had meant him to follow!

Everybody laughed, and Aunty pointed to Toby the dog to go down again. But Toby the dog didn't seem to understand, and he got behind the piano and wouldn't come out.

So Aunty had to play and the young lady to sing with Toby the dog peeping out now and then from behind the piano, and everybody tried not to notice him, lest it should make them laugh.

But still Aunty played beautifully and the young lady sang, and Milly-Molly-Mandy clapped as hard as she could, and so did everybody else when the song was finished. In fact, they all clapped so loud that Toby the dog gave a surprised bark, and everybody laughed again.

They had another try then to get Toby the dog off the platform, but Toby the dog wouldn't come.

Then Father said, 'Milly-Molly-Mandy, you go and see if you can get him.'

So Milly-Molly-Mandy slipped off her seat, past the people's knees, and climbed up the steps on to the platform (in front of all the audience).

And she said, 'Toby, come here!' round the corner of the piano, and Toby the dog put out his nose and sniffed her hand, and Milly-Molly-Mandy was able to catch hold of his collar and pull him out.

She walked right across the platform with Toby the dog in her arms, and everybody laughed, and somebody (I think it was the Blacksmith) called out, 'Bravo! Encore!' and clapped.

And Milly-Molly-Mandy (feeling very hot) hurried down the steps, with Toby the dog licking all over one side of her cheek and hair.

There was only a little bit of the concert to come after that, so Milly-Molly-Mandy stood at the back of the hall with Toby the dog till it was finished. Then everybody started crowding to the door. Most of them smiled at Milly-Molly-Mandy and Toby

She walked right across the platform

the dog as they stood waiting for Father and Mother and Grandpa and Grandma and Uncle and Aunty to come.

Mr Jakes the Postman, passing with Mrs Jakes, said, 'Well, well! I didn't expect to see you turning out a public character just yet awhile, young lady.' And Milly-Molly-Mandy laughed with Mr Jakes.

Then Mr Rudge, the Blacksmith, passed, and he said solemnly, 'You and Toby gave us a very fine performance indeed. If I'd known beforehand I'd have sent you up a bouquet each.' Milly-Molly-Mandy liked the Blacksmith – he was a nice man.

'Well,' said Aunty, as they all walked home together in the dark, 'I think if we'd known Toby was going to perform up on the platform tonight we'd have given him a bath and a new collar first!'

5. *Milly-Molly-Mandy Has her Photo Taken*

Once upon a time, when Milly-Molly-Mandy went down to the village with a list of things Mother wanted from the Grocer's, she saw something new in the middle of Mr Smale the Grocer's shop-window.

It was a board with some photographs of people pinned on, and underneath them was written that Mr D. Hammett would be there to take tasteful and artistic photos for one week only at prices strictly moderate.

When Milly-Molly-Mandy went up the step into

the shop (which always had such a smell of its own, a cardboardy, bacony sort of smell) she looked about, wondering where Mr D. Hammett was and what his camera was like.

She guessed he must be in the little room at the back of the shop, for there was a notice on the door, though it was too dark to read it; and through the door (which was a bit open) she could see part of what looked like a sheet hung up, with grey bulrushes painted on it.

While Mr Smale was taking her order (the raisins and baking-powder she was to bring, as Mother was wanting them, but the other things were too heavy, so Mr Smale was please to send them later) Milly-Molly-Mandy kept her eye on the door at the back of the shop. And presently it opened, and a young man with a pink face (he had just had his photo taken) hurried out of the shop; while another man with a small moustache and his hair parted in the middle said, 'Good morning to you, sir,' from the doorway.

Milly-Molly-Mandy guessed this must be Mr D. Hammett himself, but she did not stare at him.

Mr D. Hammett said, 'Good morning, young lady. Wouldn't you like to have your photo taken?'

Milly-Molly-Mandy said, 'No, thank you,' but she took one of his handbills which he gave her.

And while she was walking back along the white road with the hedges each side she read it all through.

And she found the price for one person alone was one shilling each photograph, artistically mounted. (If you wanted a group it was more money.) Milly-Molly-Mandy had exactly one shilling in her money-box, which was very funny. She had counted it only yesterday, all in pennies.

When Milly-Molly-Mandy got home to the nice white cottage with the thatched roof, she was just going to give Mother the handbill, with the raisins and baking-powder, when all of a sudden she thought she wouldn't, for she had an idea! It was a very exciting idea indeed! Milly-Molly-Mandy wondered if she could ever do it – it was such an exciting idea!

And this is what the idea was: She would have her photo taken all by herself, without telling anybody, and give it to Mother for a surprise present!

That very afternoon Milly-Molly-Mandy slipped up to her little bedroom, and brushed her hair and put on her hat and pulled up her socks and washed her hands and face and got the pennies out of her money-box. And she was just creeping downstairs when Aunty called:

'Milly-Molly-Mandy! Uncle is driving me into the town to get some material. Do you want to come too?'

Milly-Molly-Mandy didn't like to say no, because they would wonder why, as she generally liked the chance of a drive in the pony-trap to see all the shops and things. So she had to put off going to the photographer's that day.

Next day Milly-Molly-Mandy tidied up again and swung on the gate for a little while before she went down to the village, so that nobody should wonder where or why she was going.

But when she got to the village, whom should she meet but Miss Muggins's niece, Jilly. And Miss Muggins's Jilly said, 'Hullo, Milly-Molly-Mandy! Where're you going?'

Milly-Molly-Mandy didn't want to tell Miss Muggins's Jilly her secret, so they stood and talked for a bit. But Miss Muggins's Jilly didn't seem as if she would go, so at last Milly-Molly-Mandy had just to walk back home again, with her pennies still in her hand!

The next day Grandma wanted Milly-Molly-Mandy to get her some wool from Miss Muggins's shop, and Milly-Molly-Mandy thought she might perhaps manage to be photographed at the same time. So she tidied herself carefully and set off.

But as she passed the Moggs's cottage little-friend-Susan popped her head over the wall and said, 'Hullo, Milly-Molly-Mandy! Where're you going? Wait for me!' So they went on together.

When Milly-Molly-Mandy had got the wool from Miss Muggins's shop, she said, 'You'd better not wait for me, Susan – I think perhaps I'm going to the Grocer's next.'

But little-friend-Susan said, 'Oh, I don't mind waiting. You won't be long, will you?'

Milly-Molly-Mandy thought a moment. After all, little-friend-Susan was a 'best friend'. So she said in a whisper, 'Susan, if you won't say a single tiny word I'll tell you a great secret! I'm going to get my photo taken for Mother! But you're not to say a single tiny word, Susan.'

Little-friend-Susan solemnly promised not to say a single tiny word about it, and then she waited patiently while Milly-Molly-Mandy went into Mr Smale the Grocer's shop, holding her pennies very tight.

Mr D. Hammett said he was fortunately disengaged at that moment, so he took her straight into the back room where the bulrush sheet was hanging. Milly-Molly-Mandy gave him her handful of pennies lest she should drop them in the middle of the photographing.

And then Mr D. Hammett stood her by a little table in front of the bulrush sheet, and he took some flowers out of a vase and gave them to her to hold. (Milly-Molly-Mandy didn't much like it, because the stalks were wet!)

Then Mr D. Hammett put a black cloth over his head and moved his camera's long legs about. And then he said, 'Do you think you could manage a smile – just a very little one?' But Milly-Molly-Mandy felt as if she didn't know a bit how to smile – it all felt so solemn and queer. So Mr D. Hammett took the photo as she was.

And then he took the flowers from her hand and said that the photo would be ready on the morrow, if she would kindly call for it, and he bowed her out. And Milly-Molly-Mandy felt very glad that little-friend-Susan was outside waiting for her.

After breakfast next day Milly-Molly-Mandy said to Mother, 'Mother, would you like something nice to happen today?'

And Mother said, 'I always like something nice to happen, Milly-Molly-Mandy!'

Then Milly-Molly-Mandy said, 'I think – I'm not sure, but I *think* – something extra nice is going to happen today!' And Mother was very pleased.

When Milly-Molly-Mandy went down to the village it was too early, and the photo wasn't

'Do you think you could manage a smile?'

finished yet, but Mr D. Hammett said it would be ready that afternoon.

At dinner-time Mother said, 'Milly-Molly-Mandy, hasn't the nice thing happened yet? I'm getting so excited.'

And Milly-Molly-Mandy said, 'It's very nearly happened. I wonder if you're going to like it!' Mother was quite sure that she was; and Father and Grandpa and Grandma and Uncle and Aunty were all very curious.

That afternoon Mr D. Hammett had the photo ready for her, wrapped in paper, and Milly-Molly-Mandy ran nearly all the way home with it. (She stopped a minute at the Moggs's cottage to show it to little-friend-Susan, who thought it was lovely.)

She ran straight into the kitchen and put it in Mother's lap, on the darning-bag, and stood holding herself in very tight.

Mother said, 'Oh, Milly-Molly-Mandy! I do believe the nice thing has really happened!' She opened the paper very slowly and carefully, and took out the photograph, stuck on a beautiful card with crinkled edges.

And when Mother looked at the photograph she said: 'Why! If it isn't a picture of my little Milly-Molly-Mandy, looking as solemn as a little owl!'

And Mother and Milly-Molly-Mandy laughed

and hugged each other, while Father and Grandpa and Grandma and Uncle and Aunty all looked at the photograph in turn.

Then Mother wanted it back, and she put it on the mantelpiece where they could all see it.

And Mother thought it was a lovely surprise present, though she couldn't help laughing each time she looked at it. But that, said Mother, was only because she was so *very pleased*!

6. Milly-Molly-Mandy Goes to the Pictures

Once upon a time Milly-Molly-Mandy found out there was a moving-picture show every Saturday evening in the next village. (It was the young lady who helped Mrs Hubble in the Baker's shop who told her.)

Milly-Molly-Mandy told Father and Mother and Grandpa and Grandma and Uncle and Aunty directly she got home to the nice white cottage with the thatched roof. And Father and Mother and Grandpa and Grandma and Uncle and Aunty thought they might go one Saturday evening for a special treat (with Milly-Molly-Mandy of course), in the red bus that ran between their village and the next.

So one Saturday evening, early, they all put on their hats and coats and walked down through the village to the crossroads (where the red bus always stopped).

As they passed the Moggs's cottage little-friend-Susan was swinging on her swing, and Milly-Molly-Mandy waved to her and said, 'Hullo, Susan! We're going in the bus to the pictures!'

And little-friend-Susan waved back and said, 'We're going next Saturday!' So Milly-Molly-Mandy felt very glad for little-friend-Susan.

As they passed Mr Blunt's corn-shop Billy Blunt was making himself a scooter in the little garden at the side, and Milly-Molly-Mandy waved to him and said, 'Hullo, Billy! We're going in the bus to the pictures!'

And Billy Blunt looked round with a grin and said, 'I went last Saturday!' So Milly-Molly-Mandy felt very glad for Billy Blunt.

When they came to the crossroads the red bus was just in sight, and Milly-Molly-Mandy gave a little skip, because it was very exciting.

Then the red bus came close and pulled up, and they all crowded to the steps, Father and Mother and Grandpa and Grandma and Uncle and Aunty and Milly-Molly-Mandy.

But the Conductor put out his hand and said loudly. 'Only room for two!'

So they had to decide quickly who should go. Uncle and Aunty wanted Grandpa and Grandma to go, and Grandpa and Grandma wanted Father and Mother to go, and Father and Mother wanted not to go at all if they couldn't all go together.

Then Grandpa and Grandma and Uncle and Aunty said, 'Milly-Molly-Mandy will be so disappointed if she doesn't see the pictures. You take her, Father and Mother – there'll be room for her on your lap.'

Then the Conductor said, 'Hurry up, please!' (but quite kindly), so Father and Mother with Milly-Molly-Mandy hurried up into the red bus and squeezed past the other people into the two seats.

And Milly-Molly-Mandy, standing between Father's knees while he got the money out of his pocket, watched Grandpa and Grandma and Uncle and Aunty getting smaller and smaller in the distance, until she couldn't see them any more.

And Milly-Molly-Mandy felt very sorry indeed they weren't coming to the pictures too.

Then Mother said, 'Well, Milly-Molly-Mandy,

we must enjoy ourselves all we can, or Grandpa and Grandma and Uncle and Aunty will be so disappointed, because they wanted us to enjoy ourselves.'

So Milly-Molly-Mandy cheered up and began to look out of the windows, and at the other people in the bus. Mr Rudge, the Blacksmith, was sitting in the farther corner, and he smiled a nice twinkly smile at Milly-Molly-Mandy, and Milly-Molly Mandy smiled back. (They couldn't talk because the bus made such a rattly noise.)

Then they came to the next village and got down.

The coloured posters outside the place where the

picture show was to be looked very exciting, and
Milly-Molly-Mandy did wish Grandpa and Grandma and Uncle and Aunty could see them. But she
thought she would look at everything and remember
very carefully, so that she could tell them all about
it when they got home.

The pictures were lovely! There was a very nice
man who rescued a lady just in time (Milly-Molly-
Mandy knew he would); and there was a funny man
who ran about a lot and fell into a dust-bin; and
there was a quite close-up picture of the Prince of
Wales, and someone with feathers on his hat, whom
Father said was the King (the people clapped a lot,
and so did Milly-Molly-Mandy).

The light went out once, and they had to turn up
the gas for a little while, till they got it right; and
Milly-Molly-Mandy could see where the Blacksmith
was sitting. And there was a lady who looked
awfully like Aunty over on the other side (only she
had a little boy with her), and someone who might
easily have been Grandpa. And then the light came
again and they turned off the gas, and the picture
went on till the end.

Milly-Molly-Mandy was sorry when it was all
over. If only Grandpa and Grandma and Uncle and
Aunty could have been there it would have been
just perfect.

They went out quite close to the lady who looked like Aunty, and she really did look like Aunty, back view.

And then Milly-Molly-Mandy heard Father and Mother talking to someone and exclaiming; and she looked up, and there was Uncle! And Grandpa and Grandma were just behind! And the lady who looked like Aunty turned round, and it *was* Aunty! And she wasn't with the little boy at all, he belonged to somebody else.

And then Grandpa and Grandma and Uncle and Aunty explained how the lady who lived at the Big House with the iron railings near the crossroads was taking her little girl in their car to the pictures (the same little girl who helped Milly-Molly-Mandy that time when she got stuck up in a tree); and she passed while they were watching the red bus go out of sight, and offered them a lift. So they had a lovely ride, and arrived in time not to miss any of the pictures!

And when Father and Mother and Grandpa and Grandma and Uncle and Aunty and Milly-Molly-Mandy came out into the street, there was the car outside, and the lady who lived at the Big House with the iron railings smiled to them all and said, 'There's room for four going back, if you don't mind sitting close!'

Father and Mother and Grandpa and Grandma got in

And the little girl with her said, 'There's room for Milly-Molly-Mandy too, isn't there?'

So Father and Mother and Grandpa and Grandma got in, and the little girl and Milly-Molly-Mandy sat on their laps. (Uncle and Aunty went back by the red bus.)

And they had the loveliest possible ride home – just like the wind, and without any rattly noise. Milly-Molly-Mandy only wished it could have been twice as long.

So altogether it was very nice indeed that there had been only room for two on the bus going in!

7. Milly-Molly-Mandy Goes for a Picnic

Once upon a time, one fine morning, Milly-Molly-Mandy met little-friend-Susan. (She was eating hawthorn berries from the hedge by the roadside.)

Milly-Molly-Mandy said, 'Hullo, Susan' (eating a hawthorn berry too, in a friendly way).

And little-friend-Susan said, 'Hullo, Milly-Molly-Mandy! What do you think I'm going to do today? I'm going to take my dinner out, because Mother's busy. Look at my pockets!'

So Milly-Molly-Mandy looked, and in one of little-friend-Susan's coat pockets was a packet of bread-and-butter, and in the other was a hard-

boiled egg and an apple. Milly-Molly-Mandy thought it was a very nice thing to do indeed, and she began to feel hungry straight away.

Little-friend-Susan said, 'Couldn't you go and

see if your mother is busy? Maybe she'd like you to take your dinner out too.'

So Milly-Molly-Mandy gave a little skip, and ran back to the nice white cottage with the thatched roof to ask Mother.

And Mother looked at Milly-Molly-Mandy consideringly, and said, 'Well, maybe I can manage to be too busy to give you your dinner properly today, Milly-Molly-Mandy.'

And Milly-Molly-Mandy gave another little skip, because she was so pleased.

So Mother gave her a packet of bread-and-butter to put in one coat pocket, and a hard-boiled egg and an apple to put in the other, and told her to take her scarf and not to go in damp places and get muddy. And then Milly-Molly-Mandy gave Mother a kiss for good-bye and thank-you, and ran out to little-friend-Susan, and they started off down the road with their bulging pockets.

When they came near the village they met Billy Blunt walking along, and Milly-Molly-Mandy said, 'Hullo, Billy! Where're you going?'

And Billy Blunt said, 'Home to dinner.'

Then Milly-Molly-Mandy said, 'Susan and I are taking our dinners out because our mothers are busy. Look at our pockets!'

So Billy Blunt looked and saw the packets of

bread-and-butter in one of their coat-pockets, and the hard-boiled eggs and apples in the other, and he thought it was a very nice thing to do indeed, and he began to feel even more hungry than he did before.

Milly-Molly-Mandy said, 'Couldn't you go and see if your mother is busy? Perhaps she'd like you to take your dinner out too!'

So Billy Blunt thought a moment, and then he went in to ask his mother. And Mrs Blunt said, yes, he could if he liked; and she gave him a packet of bread-and-butter to put in one coat-pocket, and a hard-boiled egg and an apple for the other. And Billy Blunt came out and joined Milly-Molly-Mandy and little-friend-Susan, all having bulging pockets.

Then Billy Blunt said, 'Where're you planning to go?'

And Milly-Molly-Mandy and little-friend-Susan said, 'Down by the crossroads and along to the woods'.

Billy Blunt thought a moment, but he couldn't think of anywhere better, so they all started off with their bulging pockets.

As they passed the Big House with the iron railings by the crossroads the lady who lived there (her name was Mrs Green) was just getting her motor-

The little girl Jessamine said, 'Hullo, Milly-Molly-Mandy!'

car out; and the little girl (her name was Jessamine) was waiting by the gate.

Milly-Molly-Mandy smiled as they passed, and the little girl Jessamine said, 'Hullo, Milly-Molly-Mandy! Mother and I are taking our dinners out because Cook's away. Look at our basket!'

So Milly-Molly-Mandy said, 'We're taking our dinners out too! Look at our pockets!'

And then Mrs Green came up and said, 'Are we all taking our dinners out? What fun! Wouldn't you like to come with us and eat them on the Downs?'

That meant going for a ride in the motor-car, so of course Milly-Molly-Mandy and little-friend-Susan and Billy Blunt said 'Yes!' and Billy Blunt added 'Thank you!' so Milly-Molly-Mandy and little-friend-Susan added 'Thank you!' too.

So Mrs Green went back for three more mugs and some rugs and scarves and things. And then she said, 'Pile in!'

So they all piled into the car – the little girl Jessamine and Milly-Molly-Mandy and little-friend-Susan in the back (because they wanted to be together), and Billy Blunt in front beside Mrs Green (because he wanted to see how she drove) – and off they all started.

And it was fun!

Milly-Molly-Mandy hadn't been for a drive in a real car before, except once when Mrs Green had given Father and Mother and Grandpa and Grandma and herself a lift home from the pictures. Of course she had been in the red bus several times, and once the man who drove the milk-cans to the station every morning had given her a ride just for fun. But that was very rattly and different.

Mrs Green's car went so quickly, and the sun shone and the wind blew (how it did blow), and Milly-Molly-Mandy felt she wanted to shout at the top of her voice because she was so happy. Only of course she didn't – she just talked with the little girl Jessamine and little-friend-Susan about the Downs, and their favourite cakes, and that sort of thing. And Billy Blunt talked with Mrs Green (sometimes), asking what different bits of machinery were for, and watching what she did with them, and longing to have a try at driving himself.

When they came to the Downs they had a lovely time. They made a fire of sticks, not too close to a tree (for trees don't like their leaf-hair singed or their bark-clothes burned), and not too close to the bracken (for dry bracken sometimes burns more than you mean it to), but just in a nice sensible place.

Then Mrs Green made hot cocoa in a saucepan

187

and poured it into their mugs, and everybody brought out their packets of food. (Mrs Green and the little girl Jessamine had bread-and-butter and

hard-boiled eggs and apples too.) And Mrs Green cut up a cherry cake into big slices, and they all had to help to eat it up.

It was a lovely meal. Milly-Molly-Mandy couldn't think why anybody wanted to eat their dinner indoors.

Afterwards they carefully buried all their egg-shells and papers, and put the fire quite out, and left everything tidy, and then they set to work filling their empty pockets with acorns and conkers. But

Milly-Molly-Mandy collected fir-cones, because Father and Mother and Grandpa and Grandma and Uncle and Aunty did like a fir-cone fire; and she got her pockets and her bread-and-butter bag and her hat quite full.

When the time came to go home, Mrs Green drove them back to the village. And when Milly-Molly-Mandy and little-friend-Susan and Billy Blunt said good-bye and thank you, Mrs Green said:

'You must all come and have games with Jessamine some evening soon.'

The little girl Jessamine gave a skip, because she was pleased, and Milly-Molly-Mandy and little-friend-Susan and Billy-Blunt said 'Thank you very much!' again, though they didn't skip because they didn't feel they knew Mrs Green quite well enough just yet.

But they skipped like anything *inside*. (And after all, that's the best place to do it!)

8. Milly-Molly-Mandy Looks for a Name

Once upon a time something very surprising happened. Milly-Molly-Mandy couldn't remember anything happening before that was quite so surprising.

She came down to breakfast one morning and Aunty wasn't there, and Mother said Aunty had gone round to help Mrs Moggs.

Milly-Molly-Mandy wondered why Mrs Moggs should want helping, and Grandma said someone had come to stay at the Moggs's cottage, and little-friend-Susan would probably be wanting to tell Milly-Molly-Mandy all about it herself soon.

Milly-Molly-Mandy said, 'Is it someone Susan likes to have staying in their house?' And Mother and Grandma both said they were sure little-friend-Susan was very pleased indeed. Milly-Molly-Mandy couldn't think who it could possibly be.

But directly after breakfast little-friend-Susan came round to call for Milly-Molly-Mandy, because she couldn't wait till Milly-Molly-Mandy came to call for her on the way to school.

And little-friend-Susan was so bursting with excitement and importance that she could hardly speak at first. And then she held Milly-Molly-Mandy tight and said:

'Milly-Molly-Mandy, I've got a little baby sister come to live in our house and it's too small to have a name yet and it hasn't got any hair!'

Milly-Molly-Mandy was so surprised that she couldn't say anything at first except 'Susan!' And then she did so wish it could have been her little baby sister. But little-friend-Susan said generously, 'You can share it, Milly-Molly-Mandy, and it can be your nearly-sister, and we'll take it out riding in the pram together!'

Then Milly-Molly-Mandy asked about its name,

191

and little-friend-Susan said they were looking out
for a nice one for it; so Milly-Molly-Mandy said she
would help to look too, because they must find an
extra-specially nice name.

Milly-Molly-Mandy walked all the way to school
almost without saying anything, because she was so
busy thinking about the little baby sister and what
its name was to be.

When Miss Muggins's niece Jilly caught them up
at the school gate, Milly-Molly-Mandy said,
'Susan's got a new little baby sister!'

And Miss Muggins's Jilly said, 'Has she? I've got
a new kite, and it's got a tail that long!' (which was
rather disappointing of Miss Muggins's Jilly).

Little-friend-Susan said, 'It hasn't got any name
yet.'

And Miss Muggins's Jilly said, 'Hasn't it? My
doll's name's Gladys.' But Milly-Molly-Mandy
didn't like that name much.

After school they met Billy Blunt going home,
and Milly-Molly-Mandy said, 'Susan's got a new
little baby sister!'

And Billy Blunt said, 'I'd rather have a puppy.'
(Which sounded rather queer of Billy Blunt; but
anyhow, next day when Mrs Blunt sent him to the
Moggs's cottage with a bag of oranges for Mrs
Moggs, he bought a little pink rattle at Miss Mug-

gins's shop and put it in the bag. And nobody knew it was from Billy Blunt till they thanked Mrs Blunt for it and she said she didn't know anything about it.)

When they passed the forge the Blacksmith was working the handle of the great bellows up and down to make the fire roar, and after watching for a minute or two Milly-Molly-Mandy couldn't help saying to him, 'Susan's got a new little baby sister!'

And the Blacksmith said, 'Well, well, well! You don't say!' and almost dropped the handle (which was very satisfactory of the Blacksmith).

Then little-friend-Susan said, 'It hasn't got a name yet!'

And the Blacksmith (whose name was Mr Thomas Rudge) said, 'Ah! Thomas is the very best name I know. If she's a young lady you call her Thomasina!'

Milly-Molly-Mandy and little-friend-Susan didn't like that name very much, but they liked the Blacksmith – his eyes were so twinkly.

When Milly-Molly-Mandy got home to the nice white cottage with the thatched roof she saw Mrs Hurley's little hand-cart just outside the gate, and Mrs Hurley standing at the side of it cutting up fish.

Mrs Hurley came round every month selling fish (the in-between times she was selling fish in other villages), and she was very nice and fat and red-cheeked, and she cleaned the fish and slapped them about on the board on top of her cart so quickly that Milly-Molly-Mandy always loved to watch her.

So now she stopped and said, 'Hullo, Mrs Hurley!'

And Mrs Hurley said, 'Well, my darlin', and I'm glad to see you!' (Mrs Hurley always called people darlin'.)

So Milly-Molly-Mandy stood and watched Mrs Hurley slap the fish about briskly as she cleaned them with her red hands (for the wind was sometimes very cold and so were the fish, though Mrs Hurley never minded). And then Milly-Molly-Mandy said, 'Little-friend-Susan's got a new little baby sister!'

And Mrs Hurley wiped her knife on a piece of newspaper and reached for another fish and said, 'You don't tell me that! Well, to be sure! That's fine, that is!'

And Milly-Molly-Mandy said, 'Yes, isn't it? And it hasn't got a name yet, and it's my nearly-sister, so I'm looking out for one. What are your children's names, Mrs Hurley?'

'*What are your children's names, Mrs Hurley?*'

Mrs Hurley said, 'There's Sally (she's my eldest), and Rosy, and Minty (her name's Ermyntrude), and Gerty, and Poppy, and – let me see, all the rest is boys, so that's no good to you.'

But Milly-Molly-Mandy didn't like any of those names very much. 'I thought of Mayflower, which is a princess's name in a book, but it spoils it to put Moggs after it,' said Milly-Molly-Mandy. 'It's quite difficult to find a name for a baby, isn't it, Mrs Hurley?'

But Mrs Hurley, putting the fish which Milly-Molly-Mandy's mother had bought on to a plate, said cheerfully, 'Well, then, you can be thankful it's only one, my darlin'. I had to find eleven for mine, bless their hearts!'

And then she gave Milly-Molly-Mandy a little fish just for her very own self to eat for her supper – 'to celebrate the new little friend,' Mrs Hurley said. Milly-Molly-Mandy *was* pleased!

While she was eating her little fish (nicely fried) for supper, and enjoying it very much, and Father and Mother and Grandpa and Grandma and Uncle and Aunty were eating their ordinary fish (and enjoying it too), they all talked about names.

Grandpa said, 'I guess Emily's a nice enough name for anybody.' (Emily was Grandma's name.)

But somehow Milly-Molly-Mandy didn't think it would suit the new little baby.

Grandma said, 'I used to know a little girl called Holly – she always had her dresses trimmed with red or green.' Milly-Molly-Mandy thought that was quite a nice name.

Father said, 'I prefer Polly to Holly, myself.' But Milly-Molly-Mandy didn't want the baby to have a name which really belonged to Mother.

Mother said, 'How do you like Primrose? It sounds fresh and pretty.' Milly-Molly-Mandy thought it sounded a very nice name.

Uncle said, 'What about Sarah Jane?' But Milly-Molly-Mandy didn't like that name at all.

Aunty said, 'Try Amaryllis!' But Milly-Molly-Mandy couldn't say it very easily.

So she thought over Holly and Primrose, which she liked best. And then she decided, as the baby had come in the spring-time, it had better be Primrose.

So next morning she went round earlier to the Moggs's cottage on the way to school, to ask little-friend-Susan if the baby could be named Primrose.

But what do you think? Mrs Moggs had got a name for the baby already.

And it was Doris Moggs!

And though Milly-Molly-Mandy would much, *much* rather it had been called Primrose, yet when she was allowed to see it, and it held her tightly by

one finger (with its eyes closed), she felt she didn't care a bit what it was named – it was so sweet just as it was! (And, anyhow, it was Mrs Moggs's own baby, after all!)

9. Milly-Molly-Mandy Gets Locked In

Once upon a time Milly-Molly-Mandy got locked in her little bedroom (which had been the little storeroom up under the thatched roof).

No, she hadn't been naughty or anything like that, and nobody locked her in. But the latch on the door had gone just a bit wrong, somehow, so that once or twice Milly-Molly-Mandy had had to turn the handle several times before she could open it; so Mother said perhaps she had better not close it quite, till Father found time to mend it.

But one Saturday morning, when Milly-Molly-Mandy had helped Mother with the breakfast things and Aunty with the beds, she went up to her own little room to make the bed there, and Topsy the cat ran up with her.

Now Topsy the cat just loved Milly-Molly-Mandy to make her bed on Saturday mornings.

She would jump into the middle of the mattress and crouch down; and then Milly-Molly-Mandy would pretend not to know Topsy the cat was there at all. And she would thump the pillows and roll

Topsy the cat about with them, and whisk the sheets and blankets over and pretend to try to smooth out the lump that was Topsy the cat underneath; and Topsy the cat would come crawling out,

looking very untidy, and make a dive under the next blanket. (And it took quite a long while to make that bed sometimes!)

Well, Milly-Molly-Mandy had got the bed made at last, and then she was so out of breath she backed up against the door to rest a bit, while Topsy the cat sat in the middle of the coverlet to tidy herself up.

And it wasn't until Milly-Molly-Mandy had tidied her own hair and had wrapped her duster round Topsy the cat (so as to carry them both downstairs together) that she found she couldn't open the door, which had shut with a bang when she leaned against it!

'Well!' said Milly-Molly-Mandy to Topsy the cat, 'now what are we going to do?' She put Topsy the cat down and tried the door again.

But she couldn't open it.

Then she called 'Mother!' But Mother was downstairs in the kitchen, getting bowls and baking-tins ready for making cakes (as it was Saturday morning).

Then Milly-Molly-Mandy called 'Aunty!' But Aunty was in the parlour, giving it an extra good dusting (as it wouldn't get much next day, being Sunday).

Then Milly-Molly-Mandy called 'Grandma!' But Grandma was round by the back door, sprinkling crumbs for the birds (as it was just their busy time with all the hungry baby-birds hatching out).

'Well!' said Milly-Molly-Mandy to Topsy the cat, 'this *is* a waste of a nice fine Saturday!'

She went to the little low window, but the only person she could see was Uncle, looking like a little speck at the farther end of the meadow, doing something to his chicken-houses. Father, she knew, had gone to the next village to give someone advice about a garden; and Grandpa had gone to market.

'Well!' said Milly-Molly-Mandy to Topsy the cat, 'if I'd only got legs like a grasshopper I could just jump down – but I'd rather have my own legs, anyhow!'

Then she thought if she had a long enough piece of string she could touch the ground that way, and if she dangled it someone might see from the downstairs windows.

So she took the cord from her dressing-gown, and then she tied to it a piece of string from her coat-pocket. And a piece of mauve ribbon which Aunty had given her. And the belt from her frock. And her two boot-laces (Topsy the cat got quite interested). And then she tied her little yellow basket on the end, and dangled and swung it out of the window backward and forward in front of the scullery window below.

But nobody came, and at last Milly-Molly-Mandy got tired of this and tied the end of the line on to the window-catch, and drew her head in again.

'Well!' said Milly-Molly-Mandy to Topsy the cat. 'It's a good thing I've got such a nice little bedroom to be shut up in, anyhow!' Topsy the cat just turned herself round and round on the bed and settled down for a sleep.

Then Milly-Molly-Mandy suddenly remembered her crochet work, carefully wrapped up in a handkerchief on her little green chest of drawers. It was to be a bonnet for Baby Moggs (little-friend-Susan's new little sister and her own nearly-sister). It was of pale pink wool, and she was making it rather big because Mother thought Baby Moggs might grow a bit before the bonnet was finished. (Milly-Molly-Mandy did hope Baby Moggs wouldn't grow too fast.)

So Milly-Molly-Mandy sat in the middle of the floor and began crocheting.

Crocheting is quite hard work when you've done only three and a half rows in all your life before, but Milly-Molly-Mandy crocheted and crocheted until she reached the end of the row; and then she turned round and crocheted and crocheted all the way back. So that was a row and a half.

Then she heard the window-catch on which her line was tied give a little click, and she jumped up and looked out to see if someone were touching her line. But nobody was about, though she called.

But it looked as if there were something in the little yellow basket, so Milly-Molly-Mandy pulled it up in a hurry. And what do you think? In the little yellow basket was a little paperful of that nice crunchy sugar which comes inside the big lumps of peel you put in cakes. (Mother had thought the basket and line was just a game of Milly-Molly-Mandy's, and she popped the sugar in for a surprise.)

'How nice!' thought Milly-Molly-Mandy, and she dropped the little yellow basket outside again (hoping something else would be put in it) and went back to her crochet-work. And she crocheted and crunched, and crunched and crocheted, until she had done four whole rows and eaten up all the paperful of sugar.

Then, after all this time, Milly-Molly-Mandy heard Mother's voice calling outside:

'Milly-Molly-Mandy!'

And when Milly-Molly-Mandy jumped up and looked out, Mother (who had come to see if there was enough rhubarb up yet to make a tart) said, 'What are you doing, dear? You ought to be outdoors!'

So Milly-Molly-Mandy was able to tell Mother all about it; and then Mother came running up to Milly-Molly-Mandy's bedroom door.

But Mother couldn't open it, though she tried hard – and neither could Aunty.

So Mother kissed Milly-Molly-Mandy through the crack, and said she must just wait till Father came home and then he would get her out. And Milly-Molly-Mandy kissed Mother back through the crack, and sat down to her crochet-work again.

Presently the line outside the window clicked at the catch again, and Milly-Molly-Mandy looked out just in time to see Mother whisking out of sight round the corner of the cottage, and there was a big red apple in the little yellow basket! So Milly-Molly-Mandy pulled it up again, and then went back and did her crocheting between big bites at the big red apple.

And she crocheted and she crocheted and she crocheted.

Just before dinner-time Father came back, and Mother took him straight up to Milly-Molly-Mandy's bedroom door, and they tinkered about with the lock for a while, rattling and clicking and tapping.

And Milly-Molly-Mandy went on crocheting.

Then Father said through the crack, 'I'll have to break the lock, Milly-Molly-Mandy, so you mustn't mind a noise!'

Milly-Molly-Mandy put her crochet-work down, and said, 'No, Father!' (It was rather exciting!)

Then Father fetched a great big hammer, and he gave some great big bangs on the lock, and the door came bursting open in a great hurry, and Father and Mother came in. (They had to stoop their heads in Milly-Molly-Mandy's room, because it was so little and sloping.)

Milly-Molly-Mandy was so pleased to see them.

She held up her crochet-work and said, 'Look! I've crocheted nine whole rows and I haven't dropped one single stitch! Don't you think it's enough now, before you start doing it different to make it fit at the back?'

And Mother said, 'That's fine, Milly-Molly-Mandy! I'll look at it directly after dinner and see, but you'd better come downstairs now.'

So Milly-Molly-Mandy came downstairs, and they all had dinner and talked about locks and about getting new ones.

And then Mother looked at Milly-Molly-Mandy's crochet-work. And it only wanted just a little more doing to it (most of which Mother showed Milly-Molly-Mandy how to do, but some she had to do herself); and quite soon the bonnet was finished, and Milly-Molly-Mandy took it round to the Moggs's cottage in tissue paper.

It just fitted Baby Moggs perfectly!

Mrs Moggs and little-friend-Susan looked at it most admiringly, and then Mrs Moggs put it on Baby Moggs's head and tied it under her soft little chin.

And it just fitted Baby Moggs perfectly!

(But, you know, as Milly-Molly-Mandy crocheted very tightly indeed – being her first try – it was a good thing she had planned to leave enough room for Baby Moggs to grow, and a very good thing she got locked in and finished it before Baby Moggs had any time to grow, for the bonnet was only just big enough.

But you can't *think* what a darling Baby Moggs looked in it!)

10. Milly-Molly-Mandy's Mother Goes Away

Once upon a time Milly-Molly-Mandy's Mother went away from the nice white cottage with the thatched roof for a whole fortnight's holiday.

Milly-Molly-Mandy's Mother hardly ever went away for holidays – in fact, Milly-Molly-Mandy could only remember her going away once before, a long time ago (and that was only for two days).

Mrs Hooker, Mother's friend in the next town, invited her. Mrs Hooker wanted to have a holiday by the sea, and she didn't want to go alone, as it isn't so much fun, so she wrote and asked Mother to come with her.

When Mother read the letter first, she said it was very kind of Mrs Hooker, but she couldn't possibly go, as she didn't see how ever Father and Grandpa and Grandma and Uncle and Aunty and Milly-Molly-Mandy would get on without her to cook dinners for them, and wash clothes for them, and see after things.

But Aunty said she could manage to do the cooking and the washing, somehow; and Grandma said she could do Aunty's sweeping and dusting; and Milly-Molly-Mandy said she would help all she knew how; and Father and Grandpa and Uncle said they wouldn't be fussy, or make any more work than they could help.

And then they all begged Mother to write to Mrs Hooker and accept. So Mother did, and she was quite excited (and so was Milly-Molly-Mandy for her!).

Then Mother bought a new hat and a blouse and a sunshade, and she packed them in her trunk with all her best things (Milly-Molly-Mandy helping).

And then she kissed Grandpa and Grandma and Uncle and Aunty good-bye, and hugged Milly-Molly-Mandy. And then Father drove her in the pony-trap to the next town to the station to meet Mrs Hooker and go with her by train to the sea. (She kissed Father good-bye at the station.)

And so Father and Grandpa and Grandma and

Uncle and Aunty and Milly-Molly-Mandy had to manage as best they could in the nice white cottage with the thatched roof for a whole fortnight without Mother. It did feel queer.

Milly-Molly-Mandy kept forgetting, and she would run in from school to tell Mother all about something, and find it was Aunty in Mother's apron bending over the kitchen stove instead of Mother herself. And Father would put his head in at the kitchen door and say, 'Polly, will you –' and then suddenly remember that 'Polly' was having a lovely holiday by the sea (Polly was Mother's other name, of course). And they felt so pleased when they remembered, but it did seem a long time to wait till she came back.

Then one day Father said, 'I've got a plan! Don't you think it would be a good idea, while Polly's away, if we were to –'

And then Father told them all his plan; and Grandpa and Grandma and Uncle and Aunty thought it was a very fine plan, and so did Milly Molly-Mandy. (But I mustn't tell you what it was, because it was to be a surprise, and you know how secrets do get about once you start telling them! But I'll just tell you this, that they made the kitchen and the scullery and the passage outside the kitchen most dreadfully untidy, so that nothing was in its proper place, and they had to have meals like picnics, only not so nice – though Milly-Molly-Mandy thought it quite fun.)

Well, they all worked awfully hard at the plan in all their spare time, and nobody really minded having things all upset, because it was such fun to think how surprised Mother would be when she came back!

Then another day Grandpa said: 'There's something I've been meaning to do for some time, to please Polly; I guess it would be a good plan to set about it now. It is –'

And then Grandpa told them all his plan; and Father and Grandma and Uncle and Aunty thought it was a very fine plan, and so did Milly-Molly-Mandy. (But I mustn't tell you what it was! – though I will just tell you this, that Grandpa was very busy digging up things in the garden and planting them again, and bringing things home in a box at the back of the pony-trap on market-day. And Milly-Molly-Mandy helped him all she could.)

Then Uncle had a plan, and Father and Grandpa and Grandma and Aunty thought it was a very fine plan, and so did Milly-Molly-Mandy. (It's a secret, remember! – but I will just tell you this, that Uncle got a lot of bits of wood and nails and a hammer, and he was very busy in the evenings after he had shut up his chickens for the night – which he called 'putting them to bed'.

Then Grandma and Aunty had a plan, and Father and Grandpa and Uncle thought it was a very fine plan, and so did Milly-Molly-Mandy. (But I can only just tell you this, that Grandma and Aunty and Milly-Molly-Mandy, who helped too, made themselves very untidy and dusty indeed, and nobody had any cakes for tea at all that week, what with Aunty being so busy and the kitchen so upset. But nobody really minded, because it was such fun to think how pleased Mother would be when she came back!)

And then the day arrived when Mother was to return home!

They had all been working so hard in the nice white cottage with the thatched roof that the two weeks had simply flown. But they had just managed to get things straight again, and Aunty had baked a cake for tea, and Milly-Molly-Mandy had put flowers in all the vases.

When Father helped Mother down from the pony-trap it almost didn't seem as if it could be Mother at first; but of course it was! – only she had on her new hat, and she was so brown with sitting on the beach, and so very pleased to be home again!

She kissed them all round and just hugged Milly-Molly-Mandy!

And then they led her indoors.

And directly Mother got inside the doorway – she saw a beautiful new passage, all clean and painted! And she was surprised!

Then she went upstairs and took off her things, and came back down into the kitchen. And directly Mother got inside the door – she saw a beautiful new kitchen, all clean and sunny, with the ceiling whitewashed and the walls freshly painted! And she was surprised!

When they had had tea (Aunty's cake was very good, though not quite like Mother's) she helped to carry the cups and plates out into the scullery. And directly Mother got through the doorway – she saw a beautiful new scullery, all clean and white-washed! And she was surprised!

And she was surprised!

She put the cups down on the draining board, and directly she looked out of the window – she saw a beautiful new flower garden just outside, and a rustic trellis-work hiding the dust-bin! And she was surprised!

Then Mother went upstairs to unpack. And when her trunk was cleared, Grandpa carried it up to the attic and Mother went first to open the door. And directly she opened it – Mother saw a beautifully tidy, spring-cleaned attic!

And then Mother couldn't say anything, but that they were all very dear, naughty people to have worked so hard while she was being lazy! And Father and Grandpa and Grandma and Uncle and Aunty and Milly-Molly-Mandy were all very pleased, and said they liked being naughty!

Then Mother brought out the presents she had got for them. And what do you think Milly-Molly-Mandy's present was (besides some shells which Mother had picked up on the sand)?

It was a beautiful little blue dressing-gown, which Mother had sewed and sewed for her while she sat on the beach under her new sunshade with Mrs Hooker listening to the waves splashing!

Then Father and Grandpa and Grandma and Uncle and Aunty and Milly-Molly-Mandy all said Mother was very naughty to have worked when she might have been having a nice lazy time!

But Mother said *she* liked being naughty too! – and Milly-Molly-Mandy was so pleased with her new little blue dressing-gown that she couldn't help wearing it straight away!

And then Mother put on her apron and insisted on setting to work to make them something nice for supper, so that she should feel she was really at home.

For it had been a perfect holiday, said Mother, but it was really like having another one to come home again to them all at the nice white cottage with the thatched roof.

11. *Milly-Molly-Mandy Goes to the Sea*

Once upon a time – what *do* you think? – Milly-Molly-Mandy was going to be taken to the seaside!

Milly-Molly-Mandy had never seen the sea in all her life before, and ever since Mother came back from her seaside holiday with her friend Mrs Hooker, and told Milly-Molly-Mandy about the splashy waves and the sand and the little crabs, Milly-Molly-Mandy had just longed to go there herself.

Father and Mother and Grandpa and Grandma and Uncle and Aunty just longed for her to go too, because they knew she would like it so much. But they were all so busy, and then, you know, holidays cost quite a lot of money.

So Milly-Molly-Mandy played 'seaside' instead, by the little brook in the meadow, with little-friend-Susan and Billy Blunt and the shells Mother had brought home for her. (And it was a very nice game indeed, but still Milly-Molly-Mandy did wish sometimes that it could be the real sea!)

Then one day little-friend-Susan went with her mother and baby sister to stay with a relation who let lodgings by the sea. And little-friend-Susan wrote Milly-Molly-Mandy a postcard saying how lovely it was, and how she did wish Milly-Molly-Mandy was there; and Mrs Moggs wrote Mother a postcard saying couldn't some of them manage to come down just for a day excursion, one Saturday?

Father and Mother and Grandpa and Grandma and Uncle and Aunty thought something really ought to be done about that, and they talked it over, while Milly-Molly-Mandy listened with all her ears.

But Father said he couldn't go, because he had to get his potatoes up; Mother said she couldn't go, because it was baking day, and, besides, she had just had a lovely seaside holiday; Grandpa said he couldn't go, because it was market-day; Grandma said she wasn't really very fond of train journeys; Uncle said he oughtn't to leave his cows and chickens.

But then they all said Aunty could quite well leave the sweeping and dusting for that one day.

So Aunty only said it seemed too bad that she should have all the fun. And then she and Milly-Molly-Mandy hugged each other, because it was so very exciting.

Milly-Molly-Mandy ran off to tell Billy Blunt at once, because she felt she would burst if she didn't tell someone. And Billy Blunt did wish he could be going too, but his father and mother were always busy.

Milly-Molly-Mandy told Aunty, and Aunty said, 'Tell Billy Blunt to ask his mother to let him come with us, and I'll see after him!'

So Billy Blunt did, and Mrs Blunt said it was very kind of Aunty and she'd be glad to let him go.

Milly-Molly-Mandy hoppity-skipped like anything, because she was so very pleased; and Billy Blunt was very pleased too, though he didn't hoppity skip, because he always thought he was too old for such doings (but he wasn't really!).

So now they were able to plan together for Saturday, which made it much more fun.

Mother had an old bathing-dress which she cut down to fit Milly-Molly-Mandy, and the bits over she made into a flower for the shoulder (and it looked a very smart bathing-dress indeed). Billy Blunt borrowed a swimming-suit from another boy at school (but it hadn't any flower on the shoulder, of course not!).

Then Billy Blunt said to Milly-Molly-Mandy, 'If you've got swimming-suits you ought to swim. We'd better practise.'

But Milly-Molly-Mandy said, 'We haven't got enough water.'

Billy Blunt said, 'Practise in air, then – better than nothing.'

So they fetched two old boxes from the barn out into the yard, and then lay on them (on their fronts) and spread out their arms and kicked with their legs just as if they were swimming. And when Uncle came along to fetch a wheelbarrow he said it really made him feel quite cool to see them!

He showed them how to turn their hands properly, and kept calling out, 'Steady! steady! Not so fast!' as he watched them.

And then Uncle lay on his front on the box and showed them how (and he looked so funny!), and then they tried again, and Uncle said it was better that time.

So they practised until they were quite out of breath. And then they pretended to dive off the boxes, and they splashed and swallowed mouthfuls of air and swam races to the gate and shivered and dried themselves with old sacks – and it was almost as much fun as if it were real water!

Well, Saturday came at last, and Aunty and Milly-Molly-Mandy met Billy Blunt at nine o'clock by the crossroads. And then they went in the red bus to the station in the next town. And then they went in the train, *rumpty-te-tump*, *rumpty-te-tump*, all the way down to the sea.

And you can't imagine how exciting it was, when they got out at last, to walk down a road knowing they would see the real sea at the bottom! Milly-Molly-Mandy got so excited that she didn't want to look till they were up quite close.

So Billy Blunt (who had seen it once before) pulled her along right on to the edge of the sand, and then he said suddenly, 'Now look!'

And Milly-Molly-Mandy looked.

And there was the sea, all jumping with sparkles in the sunshine, as far as ever you could see. And

little-friend-Susan, with bare legs and frock tucked up, came tearing over the sand to meet them from where Mrs Moggs and Baby Moggs were sitting by a wooden breakwater.

Wasn't it fun!

They took off their shoes and their socks and their hats, and they wanted to take off their clothes and bathe, but Aunty said they must have dinner first. So they sat round and ate sandwiches and cake and fruit which Aunty had brought in a basket. And the Moggs's had theirs too out of a basket.

Then they played in the sand with Baby Moggs (who liked having her legs buried), and paddled a bit and found crabs (they didn't take them away from the water, though).

And then Aunty and Mrs Moggs said they might bathe now if they wanted to. So (as it was a very quiet sort of beach) Milly-Molly-Mandy undressed behind Aunty, and little-friend-Susan undressed behind Mrs Moggs, and Billy Blunt undressed behind the breakwater.

And then they ran right into the water in their bathing-dresses. (And little-friend-Susan thought Milly-Molly-Mandy's bathing-dress *was* smart, with the flower on the shoulder!)

But, dear me! water-swimming feels so different

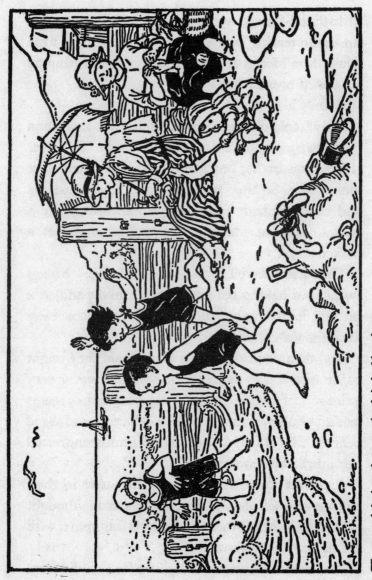

They ran right into the water in their bathing-dresses

from land-swimming, and Milly-Molly-Mandy couldn't manage at all well with the little waves splashing at her all the time. Billy Blunt swished about in the water with a very grim face, and looked exactly as if he were swimming; but when Milly-Molly-Mandy asked him, he said, 'No! my arms swim, but my legs only walk!'

It was queer, for it had seemed quite easy in the barnyard.

But they went on pretending and pretending to swim until Aunty called them out. And then they dried themselves with towels and got into their clothes again; and Billy Blunt said, well, anyhow, he supposed they were just that much nearer swimming properly than they were before; and Milly-Molly-Mandy said she supposed next time they might p'r'aps be able to lift their feet off the ground for a minute at any rate; and little-friend-Susan said she was sure she had swallowed a shrimp! (But that was only her fun!)

Then they played and explored among the rockpools and had tea on the sand. And after tea Mrs Moggs and Baby Moggs and little-friend-Susan walked with them back to the station; and Aunty and Milly-Molly-Mandy and Billy Blunt went in the train, *rumpty-te-tump, rumpty-te-tump,* all the way home again.

And Milly-Molly-Mandy was so sleepy when she got to the nice white cottage with the thatched roof that she had only just time to kiss Father and Mother and Grandpa and Grandma and Uncle and Aunty good night and get into bed before she fell fast asleep.

12. *Milly-Molly-Mandy Finds a Nest*

Once upon a time, one warm summer morning, Uncle came quickly in at the back door of the nice white cottage with the thatched roof and shouted from the kitchen, 'Milly-Molly-Mandy!'

Milly-Molly-Mandy, who was just coming downstairs carrying a big bundle of washing for Mother, called back, 'Yes, Uncle?'

'Hi! quick!' said Uncle, and went outside the back door again.

Milly-Molly-Mandy couldn't think what Uncle wanted with her, but it had such an exciting sound she dropped the big bundle on the stairs in a hurry and ran down to the passage. But when she got to the passage she thought she ought not to leave the big bundle on the stairs, lest someone trip over it in the shadow; so she ran back again in a hurry and fetched the big bundle down, and ran along to the kitchen with it. But she was in such a hurry she dropped some things out of the big bundle and had to run back again and pick them up.

But at last she got them all on to the kitchen table, and then she ran out of the back door and said, 'Yes, Uncle? What is it, Uncle?'

Uncle was just going through the meadow gate, with some boards under one arm and the tool-box on the other. He beckoned to Milly-Molly-Mandy with his head (which was the only thing he had loose to do it with), so Milly-Molly-Mandy ran after him down the garden path to the meadow.

'Yes, Uncle?' said Milly-Molly-Mandy.

'Milly-Molly-Mandy,' said Uncle, striding over the grass with his boards and tool-box, 'I've found a nest.'

'What sort of a nest?' said Milly-Molly-Mandy, hoppity-skipping a bit to keep up with him.

'Milly-Molly-Mandy,' said Uncle, 'I rather think it's a Milly-Molly-Mandy nest.'

Milly-Molly-Mandy stopped and stared at Uncle,

but he strode on with his boards and tool-box as if nothing had happened.

Then Milly-Molly-Mandy began jumping up and down in a great hurry and said, 'What's a Milly-Molly-Mandy nest, Uncle? What's it like, Uncle? Where is it, Uncle? DO-O tell me!'

'Well,' said Uncle, 'you ought to know what a Milly-Molly-Mandy nest is, being a Milly-Molly-Mandy yourself. It's up in the big old oak-tree at the bottom of the meadow.'

So Milly-Molly-Mandy tore off to the big old oak-tree at the bottom of the meadow, but she couldn't see any sort of a nest there, only Uncle's ladder leaning against the tree.

Uncle put the boards and tool-box carefully down on the ground, then he settled the ladder against the big old oak-tree, then he picked up Milly-Molly-Mandy and carried her up the ladder and sat her on a nice safe branch.

And then Milly-Molly-Mandy saw there was a big hollow in the big old oak-tree (which was a very big old oak-tree indeed). And it was such a big hollow that Uncle could get right inside it himself and leave quite a lot of room over.

'Now, Milly-Molly-Mandy,' said Uncle, 'you can perch on that branch and chirp a bit while I put your nest in order.'

Then Uncle went down the ladder and brought up some of the boards and the tool-box, which he hung by its handle on a sticking-out bit of branch. And Milly-Molly-Mandy watched while Uncle measured off boards and sawed them and fitted them and hammered nails into them, until he had made a beautiful flat floor in the hollow in the big old oak-tree, so that it looked like the nicest little fairy-tale room you ever saw!

Then he hoisted Milly-Molly-Mandy off the branch, where she had been chirping with excitement like the biggest sparrow you ever saw (only that you never saw a sparrow in a pink-and-white striped cotton frock), and heaved her up into the hollow.

And Milly-Molly-Mandy stood on the beautiful flat floor and touched the funny brown walls of the big old oak-tree's inside, and looked out of the opening on to the grass down below, and thought a Milly-Molly-Mandy nest was the very nicest and excitingest place to be in in the whole wide world!

Just then whom should she see wandering along the road at the end of the meadow but little-friend-Susan!

'Susan!' called Milly-Molly-Mandy as loud as ever she could, waving her arms as hard as ever she could. And little-friend-Susan peeped over the hedge.

At first she didn't see Milly-Molly-Mandy up in her nest, and then she did, and she jumped up and down and waved; and Milly-Molly-Mandy beckoned, and little-friend-Susan ran to the meadow-

gate and couldn't get it open because she was in such a hurry, and tried to get through and couldn't because she was too big, and began to climb over and couldn't because it was rather high. So at last she squeezed round the side of the gate-post through a little gap in the hedge and came racing across the meadow to the big old oak-tree, and Uncle helped her up.

And then Milly-Molly-Mandy and little-friend-Susan sat and hugged themselves together, up in the Milly-Molly-Mandy nest.

Just then Father came by the big old oak-tree,

and when he saw what was going on he went and got a rope and threw up one end to Milly-Molly-Mandy. And then Father tied an empty wooden box to the other end, and Milly-Molly-Mandy pulled it up and untied it and set it in the middle of the floor like a little table.

Then Mother, who had been watching from the gate of the nice white cottage with the thatched roof, came and tied an old rug to the end of the rope, and little-friend-Susan pulled it up and spread it on the floor like a carpet.

Then Grandpa came along, and he tied some fine ripe plums in a basket to the end of the rope, and Milly-Molly-Mandy pulled them up and set them on the little table.

Then Grandma came across the meadow bringing some old cushions, and she tied them to the end of the rope, and little-friend-Susan pulled them up and arranged them on the carpet.

Then Aunty came along, and she tied a little flower vase on the end of a rope, and Milly-Molly-Mandy pulled it up and set it in the middle of the table. And now the Milly-Molly-Mandy nest was properly furnished, and Milly-Molly-Mandy was in such a hurry to get Billy Blunt to come to see it that she could hardly get down from it quickly enough.

Up in the Milly-Molly-Mandy nest

Mother said, 'You may ask little-friend-Susan and Billy Blunt to tea up there if you like, Milly Molly-Mandy.'

So Milly-Molly-Mandy and little-friend-Susan ran off straight away, hoppity-skip, to the Moggs's cottage (for little-friend-Susan to ask Mrs Moggs's permission), and to the village to Mr Blunt's corn-shop (to ask Billy Blunt), while Uncle fixed steps up the big old oak-tree, so that they could climb easily to the nest.

And at five o'clock that very afternoon Milly-Molly-Mandy and little-friend-Susan and Billy Blunt were sitting drinking milk from three little mugs and eating slices of bread-and-jam and gin-gerbread from three little plates, and feeling just as excited and comfortable and happy as ever they could be, up in the Milly-Molly-Mandy nest!

13. Milly-Molly-Mandy Has Friends

Once upon a time Milly-Molly-Mandy heard the Postman's knock on the door, and when she ran to look in the letterbox there was a letter for Milly-Molly-Mandy herself!

It looked rather the same kind of writing as Milly-Molly-Mandy's own, and Milly-Molly-Mandy couldn't think whom it was from. She ran to Mother who was ironing in the kitchen, and Mother looked on while Milly-Molly-Mandy tore open the envelope.

And when she pulled out the letter, two little paper girls fell out and fluttered to the floor. And Milly-Molly-Mandy said excitedly, 'Oh, I know! – it's from Milly-next-door-to-Mrs Hooker!'

Mother remembered Milly-Molly-Mandy telling her about when she went to stay with Mrs Hooker

(the old friend of Mother's in the next town), and how a little girl, Milly-next-door, had come in to play, and they had painted and cut out paper dolls together from a fashion book.

'You had better read what the letter says,' said Mother.

So Milly-Molly-Mandy set the two little paper girls up on the ironing-board and opened the letter. And this is what the letter said:

DEAR MILLY-MOLLY-MANDY,

I am sending you some paper dolls. I hope you will like them. I am coming to see you one day. Father says he will bring me when he comes to buy chickens from your uncle. I hope you will write to me. With love from

MILLY

Milly-Molly-Mandy was pleased!

Mother said, 'You must write and tell Milly-next-door to get her father to bring her over to tea with you.'

So Milly-Molly-Mandy wrote a letter to Milly-next-door, on her best fancy notepaper, and posted it herself.

Next Saturday Uncle said Mr Short was coming over to fetch some chickens that afternoon. (Mr Short was Milly-next-door's father.) So when Mother baked the cakes, which she always did on a

Saturday morning, she made a little cherry cake specially for Milly-Molly-Mandy and Milly-next-door.

And when the Muffin-man came past with his bell on the way down to the village Mother sent Milly-Molly-Mandy out to stop him. And Milly-Molly-Mandy ran and said, 'Please, we want some muffins. I've got a little friend coming to tea with me!'

So the Muffin-man came hurrying round to the back door and took the tray of muffins off his head and lifted the green baize cloth off the top, and then the nice white cloth which was underneath it. And Mother bought some muffins, while Milly-Molly-Mandy looked at the Muffin-man's bell, and rang it just a bit (it was quite heavy).

And when little-friend-Susan came along the road outside the nice white cottage with the thatched roof, to see if Milly-Molly-Mandy were coming out to play, Mother asked Milly-Molly-Mandy if she wouldn't like to invite little-friend-Susan to meet Milly-next-door.

So Milly-Molly-Mandy ran hoppity-skipping out and said to little-friend-Susan, 'Mother says will you come to tea to-day? Milly-next-door is coming!'

So little-friend-Susan ran hoppity-skipping home down the road to ask her mother; and then she ran hoppity-skipping back to Milly-Molly-Mandy and said, 'Mother says thank you very much. I'd love to come!'

That afternoon Milly-Molly-Mandy was very busy. She tidied her little bedroom, and she brushed Toby the dog and Topsy the cat as long as they would let her, and she helped to lay the table with cups and saucers and plates, and fetched a pot of strawberry jam and a pot of honey from the storeroom (outside the back door), and picked chrysanthemums for the vase in the centre of the table.

And then little-friend-Susan came in (in her Sunday frock), and she helped Milly-Molly-Mandy to arrange her dolls.

And then there was a sound of voices outside, and they looked out of the window and saw Uncle talking to Mr Short and Milly-next-door, so Mother and Milly-Molly-Mandy went out and brought Milly-next-door in, while Uncle and Mr Short went off together to the chicken enclosure.

Milly-Molly-Mandy was very glad she had a nice little bedroom of her own now to take her friends up to. Milly-next-door thought it was very pretty indeed, and she loved the robin cloth on the little green chest of drawers.

When they came downstairs again Mother had

lighted the lamp, and Aunty had drawn the curtains, and Grandma was beginning to toast the muffins before the blazing fire. Milly-Molly-Mandy and Milly-next-door and little-friend-Susan all said they would do it for Grandma.

So they sat in a row before the blazing fire and toasted muffins on forks, and little-friend-Susan and Milly-next-door quite got over feeling shy with each other, and they talked about school and paper dolls and all sorts of things. And as they toasted the muffins Grandma buttered them and stood them in the muffin dish on the stove to keep hot.

Just then there came a knock on the back door, and when Mother opened it there was Billy Blunt with a note from Mrs Blunt. (It was a recipe for ginger biscuits which Mother wanted.)

So Mother thanked Billy Blunt and said, 'You're just in time to have tea with us!'

Billy Blunt said, 'I've just had tea, really.'

But he grinned and looked quite pleased when Mother said, 'Well, come in and have another!' And he came in, and Milly-Molly-Mandy gave him her fork and he toasted muffins, while Milly-Molly-Mandy helped Grandma to butter them.

And what with the hot muffins, and the cherry cake, and the ordinary cake, and the big dish of strawberry jam, and the honey, and the new brown

'You're just in time to have tea with us!'

loaf and the white loaf, the kitchen began to smell very nice indeed.

And when Father came in from the garden, and Grandpa came in from the stable, and Uncle and Mr Short came in from the chicken enclosure, they felt very ready indeed for their tea.

Milly-Molly-Mandy and Milly-next-door and little-friend-Susan and Billy Blunt had a low table all to themselves, with the cherry cake in the middle, which Milly-Molly-Mandy cut, and the grown-ups sat round the big table. (Toby the dog and Topsy the cat liked to be by the little table best.)

And then everybody talked and laughed and ate, and the fire blazed and crackled. And every single one of the toasted muffins was eaten up. (Toby the dog got the last half muffin, but Topsy the cat would only eat cherry cake with the cherries picked out.)

As soon as everyone had finished Mr Short and Milly-next-door had to go, as the last bus left the village at a quarter past six in winter-time. So they said good-bye to Father and Mother and Grandpa and Grandma and Uncle and Aunty and Milly-Molly-Mandy and little-friend-Susan and Billy Blunt, and hoped Milly-Molly-Mandy would come to see them next time she came to stay with Mrs Hooker.

And then Mr Short and Milly-next-door went

out into the dark with two sleepy chickens in a basket (who were going to live in Mr Short's back garden now).

When they were gone there was quite a lot of washing up to be done, and Mother and Aunty began clearing the table. So little-friend-Susan said please might she stay and help. Billy Blunt didn't say anything at all, but he started putting the crumby plates together, and Milly-Molly-Mandy collected the cups and saucers.

So everybody set to work, and they had a regular clearing-up party all to themselves, each one seeing how quick and tidy they could be. Mother washed up in a big bowl of steamy water; Aunty and little-friend-Susan dried with tea-cloths; and Milly-Molly-Mandy and Billy Blunt ran backward and forward between scullery and kitchen, putting the china away in the cupboard and the spoons and knives in the basket, and Toby the dog ran backward and forward with them, and got quite excited (he thought it was some sort of a new game!).

Grandma sat knitting by the fire with Topsy the cat on her lap, because, she said, they were better out of the way with all those busy, bustling people about.

Very soon indeed everything was done, and Mother took off her apron and thanked all her helpers. And then Mr Moggs came to fetch little-friend-Susan home.

And after Milly-Molly-Mandy had seen them off down the path (Billy Blunt with them), she came back and stood in the middle of the tidy kitchen and thought how VERY nice it was to have real friends to come visiting!

Further Doings of
Milly-Molly-Mandy

Contents

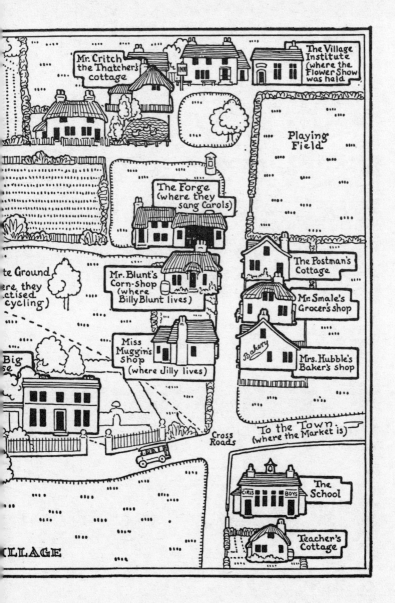

Mr. Critch the Thatcher's cottage

INN

The Village Institute (where the Flower Show was held)

Playing Field

The Forge (where they sang Carols)

...te Ground ...ere they ...ctised ...cycling)

Mr. Blunt's Corn-shop (where Billy Blunt lives)

The Postman's Cottage

Mr. Smale's Grocer's shop

Big ...se

Miss Muggins' Shop (where Jilly lives)

Bakery

Mrs. Hubble's Baker's shop

Cross Roads

To the Town (where the Market is)

GIRLS BOYS

The School

Teacher's Cottage

...LLAGE

1. Milly-Molly-Mandy Has a Tea-Party

Once upon a time Milly-Molly-Mandy had a nice little surprise.

Uncle came back from market one Saturday with a square cardboard box under the seat of the pony-trap, and he gave it to Milly-Molly-Mandy to hold while he got his other parcels out. It was a neat little whity-brown box, tied round with string, and it wasn't very heavy, and it didn't rattle much, and it didn't smell of anything except cardboard, and Milly-Molly-Mandy couldn't guess what was in it. So she asked Uncle.

And Uncle said, 'Oh, just some odd bits of things I want to get rid of. Throw them away for me, Milly-Molly-Mandy.'

Milly-Molly-Mandy looked at Uncle in surprise, for it didn't seem the sort of box to be thrown away. She thought Uncle was looking a bit twinkly, so she said, 'I'd better just peep in it first before I throw it away, hadn't I, Uncle?'

And Uncle, gathering up his parcels said, 'Oh, yes, yes. We don't want to make any mistake about it,' and went off with them towards the kitchen door.

So Milly-Molly-Mandy picked the knot undone, and when she got the box open what DO you think she saw inside? The sweetest little dolls' tea-set, with cups and plates and milk-jug and all complete, fitted neatly in holes cut in the cardboard so that they shouldn't rattle about!

Milly-Molly-Mandy gave a squeak of excitement and put the box down on the ground in a hurry, while she ran after Uncle, crying, 'Oh, Uncle, thank you! Is it for me? Oh, thank you, Uncle!' And Uncle pretended to be surprised, and said, 'What's that? Wasn't it rubbish after all? Well, well, what a good thing you looked!' and went indoors with his parcels; and Milly-Molly-Mandy ran back to her tea-set.

It was the prettiest little tea-set, with a teapot that would really pour, and a sugar-basin with a tiny lid, and two little cups and saucers and plates – 'One for me, and one for Susan,' thought Milly-Molly-Mandy to herself. 'I'll ask Mother if I can ask Susan to tea today.'

So she carried the box into the kitchen (where Mother was busy taking the cakes out of the oven), and asked. And Mother admired the tea-set, and said, 'Certainly, Milly-Molly-Mandy. And you may have this little cake on a saucer, and one of these little bread rolls to look like a loaf.'

So that afternoon Milly-Molly-Mandy laid a small cloth on the garden table and arranged her tea-set on it, with a little vase of flowers in the centre, and all the good things Mother had given her to eat; and when everything was ready she ran down the white road with the hedges each side to ask little-friend-Susan to come to the tea-party.

But what do you think?

Before she got as far as the Moggs's cottage (where little-friend-Susan lived) she met little-friend-Susan herself coming up to the nice white cottage with the thatched roof (where Milly-Molly-Mandy lived). And Milly-Molly-Mandy said, 'Hullo, Susan! I was just coming to ask you to a dolls' tea-party. I've got a new tea-set!' And little-friend-Susan said just at the same moment, 'Hullo, Milly-Molly-Mandy! I've got a new tea-set – will you come to a dolls' tea-party with me?' So then they both stopped still and stared at each other.

'Mine's a perfectly new tea-set,' said Milly-Molly-

Mandy. 'Uncle brought it to me from market, and it's pink.'

'I only had mine today,' said little-friend-Susan. 'Father brought it home from market, and it's blue.'

'But I've got a special little cake and a proper loaf,' said Milly-Molly-Mandy. 'Do come!'

'No you come!' said little-friend-Susan. 'I've got a tiny little tart and a weeny little pot of strawberry jam!'

'I've got lots of bread-and-jam on an ordinary plate for us to eat,' said Milly-Molly-Mandy, 'and it is such a sweet little tea-set!'

'Oh, Milly-Molly-Mandy,' said little-friend-Susan 'mine's all laid in the summer-house, and there's a daisy beside each plate, and lots and lots of bread-and-dripping, and my tea-set is simply beautiful too!'

It was very difficult indeed to know what to do, for Milly-Molly-Mandy felt secretly sure that her party would be nicer, and she didn't want it wasted; and little-friend-Susan felt secretly sure too that her party would be nicer, and she didn't want it wasted either!

'Do come!' said Milly-Molly-Mandy.

'No you come!' said little-friend-Susan.

Just then they saw Billy Blunt wandering down the road, scraping a bit of stick with his knife.

Milly-Molly-Mandy and little-friend-Susan were

255

Billy Blunt stopped and said, 'What's up?'

standing looking so solemn that Billy Blunt stopped and said, 'What's up?'

So Milly-Molly-Mandy told him, and little-friend-Susan told him too. And Billy Blunt scraped away for a moment, and then said, 'Better take your things into the meadow or somewhere and have a double tea.' (And he had his mouth open to add 'And ask me too', but he thought he'd better not, in case they didn't want him, so he shut it again.)

And directly Milly-Molly-Mandy and little-friend-Susan heard that they both wondered why they hadn't thought of a double tea themselves! Milly-Molly-Mandy hopped on one leg, because she was so pleased. And she said, 'Then we shall each have a cup over, so, Billy, you must come and have tea too!'

So Milly-Molly-Mandy carried her little pink tea-set out into the meadow; and little-friend-Susan carried her little blue tea-set out into the meadow too; and they all sat round on the grass and ate off the tiny plates and drank out of the tiny cups. And Milly-Molly-Mandy poured out for little-friend-Susan, and little-friend-Susan poured out for Milly-Molly-Mandy and they both poured out for Billy Blunt (who had two cups all to himself, because he was guest at two tea-parties)!

When they had finished eating (which happened when there wasn't anything more to eat) they took the tea-things to the brook at the bottom of the meadow and washed them, and stood them on some moss to drain.

And Milly-Molly-Mandy and little-friend-Susan both thought a double tea-party was much more fun than just an ordinary one. And Billy Blunt (as the cups and plates were very small!) thought being a double guest was ever so much better than being just an ordinary single one!

So THAT was all right!

2. Milly-Molly-Mandy Minds a Baby

Once upon a time Milly-Molly-Mandy had to mind a tiny little baby.

It was the funniest, tiny little baby you could possibly imagine, and Milly-Molly-Mandy had to mind it because there didn't seem to be anybody else to do so. She couldn't find its mother or its father or any of its relations, so she had to take it home and look after it herself (because, of course, you can't leave a tiny little baby alone in a wood, with no one anywhere about to look after it).

And this is how it happened.

Milly-Molly-Mandy wanted some acorn-cups (which are useful for making dolls' bowls, and wheels for matchbox carts, and all that sort of thing, you know). So, as little-friend-Susan was busy looking after her baby sister, Milly-Molly-Mandy went off to the woods with just Toby the dog to look for some.

While she was busy looking she heard a loud chirping noise. And Milly-Molly-Mandy said to herself, 'I wonder what sort of bird that is?' And then she found a ripe blackberry, and forgot about the chirping noise.

After a time Milly-Molly-Mandy said to herself, 'How that bird does keep on chirping?' And then Toby the dog found a rabbit-hole, and Milly-Molly-Mandy forgot again about the chirping noise.

After some more time Milly-Molly-Mandy said to herself, 'That bird sounds as if it wants something.' And then Milly-Molly-Mandy went towards a brambly clearing in the wood from which the chirping noise seemed to come.

But when she got there the chirping noise didn't seem to come from a tree, but from a low bramble-bush. And when she got to the low bramble-bush the chirping noise stopped.

Milly-Molly-Mandy thought that was because it was frightened of her. So she said out loud, 'It's all right – don't be frightened. It's only me!' just as kindly as she could, and then she poked about in among the bramble-bush. But she couldn't find anything, except thorns.

And then, quite suddenly, lying in the grass on the other side of the bramble-bush, Milly-Molly-Mandy and Toby the dog together found what had been making all the chirping noise. It was so frightened that it had rolled itself into a tight little prickly ball, no bigger than the penny indiarubber ball which Milly-Molly-Mandy had bought at Miss Muggins's shop the day before.

For what DO you think it was? A little tiny weeny baby hedgehog!

Milly-Molly-Mandy *was* excited! And so was Toby the dog! Milly-Molly-Mandy had to say, 'No, Toby! Be quiet, Toby!' very firmly indeed. And then she picked up the baby hedgehog in a bracken leaf (because it was a very prickly baby, though it was so small), and she could just see its little soft nose quivering among its prickles.

Then Milly-Molly-Mandy looked about to find its nest (for, of course, she didn't want to take it away from its family), but she couldn't find it. And then the baby began squeaking again for its mother, but its mother didn't come.

So at last Milly-Molly-Mandy said comfortingly, 'Never mind, darling – I'll take you home and look after you!'

So Milly-Molly-Mandy carried the baby hedgehog between her two hands very carefully; and it unrolled itself a bit and quivered its little soft nose over her fingers as if it hoped they might be good to eat, and it squeaked and squeaked, because it was very hungry. So Milly-Molly-Mandy hurried all she could, and Toby the dog capered along at her side and at last they got home to the nice white cottage with the thatched roof.

Father and Mother and Grandpa and Grandma and Uncle and Aunty were all very interested indeed.

Mother put a saucer of milk on the stove to warm, and then they tried to feed the baby. But it was too little to lap from a saucer, and it was too little even to

They were all very interested indeed

lick from Milly-Molly-Mandy's finger. So at last they had to wait until it opened its mouth to squeak and then squirt drops of warm milk into it with Father's fountain-pen filler!

After that the baby felt a bit happier, and Milly-Molly-Mandy made it a nest in a little box of hay. But when she put it in it squeaked and squeaked again for its nice warm mother till Milly-Molly-Mandy put her hand in the box; and then it snuggled up against it and went to sleep. And Milly-Molly-Mandy stood there and chuckled softly to herself, because it felt so funny being mistaken for Mrs Hedgehog! (She quite liked it!)

When Father and Grandpa and Uncle came in to dinner the baby woke and began squeaking again. So Uncle picked it up in his big hand to have a look at it, while Milly-Molly-Mandy ran for more milk and the fountain-pen filler.

And the baby squeaked so loudly that Uncle said, 'Hul-lo, Horace! What's all this noise about?' And Milly-Molly-Mandy was pleased, because 'Horace' just seemed to suit the baby hedgehog, and no one knew what its mother had named it (but I don't suppose it was Horace!).

Milly-Molly-Mandy was kept very busy all that day feeding Horace every hour or two. He was so prickly that she had to wrap him round in an old handkerchief first – and he looked the funniest little baby in a white shawl you ever did see!

When bedtime came Milly-Molly-Mandy wanted to take the hedgehog's box up to her little room with

her. But Mother said no, he would be all right in the kitchen till morning. So they gave him a hot bottle to snuggle against (it was an ink-bottle wrapped in flannel), and then Milly-Molly-Mandy went off to bed.

But being 'mother' even to a hedgehog is a very important sort of job, and in the night Milly-Molly-Mandy woke up and thought of Horace, and wondered if he felt lonely in his new home.

And she creepy-crept in the dark to the top of the stairs and listened.

And after a time she heard a tiny little 'Squeak! squeak!' coming from the kitchen. So she hurried and pulled on her dressing-gown and her bedroom slippers, and then she hurried and creepy-crept in the dark downstairs into the kitchen, and carefully lit the candle on the dresser.

And then she fed Horace and talked to him in a comfortable whisper, so that he didn't feel lonely any more. And then she put him back to bed and blew out the candle, and creepy-crept in the dark upstairs to her own little bed. (And it did feel so nice and warm to get into again!)

Next day Horace learned to open his mouth when he felt the fountain-pen filler touch it (he couldn't see, because his eyes weren't open yet – just like a baby puppy or kitten). And quite soon he learned to suck away at the filler just as if it were a proper baby's bottle! And he grew and he grew, and in a week's time his eyes were open. And soon he grew little teeth, and could gobble bread and milk out of an egg-cup, and sometimes a little bit of meat or banana.

He was quite a little-boy hedgehog now, instead of a little baby one, and Milly-Molly-Mandy didn't need to get up in the night any more to feed him.

Milly-Molly-Mandy was very proud of him, and when little-friend-Susan used to say she had to hurry home after school to look after her baby sister, Milly-Molly-Mandy used to say she had to hurry too to look after the baby Horace. She used to give him walks in the garden, and laugh at his funny little back legs and tiny tail as he waddled about, nosing the ground. When Toby the dog barked he would roll himself up into a prickly ball in a second; but he soon came out again, and would run to Milly-Molly-Mandy's hand when she called 'Horace!' (He was quite happy with her for a mother.)

One day Horace got out of his hay-box in the kitchen, and they couldn't find him for a long time, though they all looked – Father and Mother and Grandpa and Grandma and Uncle and Aunty and Milly-Molly-Mandy. But at last where do you think they found him? – in the larder!

'Well!' said Uncle, 'Horace knows how to look after himself all right now!'

After that Horace's bed was put out in the barn, and Milly-Molly-Mandy would take his little basin of bread and milk out to him, and stay and play till it got too chilly.

And then, one frosty morning, they couldn't find Horace anywhere, though they all looked – Father and Mother and Grandpa and Grandma and Uncle and Aunty and Milly-Molly-Mandy. But at last, a day or two after, Grandpa was pulling out some hay for the pony Twinkletoes, when what do you think he found! A little ball of prickles cuddled up deep in the hay!

Horace had gone to sleep for the winter, like the proper little hedgehog he was! (Grandpa said that sort of going to sleep was called 'hibernating'.)

So Milly-Molly-Mandy put the hay with the prickly ball inside it into a large box in the barn, with a little bowl of water near by (in case Horace should wake up and want a drink).

And there she left him (sleeping soundly while the cold winds blew and the snows fell) until he should wake up in the spring and come out to play with her again!

(And that's a true story!)

3. Milly-Molly-Mandy Goes Motoring

Once upon a time Milly-Molly-Mandy had a lovely invitation.

The little girl Jessamine, who lived in the Big House with the iron railings by the cross-roads, came round to the nice white cottage with the thatched roof one Saturday morning to see Milly-Molly-Mandy.

She walked up the path and knocked at the door, and when Milly-Molly-Mandy (who had seen her through the window) ran to open it the little girl Jessamine said, 'Hullo, Milly-Molly-Mandy! Mother and I are going in the car to have a picnic on the Downs this afternoon, and Mother says would you like to come too?'

Milly-Molly-Mandy was pleased.

She ran to ask Mother if she might go, and then she ran back to the little girl Jessamine and said, 'Mother says thank you very much, I'd love to come!'

So the little girl Jessamine said they would fetch her about two o'clock that afternoon. And then she went back home with a basket of sweet juicy yellow gooseberries, which Father picked for her from his best gooseberry bushes.

Milly-Molly-Mandy was so excited that she wouldn't have bothered to eat any dinner at dinner-time, only Mother said she must, so she did. And then she put on her hat and coat, and Aunty lent her a nice woolly scarf, and Mother saw that her hair was tidy and that she had a clean handkerchief. And then just when she was ready she looked out of the window and saw the big motor-car drive up to the gate.

So Milly-Molly-Mandy, in a great hurry, kissed Father and Mother and Grandpa and Grandma and Uncle and Aunty good-bye (she did so wish they could have been going for a motor-ride too), and then she ran down the path to the car. And Father and Mother and Grandpa and Grandma and Uncle and Aunty all came to the door and waved, and Milly-Molly-Mandy and Mrs Green and the little girl Jessamine all waved back from the car.

And then the car went whizzing off, and the nice white cottage with the thatched roof was out of sight in a twinkling.

It was such fun to be going to the Downs! Milly-Molly-Mandy had been taken there once before by Mrs Green (with little-friend-Susan and Billy Blunt that time), and she had thought it was just the best place in the whole world for a picnic, so it was very nice to be going there again.

The little girl Jessamine and Milly-Molly-Mandy sat close together in the front seat beside Mrs Green (who drove beautifully), so that they could all see everything and talk about it together.

And they kept on seeing things all the way along. Once a partridge flew out from behind a hedge; and once a rabbit ran along in front of the car for quite a way; and once, when they were going very slowly because it was such a pretty lane with so much to see, they saw a little brown moor-hen taking her baby

chicks over the road ahead of them! Mrs Green quietly stopped the car so that they could watch, and the little mother moor-hen hurried across with three babies, and then two more followed her; and, after quite a long pause, another little fluffy ball went scurrying across the road in a great hurry, and they all went through a gap in the hedge out of sight.

'He nearly got left behind, didn't he?' said Mrs

Green, starting the car again; and they went on, all talking about the little moor-hen family out for a walk, and wondering where they were going.

Then presently in the road ahead they saw a bus (not the red bus that passed their village, though). And standing in the road or sitting on the grass by the side of the road were a lot of school-children (but none that Milly-Molly-Mandy knew). So Mrs Green had to slow down while they got out of the way.

As they passed they saw that the bus driver was under the bus doing something to the machinery, and the children were looking rather disappointed, and a lady who seemed to be their teacher (but not one from Milly-Molly-Mandy's school) was looking rather worried.

So Mrs Green stopped and called back, 'Can we help at all?'

And the lady who seemed to be their teacher (she was their teacher) came to the side of the car, while all the children crowded round and looked on.

And the lady who was their teacher said they had all been invited to a garden-party, but the bus hired to take them kept on stopping and now it wouldn't move at all, and the lady who was their teacher didn't know quite what to do.

And then one little girl with a little pigtail said in a high little voice, 'We've all got our best dresses on

273

All the children crowded round and looked on

for the garden-party, and now we shan't be able to go-o-o!'

It did seem a pity.

Mrs Green said, 'How many are there of you?'

And the lady who was their teacher said, 'Sixteen, including myself.'

Then Mrs Green got out and looked at her car and at all the children, and considered things. And Milly-Molly-Mandy and the little girl Jessamine sat and looked at Mrs Green and at all the children, and wondered what could be done about it. And all the children stood and looked at Mrs Green and at each other, and thought that something would be done about it, somehow.

Then Mrs Green turned to Milly-Molly-Mandy and the little girl Jessamine and said, 'Shall we have our tea on the Downs or see if we can take these children to their garden-party!'

And Milly-Molly-Mandy and the little girl Jessamine of course said (both together), 'Take them to the garden-party!'

So Mrs Green said, 'I don't know if we can manage it, but let's see if we can all pack in!'

So everybody in great excitement tried to make themselves as small as possible, and clambered in and squeezed and shifted and sat in each other's laps and stood on each other's toes. But still it didn't

275

seem possible for the last two to get into the car.

Mrs Green said, 'This won't do!' and she got out again and thought a bit.

And then she picked out the two smallest children and lifted them up into the folded hood at the back of the car, and she and the lady who was their teacher tied them safely in with the belt of a coat and a stout piece of string. And there they sat above all the other children, with toes together, like babes in a cradle!

And it was Milly-Molly-Mandy and the little girl with the little pigtail who were the smallest children (and weren't they just glad!).

So everybody was in, and Mrs Green slowly drove the laden car away; and Milly-Molly-Mandy

and the little girl with the little pigtail waved from their high seat to the bus driver, who stood smiling at them and wiping his oily hands on an oily rag.

Mrs Green drove very slowly and carefully until they came to the big house where the garden-party was to be. And then everybody got out, except Milly-Molly-Mandy and the little girl with the little pigtail, who had to wait to be lifted down.

The lady who was giving the garden-party was very grateful that they had been brought, as she had prepared such a lot of good things for them. And all the children were so grateful too that they stood and cheered and cheered and cheered as the car drove off with just Mrs Green and the little girl Jessamine and Milly-Molly-Mandy inside.

'Wasn't that fun!' said Mrs Green.

'Won't they enjoy their garden-party!' said the little girl Jessamine.

'Wouldn't it be nice if we could all have ridden in the hood?' said Milly-Molly-Mandy.

There wasn't time now to go to the Downs for their picnic, but they found a field and spread it out there in the sunshine (and there was a cherry cake with lots of cherries in it!).

And they had such a good time. Milly-Molly-Mandy thought that field must be the best place in

the world, after all, for a picnic; so it was very nice
indeed that they had gone there.

4. Milly-Molly-Mandy Gets a Surprise

Once upon a time, after morning school, Milly-Molly-Mandy saw Mrs Green (the lady who lived in the Big House with the iron railings, which wasn't far from the school) just getting out of her motor-car; and her little girl Jessamine was with her.

And when the little girl Jessamine saw Milly-Molly-Mandy she said, 'Hullo, Milly-Molly-Mandy! We've just come back from the town. Mother's been to the hairdresser's and had her hair cut off!'

So when Milly-Molly-Mandy got home to the nice

white cottage with the thatched roof, and was having dinner with Father and Mother and Grandpa and Grandma and Uncle and Aunty, she told them the news. And Mother and Grandma and Aunty were quite interested. Mother felt her 'bun' and said, 'I wonder what I should look like with my hair short!'

Father said, 'I like you best as you are.'

And Grandpa said, 'Nonsense, Polly!'

And Grandma said, 'You'd always have to be going to the barber's.'

And Uncle said, 'You'll be wanting us to have our beards bobbed next!'

And Aunty said, 'It wouldn't suit you!'

But Milly-Molly-Mandy said, 'Oh, *do*, Mother! Just like me! And then you'd look like my sister!' She looked at Mother carefully, trying to see her with short hair, and added, 'I think you'd make a nice sister. DO, Mother!'

Mother laughed and said, 'Oh, it wants a lot of thinking about, Milly-Molly-Mandy!'

The next evening Mother took a new cream cheese down the road to the Moggs's cottage, and Milly-Molly-Mandy ran with her. And when Mother had given the cream cheese to Mrs Moggs she said, 'Mrs Moggs, what do you think about my having my hair off?'

And when Mrs Moggs had thanked Mother for the cream cheese she said, 'Never! It would be a shame to cut your hair off. I wonder how it would suit me!'

Mother said, 'Let's go and have it done together!' And Milly-Molly-Mandy said, 'Yes do!' But Mrs Moggs wouldn't.

It was very windy, and going back up the road again Mother lost her comb, and they couldn't find it as it was getting dark and it was probably in among the grasses under the hedge. So Mother went indoors with her hair quite untidy, and she said, 'Now, if I had short hair that would not have happened!'

But Father said again, 'You're much nicer as you are.'

And Grandpa said again, 'Nonsense, Polly, you, the mother of a big girl like Milly-Molly-Mandy!'

But Grandma said, 'It would be very comfortable.'

And Uncle said, 'You can always grow it again if you want to!'

And Aunty said, 'Well, it wouldn't suit ME!'

Mother's eyebrows said, 'Shall I?' to Milly-Molly-Mandy, and Milly-Molly-Mandy's head said, 'Yes!' quite decidedly.

The next day Father said he had to drive into the town to buy some gardening tools which he couldn't get at Mr Blunt's shop in the village; and Mother said she would like to go too. (Milly-Molly-Mandy thought Father and Mother had a sort of smiley look almost as if they had a little secret between them.)

So Father and Mother drove off in the pony-trap together. And when Milly-Molly-Mandy was walking home from school that afternoon with little-friend-Susan she suddenly began to wonder if Mother was going to have her hair cut off in the town, as the little girl Jessamine's mother did. And she was in 'such a hurry to get home and see if Mother had come back that as soon as they came to the Moggs's cottage she said 'Good-bye' at once to little-friend-Susan, without stopping to look in at her baby sister, or stand and talk or anything, and ran all the rest of the way home.

And when she got into the kitchen there was Mother sitting by the fire making toast for tea; and Grandma and Aunty were looking at her in an amused sort of way all the time they were putting cups on the table or buttering the toast.

For Mother's hair was short like Milly-Molly-Mandy's and she looked so nice, and yet quite motherly still, that Milly-Molly-Mandy was as pleased as pleased!

'Has Father seen you?' she asked. And Mother and Grandma and Aunty all laughed and said, 'Yes.'

Milly-Molly-Mandy wondered why they laughed quite like that.

Then Mother said, 'Ring the bell outside the back door, Milly-Molly-Mandy, to tell the men-folk tea is ready.' So Milly-Molly-Mandy rang the bell loudly, and she could hear the men-folk's voices round by the barn. She wondered what they were laughing at.

Then everybody sat down to tea, and Milly-Molly-Mandy couldn't keep her eyes off Mother's hair. Mother looked so nice, and sort of smiley; Milly-Molly-Mandy couldn't think what she was smiling at so, as she put sugar in the cups. Uncle looked sort of smiley, too, down in his beard – everybody was looking sort of smiley!

Milly-Molly-Mandy looked round the table in surprise.

And then she saw there was a strange man sitting in Father's place! And she was so surprised that she stared hard, while everybody watched her and laughed outright.

And then Mother patted her shoulder, and said, 'Wasn't Father naughty? He went and had his beard cut off while I was having my hair done!'

And the 'strange man' who was Father stroked his chin, and said, 'Don't you think I look very nice shingled too, Milly-Molly-Mandy?'

It was quite a long time before Milly-Molly-Mandy was able to say anything. And then she wanted to know what Father and Mother thought of each other.

And Father said, 'I told you before, I like her best just as she is – so I do!'

Milly-Molly-Mandy was satisfied

And Mother said, 'I'll like him best as he is – when I get used to it!'

And when Milly-Molly-Mandy had tried how it felt kissing Father without his beard she said in a satisfied way, 'I think everybody's nicest as they are, really, aren't they?'

And Aunty, poking a hairpin back in her own hair, quite agreed.

5. *Milly-Molly-Mandy Goes on an Expedition*

Once upon a time it was a Monday-bank-holiday.
Milly-Molly-Mandy had been looking forward to
this Monday-bank-holiday for a long time, more
than a week, for she and Billy Blunt had been planning to go for a long fishing expedition on that day.

It was rather exciting.

They were to get up very early, and take their
dinners with them, and their rods and lines and jam-
jars, and go off all on their own along by the brook,
and not be back until quite late in the day.

Milly-Molly-Mandy went to bed the night before with all the things she wanted for the expedition arranged beside her bed – a new little tin mug (to drink out of), and a bottle (for drinking-water), and a large packet of bread-and-butter and an egg and a banana (for her dinner), and a jam-jar (to carry the fish in), and a little green fishing net (to catch them with), and some string and a safety-pin (which it is always useful to have), and her school satchel (to put things in). For when you are going off for the whole day you want quite a lot of things with you.

When Milly-Molly-Mandy woke up on Monday-bank-holiday morning she thought to herself, 'Oh, dear! it is a grey sort of day – I do hope it isn't going to rain!'

But anyhow she knew she was going to enjoy herself, and she jumped up and washed and dressed and put on her hat and the satchel strap over her shoulder.

And then the sunshine came creeping over the trees outside, and Milly-Molly-Mandy saw that it had only been a grey day because she was up before the sun – and she felt a sort of little skip inside, because she was so very sure she was going to enjoy herself!

Just then there came a funny gritty sound like a handful of earth on the window-pane, and when she put her head out there was Billy Blunt, eating a large piece of bread-and-butter and grinning up at her, looking very businesslike with rod and line and jam-jar and bulging satchel.

Milly-Molly-Mandy called out of the window in a loud whisper, 'Isn't it a lovely day? I'm just coming!'

And Billy Blunt called back in a loud whisper, 'Come on! Hurry up! It's getting late.'

So Milly-Molly-Mandy hurried up like anything, and picked up her things and ran creeping downstairs, past Father's and Mother's room, and Grandpa's and Grandma's room, and Uncle's and Aunty's room. And she filled her bottle at the tap in the scullery, and took up the thick slice of bread-and-

289

butter which Mother had left between two plates ready for her breakfast, and unlocked the back door and slipped out into the fresh morning air.

And there they were, off on their Monday-bank-holiday expedition!

'Isn't it lovely!' said Milly-Molly-Mandy, with a little hop.

'Umm! Come on!' said Billy Blunt,

So they went out of the back gate and across the meadow to the brook, walking very businesslikely and enjoying their bread-and-butter very thoroughly.

'We'll go that way,' said Billy Blunt, 'because that's the way we don't generally go.'

'And when we come to a nice place we'll fish,' said Milly-Molly-Mandy.

'But that won't be for a long way yet,' said Billy Blunt.

So they went on walking very businesslikely (they had eaten their bread-and-butter by this time) until they had left the nice white cottage with the thatched roof a long way behind, and the sun was shining down quite hotly.

'It seems like a real expedition when you have the whole day to do it in, doesn't it?' said Milly-Molly-Mandy. 'I wonder what the time is now!'

'Not time for dinner yet,' said Billy Blunt. 'But I could eat it.'

Off on their Monday-bank-holiday expedition!

'So could I,' said Milly-Molly-Mandy. 'Let's have a drink of water.' So they each had a little tin mugful of water, and drank it very preciously to make it last, as the bottle didn't hold much.

The brook was too muddy and weedy for drinking, but it was a very interesting brook. One place, where it had got rather blocked up, was just full of tadpoles – they caught ever so many with their hands and put them in the jam-jars, and watched them swim about and wiggle their little black tails and open and shut their little black mouths. Then farther on were lots of stepping-stones in the stream, and Milly-Molly-Mandy and Billy Blunt had a fine time scrambling about from one to another.

Billy Blunt slipped once, with one foot into the water, so he took off his boots and socks and tied them round his neck. And it looked so nice that Milly-Molly-Mandy took off one boot and sock and tried it too. But the water and the stones were *so-o* cold that she put them on again, and just tried to be fairly careful how she went. But even so she slipped once, and caught her frock on a branch and pulled the button off, and had to fasten it together with a safety-pin. (So wasn't it a good thing she had brought one with her?)

Presently they came to a big flat mossy stone beside the brook. And Milly-Molly-Mandy said, 'That's

where we ought to eat our dinners, isn't it? I wonder
what the time is now!'

Billy Blunt looked round and considered; and then
he said, 'Somewhere about noon, I should say. Might
think about eating soon, as we had breakfast early.
Less to carry, too.'

And Milly-Molly-Mandy said, 'Let's spread it out
all ready, anyhow! It's a lovely place here.'

So they laid the food out on the flat stone, with the
bottle of water and little tin mug in the middle,
and it looked so good and they felt so hungry that,
of course, they just had to set to and eat it all up
straight away.

And it *did* taste nice!

And the little black tadpoles in the glass jam-jars
beside them swam round and round, and wiggled
their little black tails and opened and shut their
little black mouths; till at last Milly-Molly-Mandy
said, 'We've taken them away from their dinners,
haven't we? Let's put them back now.'

And Billy Blunt said, 'Yes. We'll want the pots for real fishes soon.'

So they emptied the tadpoles back into the brook where they wiggled away at once to their meals.

'Look! There's a fish!' cried Milly-Molly-Mandy, pointing. And Billy Blunt hurried and fetched his rod and line, and settled to fishing in real earnest.

Milly-Molly-Mandy went a little farther downstream, and poked about with her net in the water; and soon she caught a fish, and put it in her jam-jar, and ran to show it to Billy Blunt. And Billy Blunt said, 'Huh!' But he said it wasn't proper fishing without a rod and line, so it didn't really count.

But Milly-Molly-Mandy liked it quite well that way, all the same.

So they fished and they fished along the banks, and sometimes they saw quite big fish, two or three inches long, and Billy Blunt got quite excited and borrowed Milly-Molly-Mandy's net; and they got a number of fish in their jam-jars.

'Oh, don't you wish we'd brought our teas too, so we could stay here a long, long time?' said Milly-Molly-Mandy.

'Umm,' said Billy Blunt. 'We ought to have done. Expect we'll have to be getting back soon.'

So at last as they got hungry, and thirsty too (having finished all the bottle of water), they began to pack up their things and Billy Blunt put on his socks and boots. And they tramped all the way back, scrambling up and down the banks, and jumping the stepping-stones.

When they got near home Milly-Molly-Mandy said doubtfully, 'What about our fishes?'

And Billy Blunt said, 'We don't really want 'em now, do we? We only wanted a fishing expedition.' So they counted how many there were (there were fifteen), and then emptied them back into the brook, where they darted off at once to their meals.

And Milly-Molly-Mandy and Billy Blunt went on up through the meadow to the nice white cottage with the thatched roof, feeling very hungry, and hoping they weren't too badly late for tea.

And when they got in Father and Mother and

Grandpa and Grandma and Uncle and Aunty were all sitting at table, just finishing – what DO you think?

Why, their midday dinner!

Milly-Molly-Mandy and Billy Blunt couldn't think how it had happened. But when you get up so very early to go on fishing expeditions, and get so very hungry, well, it *is* rather difficult to reckon the time properly!

6. Milly-Molly-Mandy Helps to Thatch a Roof

Once upon a time it was a very blustery night, so very blustery that it woke Milly-Molly-Mandy right up several times.

Milly-Molly-Mandy's little attic bedroom was just under the thatched roof, so she could hear the wind blowing in the thatch, as well as rattling her little low window, and even shaking her door.

Milly-Molly-Mandy had to pull the bedclothes well over her ears to shut out some of the noise before she could go to sleep at all, and so did Father and

Mother and Grandpa and Grandma and Uncle and Aunty, in their bedrooms. It was so very blustery.

The next morning, when Milly-Molly-Mandy woke up properly, the wind was still very blustery, though it didn't sound quite so loud as it did in the dark.

Milly-Molly-Mandy sat up in her little bed, thinking, 'What a noisy night it was!' And she looked toward her little low window to see if it were raining.

But what do you think she saw? Why, lots of long bits of straw dangling and swaying just outside from the edge of the thatched roof above. And when she got up and looked out of her little low window she saw – why! – lots of long bits of straw lying all over the grass, and all over the flower-beds, and all over the hedge!

Milly-Molly-Mandy stared round, thinking, 'It's been raining straw in the night!'

And then she thought some more. And suddenly she said right out loud, 'Ooh! the wind's blowing our nice thatched roof off!'

And then Milly-Molly-Mandy didn't wait to think any longer, but ran barefooted down into Father's and Mother's room, calling out, 'Ooh! Father and Mother! the wind's blowing our nice thatched roof off, and it's lying all over the garden!'

Then Father jumped out of bed, and put his boots on his bare feet, and his big coat over his pyjamas, and ran outside to look. And Mother jumped out of bed, and wrapped the down-quilt round Milly-Molly-Mandy, and went with her to the window to look (but there wasn't anything to see from there).

Then Father came back to say that one corner of the thatched roof was being blown off, and it would have to be seen to immediately before it got any worse. And then everybody began to get dressed.

Milly-Molly-Mandy thought it was kind of funny to have breakfast just the same as usual while the roof was blowing off. She felt very excited about it, and ate her porridge nearly all up before she even remembered beginning it!

'When shall you see to the roof?' asked Milly-Molly-Mandy. 'Directly after breakfast?'

And Father said, 'Yes, it must be seen to as soon as possible.'

'How will you see to it?' asked Milly-Molly-Mandy. 'With a long ladder?'

And Father said, 'No it's too big a job for me. We must send to Mr Critch the Thatcher, and he'll bring a long ladder and mend it.'

Milly-Molly-Mandy felt sorry that Father couldn't mend it himself, but it would be nice to see Mr Critch the Thatcher mend it.

Directly after breakfast Aunty put on her hat and coat to go down to the village with the message; and Milly-Molly-Mandy put on her hat and coat and went with her, because she wanted to see where Mr Critch the Thatcher lived. And as they went out of the gate the wind got another bit of thatch loose on the roof, and blew it down at them; so they hurried as fast as they could, along the white road with the hedges each side, down to the village.

But when Aunty knocked at Mr Critch the Thatcher's door (he lived in one of the little cottages just by the pond where the ducks were), Mrs Critch, the

Thatcher's wife, opened it (and her apron blew about like a flag, it was so windy).

And Mrs Critch, the Thatcher's wife, said she was very sorry, but Mr Critch had just gone off in a hurry to mend another roof, and she knew he would

not be able to come to them for a couple of days at the earliest, because he was so rushed – 'what with this wind and all,' said Mrs Critch.

'Dear, dear!' said Aunty. 'Whatever shall we do?'

Mrs Critch was sorry, but she did not know what they could do, except wait until Mr Critch could come.

'Dear, dear!' said Aunty. 'And meantime our roof will be getting worse and worse.' Then Aunty and Milly-Molly-Mandy said good morning to Mrs

Critch, and went out through her little gate into the road again.

'Father will have to mend it now, won't he, Aunty?' said Milly-Molly-Mandy.

'It isn't at all easy to thatch a roof,' said Aunty. 'You have to know how. I wonder what we can do!'

They set off back home along the white road with the hedges each side, and Aunty said, 'Well, there must be a way out, somehow.' And Milly-Molly-Mandy said, 'I expect Father will know what to do.' So they hurried along, holding their hats on.

As they passed the Moggs's cottage they saw little-friend-Susan trying to hang a towel on the line, with the wind trying all the time to wrap her up in it.

Milly-Molly-Mandy called out, 'Hullo, Susan! Our roof's being blown off, and Mr Critch the Thatcher can't come and mend it, so Father will have to. Do you want to come and see?' Little-friend-Susan was very interested, and as soon as she had got the towel up she came along with them.

When Father and Mother and Grandpa and Grandma and Uncle heard their news they all looked as if they were saying 'Dear, dear!' to themselves. But Milly-Molly-Mandy looked quite pleased, and said, 'Now you'll have to mend the roof, won't you, Father?'

And Father looked at Uncle, and said, 'Well, Joe.

How about it?' And Uncle said, 'Right, John!' in his big voice.

And then Father and Uncle buttoned their jackets (so that the wind shouldn't flap them), and fetched ladders (to reach the roof with), and a rake (to comb the straw tidy with), and wooden pegs (with which to

fasten it down). And then they put one ladder so that they could climb up *to* the thatched roof, and another ladder with hooks on the end so that they could climb up *on* the thatched roof; and then Father gathered up a big armful of straw, and he and Uncle set to work busily to mend the hole in the thatch as well as they could, till Mr Critch the Thatcher could come.

Milly-Molly-Mandy and little-friend-Susan, down below, set to work busily to collect the straw from the hedges and the flower-beds and the grass, piling it up in one corner, ready for Father when he came down for another armful. And they helped to hold the ladder steady, and handed up sticks for making the pattern round the edge of the thatch, and fetched things that Father or Uncle called out for, and were very useful indeed.

Soon the roof began to look much better.

Then Father fetched a big pair of shears, and he snip-snip-snipped the straggly ends of the straw all round Milly-Molly-Mandy's little bedroom window up under the roof. (Milly-Molly-Mandy thought it was just like the nice white cottage having its hair cut!) And then Father and Uncle stretched a big piece of wire netting over the mended place, and fastened it down with pegs. (Milly-Molly-Mandy thought it was just like the nice white cottage having a hair-net put on and fastened with hairpins!)

And then the roof was all trim and tidy again, and they wouldn't feel in any sort of a hurry for Mr Critch the Thatcher to come and thatch it properly.

'Isn't it a lovely roof?' said Milly-Molly-Mandy. 'I knew Father could do it!'

'Well, you can generally manage to do a thing when you have to, Milly-Molly-Mandy,' said Father, but he looked quite pleased with himself, and so did Uncle.

Soon the roof began to look much better

And when they saw what a nice snug roof they had now, so did Mother and Grandpa and Grandma and Aunty and Milly-Molly-Mandy!

7. Milly-Molly-Mandy Writes Letters

Once upon a time Milly-Molly-Mandy heard the postman's knock, bang-BANG! on the front door; so she ran hop-skip down the passage to look in the letter-box because she always sort of hoped there might be a letter for her!

But there wasn't.

'I do wish the postman would bring me a letter sometimes,' said Milly-Molly-Mandy, coming slowly back into the kitchen. 'He never does. There's only a business-looking letter for Father and an advertisement for Uncle.'

And then Milly-Molly-Mandy noticed that the business-looking letter was from Holland (where Father got his flower bulbs) and had a Dutch stamp on it, so that was more interesting. Milly-Molly-Mandy was collecting foreign stamps. She had collected one Irish one already, and it was stuck in Billy Blunt's new stamp album. (Billy Blunt had just started collecting stamps, so Milly-Molly-Mandy was collecting for him.)

'If you want the postman to bring you letters you'll

have to write them to other people first,' said Mother, putting the letter up on the mantelshelf till Father and Uncle should come in.

'But I haven't got any stamps,' said Milly-Molly-Mandy.

'I'll give you one when you want it,' said Grandma, pulling the kettle forward on the stove.

'But I don't know who to write to,' said Milly-Molly-Mandy.

'You'll have to think round a little,' said Aunty, clearing her sewing off the table.

'There's only Billy Blunt and little-friend-Susan and it would be silly to write to them when I see them every day,' said Milly-Molly-Mandy.

'We must just think,' said Mother, spreading the cloth on the table for tea. 'There are sure to be lots of people who would like to have letters by post, as well as you.'

Milly-Molly-Mandy hadn't thought of that. 'Do you suppose they'd run like anything to the letter-box because they thought there might be a letter from me?' she said. 'What fun! I've got the fancy note-paper that Aunty gave me at Christmas – they'll like that, won't they? Who *can* I write to?'

And then she helped to lay the table, and made a piece of toast at the fire for Grandma; and presently Father and Uncle and Grandpa came in to tea, and Milly-Molly-Mandy was given the Dutch stamp off Father's letter. She put it in her pencil-box, ready for Billy Blunt in the morning.

And then she had an idea. 'If I could write to some one not in England they'd stick foreign stamps on their letters when they wrote back, wouldn't they?'

And then Aunty had an idea. 'Why, there are my little nieces in America!' she said. (For Aunty had a brother who went to America when he was quite young, and now he had three little children, whom none of them had seen or knew hardly anything about, for 'Tom', as Aunty called him, wasn't a very good letter writer, and only wrote to her sometimes at Christmas.)

'Ooh, yes!' said Milly-Molly-Mandy, 'and I don't believe Billy has an American stamp yet. What are their names, Aunty? I forget.'

'Sallie and Lallie,' said Aunty, 'and the boy is Tom, after my brother, but they call him Buddy. They would like to have a letter from their cousin in England, I'm sure.'

So Milly-Molly-Mandy looked out the box of fancy notepaper that Aunty had given her, and kept it by her side while she did her home-lessons after tea. And then, when she had done them all, she wrote quite a long letter to her cousin Sallie (at least it looked quite a long letter, because the pink note-paper was rather small), telling about her school, and her friends, and Billy Blunt's collection, and about Toby the dog, and Topsy the cat, and what Father and Mother and Grandpa and Grandma and Uncle and Aunty were all doing at that moment in the kitchen, and outside in the barn; so that Sallie should get to know them all. And then there was just room to send her love to Lallie and Buddy, and to sign her name.

It was quite a nice letter.

Milly-Molly-Mandy showed it to Mother and Aunty, and then (just to make it more interesting) she put in a piece of coloured silver paper and two primroses (the first she had found that year), and stuck down the flap of the pink envelope.

The next morning she posted her letter in the red pillar-box on the way to school (little-friend-Susan was quite interested when she showed her the address); and then she tried to forget all about it, because she knew it would take a long while to get there and a longer while still for an answering letter to come back.

After morning school she gave the Dutch stamp to Billy Blunt for his collection. He said he had got one, as they were quite common, but that it might come in useful for exchanging with some other fellow. And after school that very afternoon he told her he had exchanged it for a German stamp; so it was very useful.

'Have you got an American stamp?' asked Milly-Molly-Mandy.

'No,' said Billy Blunt. 'What I want to get hold of is a Czechoslovakian one. Ted Smale's just got one. His uncle gave it to him.'

Milly-Molly-Mandy didn't think she could ever collect such a stamp as that for Billy Blunt, but she was glad he hadn't got an American one yet.

All that week and the next Milly-Molly-Mandy rushed to the letter-box every time she heard the postman, although she knew there wouldn't be an answer for about three weeks, anyhow. But the postman's knock, bang-BANG! sounded so exciting she always forgot to remember in time.

A whole month went by, and Milly-Molly-Mandy began almost to stop expecting a letter at all, or at least one from abroad.

And then one day she came home after school a bit later than usual, because she and little-friend-Susan had been picking wild-flowers and primroses under

They sat and wrote letters together

a hedge, very excited to think spring had really come. But when she did get in what DO you think she found waiting for her, on her plate at the table?

Why, *three* letters, just come by post! One from Sallie, one from Lallie, and one from Buddy!

They were so pleased at having a letter from England that they had all written back hoping she would write again. And they sent some snapshots of themselves, and Buddy enclosed a Japanese stamp for Billy Blunt's collection.

The next Saturday Billy Blunt came to tea with Milly-Molly-Mandy and she gave him the four

stamps, three American and one Japanese. And though he said they were not really valuable ones, he was as pleased as anything to have them!

And when the table was cleared they sat and wrote letters together – Milly-Molly-Mandy to Sallie and

Lallie, and Billy Blunt to Buddy (to thank him for the stamp), with a little P.S. from Milly-Molly-Mandy (to thank him for his letter).

Milly-Molly-Mandy does like letter-writing, because now she has got three more friends!

8. Milly-Molly-Mandy Learns to Ride

Once upon a time, when Milly-Molly-Mandy had gone down to the village to get some things for Mother at the grocer's shop, she saw Miss Muggins's little niece Jilly wheeling a bicycle out of their side door.

It was a young bicycle, not a grown-up one, and it was very new, and very shiny, and very black-and-silvery.

'Hullo!' said Milly-Molly-Mandy, looking at it interestedly, 'is that your bicycle?'

'Hullo!' said Miss Muggins's Jilly, trying to look as if nothing unusual were happening. 'Yes. My Uncle gave it to me.'

'Can you ride it?' asked Milly-Molly-Mandy.

'Oh, yes,' said Miss Muggins's Jilly, 'I ride it up and down the road. I'm just going to do it now. Good-bye.' And she got up on it and rode off (rather wobblily, but still she did it) toward the cross-roads.

Milly-Molly-Mandy went into the grocer's shop with her basket, wishing she could have a ride, but of course as it was such a beautiful new bicycle she hadn't liked to ask.

When she came out again Miss Muggins's Jilly passed her, riding back; and she got off when she came to the letter-box at the corner to turn round because she couldn't ride round without toppling over yet.

Milly-Molly-Mandy couldn't help saying to her longingly, 'I do wish I could have a little ride on it.'

But Miss Muggins's Jilly said, 'I don't expect you could if you've never learned – you'd fall off. And my Aunty says I've got to be very careful with it, because it's new. I'm going to ride back to the crossroads now. Good-bye.' And Miss Muggins's Jilly rode off again, and Milly-Molly-Mandy walked on homeward.

As she passed the duck-pond she saw Billy Blunt

hanging over the rail to see if he could see a tiddler.

And Milly-Molly-Mandy said, 'Hullo, Billy. What do you think? Jilly's got a new bicycle!'

And Billy Blunt said, 'I know. I've seen it.'

'I wish we had bicycles, don't you?' said Milly-Molly-Mandy.

'I have got one,' said Billy Blunt surprisingly.

'You haven't!' said Milly-Molly-Mandy.

'I've got two, if I wanted 'em,' said Billy Blunt.

'Where are they?' asked Milly-Molly-Mandy.

'In our shed,' said Billy Blunt.

'I don't believe it!' said Milly-Molly-Mandy. 'You're only funning. Because you'd ride them if you had them – only you wouldn't have two, anyhow!'

But Billy Blunt only grinned; and Milly-Molly-Mandy walked on homeward.

As she passed the Moggs's cottage she saw little-friend-Susan on the other side of the wall playing with her baby sister. And Milly-Molly-Mandy said, 'Hullo, Susan. What do you think? Jilly's got a new bicycle!'

'Oh!' said little-friend-Susan, 'I wish we'd got bicycles.'

And Milly-Molly-Mandy said, 'I wish we could ride, anyhow – then p'r'aps Jilly would let us have a tiny little ride on hers.' And then Milly-Molly-Mandy walked on home to the nice white cottage with the thatched roof and gave Mother her basket of groceries.

A few days later, coming home from school in the afternoon (Miss Muggins's Jilly had just gone in at Miss Muggins's side door, which they passed first) Billy Blunt stopped as he was going in at the little white gate by the corn-shop, and said to Milly-Molly-Mandy and little-friend-Susan, 'Want to see something?'

Milly-Molly-Mandy and little-friend-Susan of course said 'Yes!' at once.

And Billy Blunt said, 'Come on and see!'

So Milly-Molly-Mandy and little-friend-Susan went with him through the little white gate into the Blunt's garden.

'What is it?' asked Milly-Molly-Mandy. But Billy Blunt only led the way to the old shed at the farther end. 'Oh, I know!' said Milly-Molly-Mandy, with a sudden guess. 'It's your old bicycles – but I don't believe it!'

Billy Blunt solemnly undid the rickety door of the shed and pulled it open. 'There you are, Miss!' he said, grinning triumphantly. 'Now you can just unsay what you said.'

And there in the dusty, mouldy-smelling shed, among a lot of boxes and bottles and paint-tins and other lumber, stood two old bicycles leaning against the wall. They were covered all over with rust and cobwebs, and their tyres were falling off in rags.

'Oh-h-h!' said Milly-Molly-Mandy and little-friend-Susan together, pushing in closer to look.

'They aren't any good,' said little-friend-Susan disappointedly.

'Oh, wait! They might be! Can't we make them be?' cried Milly-Molly-Mandy excitedly.

Billy Blunt wheeled one of the bicycles out – only it wouldn't wheel because the wheels were all rusty. Milly-Molly-Mandy pulled the other one out; it was a lady's bike, and just a bit smaller (and it did make her hands dirty!).

'Oh, Billy!' said Milly-Molly-Mandy, 'if we could only make the wheels go round you could learn on that one and we could learn on this one. What fun!'

And little-friend-Susan said, 'Oh, we never could, but let's try!' and she pulled a whole mass of cobwebs off the spokes, and jumped as a big black spider ran away.

Billy Blunt put his cap and school satchel down on the grass, and started poking and scraping with a bit of stick to loosen the rust. And then the others started working the wheels backwards and forwards to make

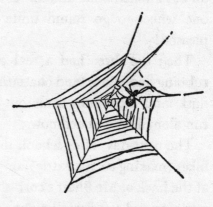

them turn. And they pulled off the ragged tyres in strips, and rubbed at the rust with bunches of grass; and they DID get dirty, all red rusty dirt! (But they enjoyed it!)

They forgot all about tea till Mrs Blunt called Billy Blunt in; then Milly-Molly-Mandy and little-friend-Susan ran off to their homes, promising to come back directly after.

Milly-Molly-Mandy ate her tea as quickly as she could, talking about bicycles all the time; and

Mother made her take an old overall to put on, and gave her a bundle of rags with which to rub the rust and dust off. And then she ran down the road to little-friend-Susan's and the two of them ran along together back to the Blunt's garden.

Billy Blunt was already hard at work again with an old kitchen knife and an oil-can, and he had got one wheel to go round quite nicely. They were pleased!

Then the three had a real set-to, scraping and rubbing and oiling (and chattering) until it got quite dusk, and Mrs Blunt came out and said they must run along home to bed now.

The next day, after school, they wheeled the two bikes (making such a rattle!) on to the waste ground at the back of Mr Blunt's corn-shop, where the grass was nice and soft for falling on (or at any rate softer than the road!). And there they started to practise cycling – Billy Blunt on the gentleman's bicycle, and Milly-Molly-Mandy and her little-friend-Susan taking turns riding and holding each other up on the lady's bicycle. (Mr Blunt had hammered the saddles down for them as low as they would go.)

It was fun!

And what a rattling, scraping, creaking noise they did make, to be sure, over the grass! And how they did keep on toppling over sideways, and calling to each other to hold them up, and falling with a crash among the buttercups! And how they did scratch and scrape and bump themselves! And HOW they did enjoy it all!

By the end of the evening Billy Blunt could ride half as far as the tree before he fell off, and Milly-Molly-Mandy and little-friend-Susan could do nearly as well (but of course they had to take turns, which made them a bit slower).

Milly-Molly-Mandy could hardly wait for the night to go, she was so keen to get back to her riding!

It was Saturday next day, so they were able to spend nearly all day in the field, rattling and bump-

What a rattling, scraping, creaking noise they did make!

ing round over the tufty grass and the molehills. And presently they started riding up and down the path by the forge, where it was easier going, only harder if you fell off (but they didn't fall off so much now).

Mr Rudge the Blacksmith laughed at them as they rattled past the open door of the forge, where he was clanging away with his big hammer; but they didn't mind. Billy Blunt even managed to wave to him once without falling off!

Miss Muggins's Jilly came and watched them for a while and presently she said, 'You are riding nicely. I'll let you have a ride on my bicycle soon, Milly-Molly-Mandy.'

Milly-Molly-Mandy thanked her very much, and thought it would be nice to know how it felt to be on a real bicycle. But all the same, she couldn't help thinking that no bicycle in the whole world could be *half* as thrilling to ride on as these rusty, rattling, creaking old bikes of Billy Blunt's!

9. *Milly-Molly-Mandy Makes a Garden*

Once upon a time Milly-Molly-Mandy was very excited.

There was to be a grand Flower and Vegetable Show in the village in a month's time (the posters telling about it were stuck on the back of the forge); and besides prizes being given for all the usual things – such as the finest potatoes and strawberries and garden flowers, and the best home-made jams and pickles – there were also to be prizes for the prettiest posy of wild flowers, and the best miniature garden (grown in a bowl).

'Ooh!' said Milly-Molly-Mandy to little-friend-Susan (they were reading the poster together after morning school); 'I wonder!'

'What!' said little-friend-Susan.

'I wonder,' said Milly-Molly-Mandy, 'if I shall grow a little garden in a bowl, and send it to the Flower Show!'

'Oh, could you?' said little-friend-Susan. 'And do you suppose I could make a posy and send it in too? Wouldn't it be lovely to win a prize?'

'I don't suppose we could,' said Milly-Molly-Mandy, 'but it would be such fun to try. I'm going to ask Mother.'

So when Milly-Molly-Mandy got home she asked if she might make a little garden and send it to the Flower Show. And Mother said, 'If you can make it nicely enough you may, Milly-Molly-Mandy. Father is going to send in some of his best gooseberries, and I am going to send some pots of jam and pickles; so we shall make a good showing, all together!'

Then Mother got out a brown pottery pie-dish

from the kitchen cupboard and asked Milly-Molly-Mandy if she thought that would do to grow her garden in; and after Milly-Molly-Mandy had considered it well she thought it would. She put some broken bits of flower pot at the bottom (to help to drain off the wet), and then she filled the dish with the brownest, softest earth she could find. And then she had to think what to plant in her garden so that it would look just like a real big one, if it weren't so very little!

It took a lot of thinking.

After school Milly-Molly-Mandy told Billy Blunt about the Flower Show in case he hadn't heard about it; but he said he had.

'Are you going to go in for any of the prizes?' asked Milly-Molly-Mandy.

''Huh!' was all Billy Blunt said; but Milly-Molly-Mandy knew he was!

'Which one?' she asked. And Billy Blunt took her into the old cycle-shed beside the corn-shop and showed her – a fine new red earthenware bowl filled with soft brown earth!

'Billy!' said Milly-Molly-Mandy. 'Fancy your going in for that one! So am I! And we can't both win the prize.'

'Don't suppose either of us will,' said Billy Blunt, 'but I mean to have a good try.'

Showed her a fine new red earthenware bowl

'So do I,' said Milly-Molly-Mandy.

'And the best one wins,' said Billy Blunt.

The next day Milly-Molly-Mandy set the first plant in her garden. It was a tiny little holly-tree which she had found growing almost in the path under the big holly-tree by the hedge. (It had grown from one of the fallen berries.) Milly-Molly-Mandy knew it would only be trodden on if left there, so she carefully dug it up and planted it in the soft brown earth in her bowl.

Next she went poking about down by the brook, and she found some nice moss-grown bits of rotten wood; one bit looked just like a little green mossy cave, so she took it home and put it in the bowl by the holly-tree; and then she planted some grass and a daisy root in the rest of the space, and it really looked quite a pretty garden. It grew so nicely, and the baby holly-tree opened out its new little leaves as if it felt quite at home there.

Billy Blunt wouldn't let anyone see his garden until he had got it arranged to his liking. And then one day he said Milly-Molly-Mandy might have a look if she liked. And he fetched it down from his bedroom to show her.

And it was pretty!

There was more room in Billy Blunt's bowl, and he had made it like a rock garden with rough-looking little stones; and a small sycamore-tree was growing between them in one place, and a wee sage-bush in another; and little tiny plants – scarlet pimpernels, and rock-roses, and lady's bedstraw – sprouted here and there. Milly-Molly-Mandy did like it.

'Oh, Billy!' she said, 'yours is much prettier than mine! Except that yours hasn't got a cave in it. You'll get the prize.'

But when Billy Blunt saw the mossy cave in Milly-Molly-Mandy's garden he wasn't so sure.

The day of the Flower Show drew near. It was to be held in the village Institute on the Saturday, and everybody who was going to send in (and nearly everybody was) was feeling very busy and important. Mr Jakes the Postman had some fine gooseberries and red-currants which he meant to enter, and little-

331

friend-Susan said her father and Mrs Green were going to show lots of flowers and vegetables from the garden at the Big House with the iron railings (Mr Moggs was gardener at Mrs Green's), and Mrs Green was making a miniature garden too.

And then, just the very day before the Show (which, of course, was sending-in day), what DO you think happened?

Billy Blunt's little sycamore-tree lost all its leaves!

Either he hadn't managed to get all its roots when he dug it up or else it had been left too long in the hot sun, without much earth to grow in; anyhow, when he came back from school there it was, with its leaves all curled up and spoiled.

Billy Blunt was dreadfully disappointed, and so was Milly-Molly-Mandy.

'Whole thing's done for now,' said Billy Blunt; 'it's nothing without that tree.'

'Can't we find another one somewhere?' said Milly-Molly-Mandy. 'Let's look!'

'I looked everywhere before I found that one,' said Billy Blunt. 'Besides, there isn't any time to look. It's got to go in. Only it's no good sending it now.'

'Oh, Billy!' said Milly-Molly-Mandy. She was as disappointed as he was. 'It won't be any fun sending mine in now. It wouldn't seem fair if I *did* get a prize.

But I don't expect I'll get one anyhow – Susan says Mrs Green is sending in a garden.'

'Hers won't have a cave in it,' said Billy Blunt.

And then, suddenly, Milly-Molly-Mandy had an idea.

'I tell you what! Couldn't we make one beautiful garden between us and send it in together? Why not? Your big bowl and garden, with my tree and the mossy cave? Couldn't we?'

Billy Blunt was very doubtful. 'I don't know that we could send in together,' he said slowly.

'Why couldn't we? Mr Moggs and Mrs Green at the Big House do,' said Milly-Molly-Mandy. 'I'll go and fetch my garden and we'll see how it would look!'

So she ran all the way home to the nice white cottage with the thatched roof and fetched her little garden; and then she walked carefully with it all the way back. And what do you think she found Billy Blunt doing? He was writing a label to see how it would look for the Flower Show: 'Sent in by Billy Blunt and Milly-Molly-Mandy.'

'Looks quite businesslike,' he said. 'Did you fetch your tree?'

The little garden in the pottery dish looked so pretty it almost seemed a pity to spoil it, but Milly-

Molly-Mandy insisted. So together they took out the little holly-tree and planted it in place of the syca-more-tree; and then they arranged the mossy bit of wood at one side of the bowl; and it looked so real you almost felt as if you could live in the little green cave, and go clambering on the rocks, or climb the tree, if you wished!

'Well!' said Milly-Molly-Mandy, sitting back on her heels, 'it just couldn't be prettier!'

'Umm!' said Billy Blunt, looking very satisfied. 'It's prettier than either of them was before. Let's take it in now.'

So they walked across to the Institute and handed in the precious miniature garden, with the sixpence entrance fee between them.

It was so hard to wait till the next day! But on Saturday, as soon as the judges had decided which things had won prizes, the Flower Show was opened and the shilling people could go in. Most people waited till the afternoon, when it cost only sixpence; Father and Mother and Grandpa and Grandma and Uncle and Aunty and Milly-Molly-Mandy (who was half-price) went then.

The place was filled with people and lovely smells of flowers and strawberries, and there was a great noise of people talking and exclaiming, and cups clattering somewhere at the back, and the village band was tuning up.

Milly-Molly-Mandy could not see Billy Blunt or the miniature gardens; but Father's gooseberries had got first prize, and his basket of vegetables second prize (Mr Moggs's got the first), and Mother had first prize for her jam, but nothing for her marrow-chutney (Mrs Critch, the Thatcher's wife, won that). Little-friend-Susan was there, skipping up and down gleefully because her wild posy had won a third prize.

And then Milly-Molly-Mandy saw Billy Blunt. He was grinning all over his face!

'Seen the gardens?' he said. 'Come on. This way.' And he pulled her through the crowd to a table at the farther end, where were arranged several minia-ture gardens of all sorts and sizes, some of them very pretty ones indeed.

But right in the middle, raised up by itself, was the prettiest one of all; and it was labelled:

'FIRST PRIZE. Sent in by Billy Blunt and Milly-Molly-Mandy'!

10. *Milly-Molly-Mandy Camps Out*

Once upon a time Milly-Molly-Mandy and Toby the dog went down to the village, to Miss Muggins's shop, on an errand for Mother; and as they passed Mr Blunt's corn-shop Milly-Molly-Mandy saw something new in the little garden at the side. It looked like a small, shabby sort of tent, with a slit in the top and a big checked patch sewn on the side.

Milly-Molly-Mandy wondered what it was doing there. But she didn't see Billy Blunt anywhere about, so she couldn't ask him.

When she came out of Miss Muggins's shop she had another good look over the palings into the Blunt's garden. And while she was looking Billy Blunt came out of their house door with some old rugs and a pillow in his arms.

'Hullo, Billy!' said Milly-Molly-Mandy. 'What's that tent-thing?'

'It's a tent,' said Billy Blunt, not liking its being called 'thing'.

'But what's it for?' asked Milly-Molly-Mandy.

'It's mine,' said Billy Blunt.

337

'Yours? Your very own? Is it?' said Milly-Molly-Mandy. 'Ooh, do let me come and look at it!'

'You can if you want to,' said Billy Blunt. 'I'm going to sleep in it tonight – camp out.'

Milly-Molly-Mandy was very interested indeed. She looked at it well, outside and in. She could only just stand up in it. Billy Blunt had spread an old

mackintosh for a ground-sheet, and there was a box in one corner to hold a bottle of water and a mug, and his electric torch, and such necessary things; and when the front flap of the tent was closed you couldn't see anything outside, except a tiny bit of sky and some green leaves through the tear in the top.

338

Milly-Molly-Mandy didn't want to come out a bit, but Billy Blunt wanted to put his bedding in.

'Isn't it beautiful! Where did you get it, Billy?' she asked.

'My cousin gave it to me,' said Billy Blunt. 'Used it when he went cycling holidays. He's got a new one now. I put that patch on, myself.'

Milly-Molly-Mandy thought she could have done it better; but still it was quite good for a boy, so she duly admired it, and offered to mend the other place. But Billy Blunt didn't think it was worth it, as it would only tear away again – and he liked a bit of air, anyhow.

'Shan't you feel funny out here all by yourself when everybody else is asleep?' said Milly-Molly-Mandy. 'Oh, I wish I had a tent too!' Then she said good-bye, and ran with Toby the dog back home to the nice white cottage with the thatched roof, thinking of the tent all the way.

She didn't see little-friend-Susan as she passed the Moggs's cottage along the road; but when she got as far as the meadow she saw her swinging her baby sister on the big gate.

'Hullo, Milly-Molly-Mandy! I was just looking for you,' said little-friend-Susan, lifting Baby Moggs down. And Milly-Molly-Mandy told her all about Billy Blunt's new tent, and how he was going to

339

sleep out, and how she wished she had a tent too.

Little-friend-Susan was almost as interested as Milly-Molly-Mandy. 'Can't we make a tent and play in it in your meadow?' she said. 'It would be awful fun!'

So they got some bean-poles and bits of sacking from the barn and dragged them down into the meadow. And they had great fun that day trying to make a tent; only they couldn't get it to stay up properly.

Next morning little-friend-Susan came to play 'tents' in the meadow again. And this time they tried with an old counterpane, which Mother had given them, and two kitchen chairs; and they managed to rig up quite a good tent by laying the poles across the chair-backs and draping the counterpane over. They fastened down the spread-out sides with stones; and the ends, where the chairs were, they hung with sacks. And there they had a perfectly good tent, really quite big enough for two – so long as the two were small, and didn't mind being a bit crowded!

They were just sitting in it, eating apples and pretending they had no other home to live in, when they heard a '*Hi!*'-ing from the gate; and when they peeped out there was Billy Blunt, with a great bundle in his arms, trying to get the gate open. So they ran across the grass and opened it for him.

'What have you got? Is it your tent? Did you sleep out last night?' asked Milly-Molly-Mandy.

'Look here,' said Billy Blunt, 'do you think your father would mind, supposing I pitched my tent in your field? My folk don't like it in our garden – say it looks too untidy.'

Milly-Molly-Mandy was quite sure Father would not mind. So Billy Blunt put the bundle down inside the gate and went off to ask (for of course you never camp anywhere without saying 'please' to the owner first). And Father didn't mind a bit, so long as no papers or other rubbish were left about.

So Billy Blunt set up his tent near the others', which was not too far from the nice white cottage with the thatched roof (because it's funny what a long way off from everybody you feel when you've got only a tent round you at night!). And then he went home to fetch his other goods; and Milly-Molly-Mandy and little-friend-Susan sat in his tent, and wished and wished that their mothers would let them sleep out in the meadow that night.

When Billy Blunt came back with his rugs and things (loaded up on his box on wheels) they asked him if it were very creepy-feeling to sleep out of doors.

And Billy Blunt (having slept out once) said, 'Oh, you soon get used to it,' and asked why they didn't try it in their tent.

So then Milly-Molly-Mandy and little-friend-Susan looked at each other, and said firmly, 'Let's ask!' So little-friend-Susan went with Milly-Molly-Mandy up to the nice white cottage with the thatched roof, where Mother was just putting a treacle-tart into the oven.

She looked very doubtful when Milly-Molly-Mandy told her what they wanted to do. Then she shut the oven door, and wiped her hands, and said, well, she would just come and look at the tent they had made first. And when she had looked and considered, she said, well, if it were still very fine and dry by the evening perhaps Milly-Molly-Mandy might sleep out there, just for once. And Mother found a rubber groundsheet and some old blankets and cushions, and gave them to her.

Then Milly-Molly-Mandy went with little-friend-Susan to the Moggs's cottage, where Mrs Moggs was just putting their potatoes on to boil.

She looked very doubtful at first; and then she said, well, if Milly-Molly-Mandy's mother had been out to see, and thought it was all right, and if it were a *very* nice, fine evening, perhaps little-friend-Susan might sleep out, just for once.

So all the rest of that day the three were very busy, making preparations and watching the sky. And when they all went home for supper the evening was beautifully still and warm, and without a single cloud.

So, after supper, they all met together again in the

meadow, in the sunset. And they shut and tied up the meadow-gate. (It was all terribly exciting!)

And Mother came out, with Father and Grandpa and Grandma and Uncle and Aunty, to see that all was right, and their ground-sheets well spread under their bedding.

Then Milly-Molly-Mandy and little-friend-Susan crawled into their tent, and Billy Blunt crawled into his tent. And presently Milly-Molly-Mandy crawled out again in her pyjamas, and ran about with bare feet on the grass with Toby the dog; and then little-friend-Susan and Billy Blunt, in their pyjamas, crawled out and ran about too (because it feels so very nice, and so sort of new, to be running about under the sky in your pyjamas!).

And Father and Mother and Grandpa and Grandma and Uncle and Aunty laughed, and looked on as if they wouldn't mind doing it too, if they weren't so grown up.

Then Mother said, 'Now I think it's time you campers popped into bed. Good night!' And they went off home.

So Milly-Molly-Mandy and little-friend-Susan called 'Good night!' and crawled into one tent, and Billy Blunt caught Toby the dog and crawled into the other.

And the trees outside grew slowly blacker and

Then little-friend-Susan and Billy Blunt crawled out

blacker until they couldn't be seen at all; and the owls hooted; and a far-away cow moo-ed; and now and then Toby the dog wuffed, because he thought he heard a rabbit; and sometimes Milly-Molly-Mandy or little-friend-Susan squeaked, because they thought they felt a spider walking on them. And once Billy Blunt called out to ask if they were still awake, and they said they were, and was he? and he said of course he was.

And then at last they all fell fast asleep.

And in no time at all the sun was shining through their tents, telling them to wake up and come out, because it was the next day.

And Billy Blunt and Milly-Molly-Mandy and little-friend-Susan DID enjoy that camping-out night!

11. Milly-Molly-Mandy Keeps House

Once upon a time Milly-Molly-Mandy was left one evening in the nice white cottage with the thatched roof to keep house.

There was something called a political meeting being held in the next village (Milly-Molly-Mandy didn't know quite what that meant, but it was something to do with voting, which was something you had to do when you grew up), and Father and Mother and Grandpa and Grandma and Uncle and Aunty all thought they ought to go to it.

Milly-Molly-Mandy said she would not mind one bit being left, especially if she could have little-friend-Susan in to keep her company.

So Mother said, 'Very well, then, Milly-Molly-Mandy, we'll have little-friend-Susan in to keep you company. And you needn't open the door if anyone knocks unless you know who it is. And I'll leave you out some supper, in case we may be a little late getting back.'

Little-friend-Susan was only too pleased to come and spend the evening with Milly-Molly-Mandy. So after tea she came in; and then Father and Mother and Grandpa and Grandma and Uncle and Aunty put on their hats and coats, and said good-bye, and went off.

And Milly-Molly-Mandy and little-friend-Susan shut the door carefully after them, and there they were, all by themselves, keeping house!

'What fun!' said little-friend-Susan. 'What'll we do?'

'Well,' said Milly-Molly-Mandy, 'if we're house-keepers I think we ought to wear aprons.'

So they each tied on one of Mother's aprons.

And then little-friend-Susan said, 'Now if we've got aprons on we ought to work.'

So Milly-Molly-Mandy fetched a dustpan and brush and swept up some crumbs from the floor; and little-friend-Susan folded the newspaper that was lying all anyhow by Grandpa's chair and put it neatly on the shelf. And then they banged the cushions and straightened the chairs, feeling very housekeeperish indeed.

Then little-friend-Susan looked at the plates of bread-and-dripping on the table, with the jug of milk and two little mugs. And she said, 'What's that for?'

And Milly-Molly-Mandy said, 'That's for our supper. But it isn't time to eat it yet, Mother says we can warm the milk on the stove, if we like, in a saucepan.'

'What fun!' said little-friend-Susan. 'Then we'll be cooks. Couldn't we do something to the bread-and dripping too?'

So Milly-Molly-Mandy looked at the bread-and-dripping thoughtfully, and then she said, 'We could toast it – at the fire!'

'Oh, yes!' said little-friend-Susan. And then she said, 'Oughtn't we to begin doing it now? It takes quite a long time to cook things.'

So Milly-Molly-Mandy said, 'Let's!' and fetched a saucepan, and little-friend-Susan took up the jug of milk, and then – suddenly – 'Bang-bang-BANG!' went the door-knocker, ever so loudly.

'Ooh!' said little-friend-Susan, 'that did make me jump! I wonder who it is!'

'Ooh!' said Milly-Molly-Mandy. 'We mustn't open the door unless we know. I wonder who it can be!'

So together they went to the door, and Milly-Molly-Mandy put her mouth to the letter-box and said politely, 'Please, who are you, please?'

Nobody spoke for a moment; and then a funny sort of voice outside said very gruffly, 'I'm Mr Snooks.'

And directly they heard that Milly-Molly-Mandy and little-friend-Susan looked at each other and said both together – 'It's Billy Blunt!' And they unlocked the door and pulled it open.

And there was Billy Blunt standing grinning on the doorstep!

Milly-Molly-Mandy held the door wide for him

to come in, and she said, 'Did you think we didn't know you?'

And little-friend-Susan said, 'You did give us a jump!' And Billy Blunt came in, grinning all over his face.

'We're all alone,' said Milly-Molly-Mandy. 'We're keeping house.'

'Look at our aprons,' said little-friend-Susan. 'We're going to cook our suppers.'

'Come on,' said Milly-Molly-Mandy, 'and we'll give you some. May you stop?'

Billy Blunt let them pull him into the kitchen, and then he said he'd seen Father and Mother and Grandpa and Grandma and Uncle and Aunty as they went past the corn-shop to the cross-roads, and

Mother had told him they were alone, and that he could go and have a game with them if he liked. So he thought he'd come and give them a jump.

'Take your coat off, because it's hot in here,' said Milly-Molly-Mandy. 'Now we must get on with the cooking. Come on, Susan!'

So they put the milk in to the saucepan on the back of the stove, and then they each took a piece of bread-and-dripping on a fork, to toast it.

But it wasn't a very good 'toasting fire' (or else there were too many people trying to toast at the same time). Billy Blunt began to think it was rather long to wait, and he looked at the frying-pan on the side of the stove (in which Mother always cooked the breakfast bacon), and said, 'Why not put' em in there and fry 'em up?'

Milly - Molly - Mandy and little - friend - Susan thought that was a splendid idea; so they fried all the bread-and-dripping nice and brown (and it did smell good!). When they had done it there was just a little fat left in the pan, so they looked round for something else to cook.

'I'll go and see if there're any odd bits of bread in the bread-crock,' said Milly-Molly-Mandy. 'We mustn't cut any, because I'm not allowed to use the bread-knife yet.'

So she went in to the scullery to look, and there

were one or two dry pieces in the bread-crock. But she found something else, and that was – a big basket of onions! Then Milly-Molly-Mandy gave a little squeal because she had a good idea, and she took out a small onion (she knew she might, because they had

lots, and Father grew them) and ran back into the kitchen with it.

And Billy Blunt, with his scout's knife, peeled it and sliced it into the pan (and the onion made him cry like anything!); and then Milly-Molly-Mandy fried it on the stove (and the onion made *her* cry like anything!) and then little-friend-Susan, who didn't want to be out of any fun stirred it up, with her head well over the pan (and the onion made her cry like anything too! – at least, she managed to get one small tear out).

And the onion smelt most delicious, all over the

353

And the onion smelt most delicious!

kitchen – only it would seem to cook all black or else not at all. But you can't *think* how good it tasted, spread on slices of fried bread!

They all sat on the hearthrug before the fire, with plates on their laps and mugs by their sides, and divided everything as evenly as possible. And they only wished there was more of everything (for of course Mother hadn't thought of Billy Blunt when she cut the bread-and-dripping).

When they had just finished the last crumb the door opened and Father and Mother and Grandpa and Grandma and Uncle and Aunty came in. And they all said together, 'Whatever's all this smell of fried onions?'

So Milly-Molly-Mandy explained, and when Mother had looked at the frying-pan to see that it wasn't burnt (and it wasn't) she only laughed and opened the window.

And Father said, 'Well, this smell makes me feel very hungry. Can't we have some fried onions for supper too, Mother?'

Then, before Father took little-friend-Susan and Billy Blunt home, Mother gave them all a piece of currant cake with which to finish their supper; and then she started frying a panful of onions for the grown-up supper.

And Milly-Molly-Mandy (when she had said

good-bye to little-friend-Susan and Billy Blunt) watched Mother very carefully, so that she should know how to fry quite properly next time she was left to keep house!

12. Milly-Molly-Mandy Goes Carol-singing

Once upon a time Milly-Molly-Mandy heard some funny sounds coming from the little garden at the side of Mr Blunt's corn-shop.

So she looked over the palings, and what should she see but Billy Blunt, looking very solemn and satisfied, blowing away on a big new shiny mouth-organ!

Milly-Molly-Mandy said, 'Hullo, Billy!' And

Billy Blunt blew 'Hullo!' into his mouth-organ (at least, Milly-Molly-Mandy guessed it was that), and went on playing.

Milly-Molly-Mandy waited a bit and listened, and suddenly she found she knew what he was playing. 'It's *Good King Wenceslas*!' said Milly-Molly-Mandy, 'isn't it? Can I have a go soon?'

'I'm practising,' said Billy Blunt, stopping for a moment and then going on again.

'Practising what?' said Milly-Molly-Mandy.

'Carols,' said Billy Blunt.

'What for?' said Milly-Molly-Mandy.

'Don't know,' said Billy Blunt, 'only it's Christmas time.'

'Then we could go caroling!' said Milly-Molly-Mandy, with a sudden thought. 'You could play on your mouth-organ, and I could sing. We could do it outside people's houses on Christmas Eve. Ooh, let's'!

But Billy Blunt only said 'Huh!' and went on blowing his mouth-organ. But he did it rather thoughtfully.

Milly-Molly-Mandy waited a bit longer, and then she was just going to say good-bye when Billy Blunt said, 'Here! You can have a go if you want to.'

So Milly-Molly-Mandy, very pleased, took the mouth organ and wiped it on her skirt, and had quite a good 'go' (and Billy Blunt knew she was playing

God Save the King). And then she wiped it again and gave it back saying, 'Good-bye, Billy. Don't forget about the carol-singing,' and went on homeward up the white road with the hedges each side.

A few days later (it was the day before Christmas Eve) Billy Blunt came up to the nice white cottage with the thatched roof, where Milly-Molly-Mandy lived, to bring a bag of meal which Uncle had ordered from Mr Blunt's corn-shop for his chickens. Milly-Molly-Mandy was watching Father cut branches

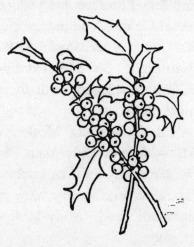

of holly from the holly-tree; but when she saw Billy Blunt she thought of the carols, and came running down to the path.

'I say,' said Billy Blunt. 'About that carol-singing.'

'Yes!' said Milly-Molly-Mandy. 'Have you been practising hard?'

'Mmm,' said Billy Blunt, 'I thought we might try 'em over now, if you're still keen on it. Where'll we do it?'

So Milly-Molly-Mandy led the way to the barn; and there in private they made plans and tried over one or two songs. They couldn't do *Hark the Herald Angels Sing* or *Christians Awake*, as the top notes in both of them went beyond the top of the mouth-organ and Billy Blunt wouldn't sing the top notes, because he said it didn't sound proper. But he could play *Noël* and *While Shepherds Watched* and *Wenceslas* beautifully. So Milly-Molly-Mandy sang while Billy Blunt played, until they could do it together quite nicely.

'I'll have to ask Mother first if I may,' said Milly-Molly-Mandy then. So they went round the back way into the kitchen, where Mother and Grandma and Aunty were mixing the Christmas pudding, and Milly-Molly-Mandy asked her question.

Just at first Mother looked a little doubtful. And then she said, 'You know Christmas-time is giving time. If you don't mean to knock at the doors and sing for money –'

Milly-Molly-Mandy said, 'No, we won't.'

'Why, that would be very nice, then,' said Mother, 'if you do it as nicely as ever you can.'

'We'll do it our very best, just for love,' said Milly-Molly-Mandy; and Billy Blunt nodded. Then Mother gave them some almonds and bits of peel-sugar, and then Billy Blunt had to go back.

The next day, directly tea was over, Milly-Molly-Mandy, very excited, slipped out of the house in her and coat and muffler, and ran down to the gate to look for Billy Blunt.

It was very dark. Presently she saw a bicycle lamp coming along the road. It was jogging up and down in a queer way for a bicycle. And then as it came near it started waving to and fro, and Milly-Molly-Mandy guessed there must be Billy Blunt with it; and she

361

skipped up and down outside the gate, because it did look so exciting and Christmassy!

'You ready? Come on,' said Billy Blunt, and the two of them set off down the road.

Soon they came to the Moggs's cottage, and began their carols. At the end of the first song little-friend-Susan's head peered from behind the window curtain and in the middle of the second she came rushing out of the door, saying, 'Oh, wait a bit while I get my hat and coat on, and let me join!'

And Mrs Moggs called from inside, 'Susan, bring them in quickly and shut that door, you're chilling the house!'

So they hurried inside and shut the door; and there was Mrs Moggs sitting by the fire with Baby Moggs in her lap, and Mr Moggs was fixing a bunch of holly over the mantelpiece. Mrs Moggs gave them each a lump of toffee, and then Milly-Molly-Mandy and Billy Blunt with little-friend-Susan went off to their caroling.

When they came to the village they meant to sing outside Mr Blunt's corn-shop, and Miss Muggins's draper's shop; but all the little shop-windows were so brightly lit up it made them feel shy.

People were going in and out of Mr Smale the Grocer's shop, and Mrs Hubble the Baker's shop, and sometimes they stopped to look in Miss

They started on their carol

Muggins's window (which was showing a lot of gay little penny toys and strings of tinsel balls, as well as gloves and handkerchiefs).

Milly-Molly-Mandy said, 'Let's wait!' and Billy Blunt said, 'Come on!' So they turned into the dark lane by the forge.

They heard the *cling-clang* of a hammer banging on the anvil. And Milly-Molly-Mandy said, 'Let's sing to Mr Rudge!' So they went up to the half-open door of the forge.

Billy Blunt blew a little note on the mouth-organ, and they started on their carol.

By the end of the first verse the Blacksmith was bringing his hammer down in time to the music, and it sounded just like a big bell chiming; and then he began joining in, in a big humming sort of voice. And when they finished he shouted out, 'Come on in and give us some more!'

So Milly-Molly-Mandy and Billy Blunt and little-friend-Susan came in out of the dark.

It was lovely in the forge, so warm and full of strange shadows and burnt-leathery sort of smells. They had a warm-up by the fire, and then began another song. And the Blacksmith sang and hammered all to time; and it sounded – as Mr Jakes the Postman popped his head in to say – 'real nice and Christmassy!'

'Go on, give us some more,' said the Blacksmith, burying his horseshoe in the fire again to make it hot so that he could punch nail-holes in it.

'We can't do many more,' said Milly-Molly-Mandy, 'because the mouth-organ isn't quite big enough.'

'Oh, never mind that,' said the Blacksmith. 'Go on, William, give us *Hark the Herald Angels Sing*!'

So Billy Blunt grinned and struck up, and everybody joined in so lustily that nobody noticed the missing top notes. While they were in the middle of it the door creaked open a little wider, and Miss Muggins's Jilly slipped in to join the fun; and later

365

on Mr and Mrs Blunt strolled over (when they had shut up shop); and then Mr Critch the Thatcher. And soon it seemed as if half the village were in and round the old forge, singing away, song after song, while the Blacksmith hammered like big bells on his anvil, and got all his horseshoes finished in good time before the holidays.

Presently who should come in but Father! He had been standing outside for quite a time, listening with Mother and Uncle and Aunty and Mr Moggs (they had all strolled down to see what their children were up to, and stopped to join the singing).

But soon Mother beckoned to Milly-Molly-Mandy from behind Father's shoulder, and Miss Muggins peeped round the door and beckoned to Billy Blunt, and Mr Moggs to little-friend-Susan. They knew that meant bed, but for once they didn't much mind, because it would make Christmas come all the sooner!

So the carols came to an end, and the Blacksmith called out, 'What about passing the hat for the carollers!'

But Billy-Blunt said with a grin, 'You sang, too – louder than we did!'

And little-friend-Susan said, 'Everybody sang!'

And Milly-Molly-Mandy said, 'We did it for love – all of us!'

And everybody said, 'So we did, now!' and wished everybody else 'Happy Christmas!'

And then Milly-Molly-Mandy said, 'Good night, see you tomorrow!' to Billy Blunt, and went skipping off home to bed, holding on to Father's hand through the dark.

" PEACE ON EARTH · GOODWILL TO MEN "

Milly-Molly-Mandy Again

Contents

The Brook
(near where M·M·M
saw the train)

The Nice White Cottage
with the Thatched Roof.
(where Milly-Molly-
Mandy lives)

The Barn

The Moggs' Cottage
(where little-friend
Susan lives)

Short cut

The Church
(where the Black-
Smith was married)

Dum-dum's
enclosure

To the Next Village

MAP of th

Joyce L. Brisley

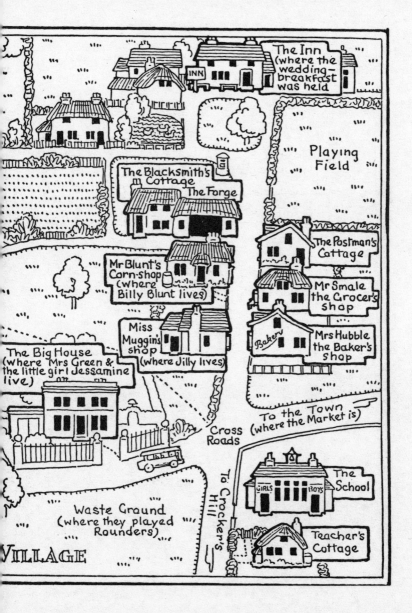

1. Milly-Molly-Mandy has a New Dress

Once upon a time Milly-Molly-Mandy was playing hide-and-seek with Toby the dog.

First Milly-Molly-Mandy threw a stone as far as she could, and then while Toby the dog was fetching it Milly-Molly-Mandy ran the other way and hid in among the gooseberry and currant bushes or behind the wall. And then Toby the dog came to look for her. He was so clever he always found her almost at once – even when she hid in the stable where Twinkletoes the pony lived (only he was out in the meadow eating grass now).

She shut the lower half of the stable door and kept quite quiet, but Toby the dog barked and scratched outside, and wouldn't go away till Milly-Molly-Mandy pushed open the door and came out.

Then Toby the dog was so pleased to see her, and so pleased with himself for finding her, that he jumped up and down on his hind legs, pawing and scratching at her skirt.

And suddenly – *rrrrrip!* – there was a great big

tear all the way down the front of Milly-Molly-Mandy's pink-and-white striped cotton frock.

'Oh dear, oh dear!' said Milly-Molly-Mandy. 'Oh, Toby, just see what you've done now!'

Then Toby the dog stopped jumping up and down, and he looked very sorry and ashamed of himself. So Milly-Molly-Mandy said, 'All right, then! Poor Toby! You didn't mean to do it. But whatever will Mother say? I'll have to go and show her.'

So Milly-Molly-Mandy, looking very solemn and holding her dress together with both hands, walked back through the barnyard where the cows were milked (only they, too, were out in the meadow eating grass now).

Uncle was throwing big buckets of water over the floor of the cowshed, to wash it. 'Now what have you been up to?' he asked, as Milly-Molly-Mandy, looking very solemn and holding her dress together with both hands, passed by.

'I tore my dress playing with Toby, and I'm going in to show Mother,' said Milly-Molly-Mandy.

'Well, well,' said Uncle, sending another big bucketful of water swashing along over the brick floor. 'Now you'll catch it. Tell Mother to send you out to me if she wants you to get a good spanking. I'll give you a proper one!'

'Mother won't let you spank me!' said Milly-Molly-Mandy (she knew Uncle was only joking). 'But she won't like having to mend such a great big tear, I expect. She mended this dress only a little while ago, and now it's got to be done all over again. Come on, Toby.'

So they went through the gate into the kitchen garden (where Father grew the vegetables) and in by the back door of the nice white cottage with the thatched roof where Father and Mother and Grandpa and Grandma and Uncle and Aunty and, of course, Milly-Molly-Mandy all lived together.

377

'Now what's the matter with little Millicent Margaret Amanda?' said Grandma, who was shelling peas for dinner, as Milly-Molly-Mandy came in, looking very solemn and holding her dress together with both hands.

'I'm looking for Mother,' said Milly-Molly-Mandy.

'She's in the larder,' said Aunty, who was patching sheets with her machine at the kitchen table. 'What have you been up to?'

But Milly-Molly-Mandy went over to the door of the larder, where Mother was washing the shelves.

'Mother,' said Milly-Molly-Mandy, looking very solemn and holding her dress together with both hands, 'I'm dreadfully sorry, but I was playing hide-and-seek with Toby, and we tore my dress. Badly.'

'Dear, dear, now!' said Grandma.

'Whatever next!' said Aunty.

'Let me have a look,' said Mother. She put down her wash-cloth and came out into the kitchen.

Milly-Molly-Mandy took her hands away and showed her frock, with the great big tear all down the front of it.

Mother looked at it. And then she said:

'Well, Milly-Molly-Mandy! That just about finishes that frock! But I was afraid it couldn't last much longer when I mended it before.'

And Grandma said, 'She had really outgrown it.'

And Aunty said, 'It was very faded.'

And Mother said, 'You will have to have a new one.'

Milly-Molly-Mandy *was* pleased to think that was all they said about it. (So was Toby the dog!)

Mother said, 'You can go out in the garden and tear it all you like now, Milly-Molly-Mandy. But don't you go tearing anything else!'

So Milly-Molly-Mandy and Toby the dog had a fine time tearing her old dress to ribbons, so that

Milly-Molly-Mandy showed her frock with the tear all down the front

she looked as if she had been dancing in a furze bush, Grandpa said. And then Mother sent her upstairs to change into her better frock (which was pink-and-white striped, too).

During dinner Mother said:

'I'm going to take Milly-Molly-Mandy down to the Village this afternoon, to buy her some stuff for a new dress.'

Father said, 'I suppose that means you want some more money.' And he took some out of his trousers' pocket and handed it over to Mother.

Grandma said, 'What about getting her something that isn't pink-and-white striped, just for a change?'

Grandpa said, 'Let's have flowers instead of stripes this time.'

Aunty said, 'Something with daisies on would look nice.'

Uncle said, 'Oh, let's go gay while we are about it, and have magenta roses and yellow sunflowers – eh, Milly-Molly-Mandy?'

But Milly-Molly-Mandy said, 'I don't 'spect Miss Muggins keeps that sort of stuff in her shop, so then I can't have it!'

After dinner Milly-Molly-Mandy helped Mother

to wash up the plates and things, and then Mother changed her dress, and they put on their hats, and Mother took her handbag, and they went together down the road with the hedges each side towards the Village.

They passed the Moggs' cottage, where little-friend-Susan lived. Little-friend-Susan was helping her baby sister to make mud pies on the step.

'Hullo, Susan,' said Milly-Molly-Mandy. 'We're going to buy me some different new dress stuff at Miss Muggins' shop, because I tore my other one!'

'Are you? How nice! What colour are you going to have this time?' asked little-friend-Susan.

'We don't know yet, but it will be something quite different,' said Milly-Molly-Mandy.

They passed the Forge, where Mr Rudge the Blacksmith and his new boy were making a big fire over an iron hoop which, when it was red-hot, they were going to fit round a broken cart-wheel to mend it. Milly-Molly-Mandy wanted to stay and watch, but Mother said she hadn't time.

So Milly-Molly-Mandy just called out to Mr Rudge, 'We're going to buy some different-coloured dress stuff, because I tore my other one!'

And Mr Rudge stopped to wipe his hot face on his torn shirt sleeve, and said, 'Well, if they'd buy

us different-coloured shirts every time we tear ours,
you'd see us going about like a couple of rainbows!
Eh, Reginald?'

And the new boy grinned as he piled more brush-
wood on the fire. (He'd got a tear in his shirt too.)

They passed Mr Blunt's corn-shop, where Billy
Blunt was polishing up his new second-hand bicycle,
which his father had just given him, on the pavement outside.

Milly-Molly-Mandy and Mother stopped a
minute to admire it shininess (which was almost
like new). And then Milly-Molly-Mandy said,
'We're going to buy me some different-coloured
dress stuff, because I tore my other!'

383

But Billy Blunt wasn't very interested (he was just testing his front brake).

Then they came to Miss Muggins' shop.

And just as they got up to the door so did two other people, coming from the other way. One was an old lady in a black cloak and bonnet, and one was a little girl in a faded flowered dress, with a ribbon round her hair. Mother pushed open the shop door for the old lady and set the little bell jangling above, and they all went in together, so that the shop seemed quite full of people, with Miss Muggins behind the counter too.

Miss Muggins didn't know quite whom to serve first. She looked towards the old lady, and the old lady looked towards Mother, and Mother said, 'No, you first.'

So then the old lady said, 'I would like to see something for a dress for a little girl, if you please – something light and summery.'

And Mother said, 'That is exactly what I am wanting, too.'

So then Miss Muggins brought out the different stuffs from her shelves for both her customers to choose from together.

Milly-Molly-Mandy looked at the little girl. She thought she had seen her before. Surely it was the new little girl who had lately come to Milly-Molly-Mandy's school. Only she was in the 'baby class', so they hadn't talked together yet.

The little girl looked at Milly-Molly-Mandy. And presently she pulled at the old lady's arm and whispered something, whereupon the old lady turned and smiled at Milly-Molly-Mandy, so Milly-Molly-Mandy smiled back.

Milly-Molly-Mandy whispered up at Mother (looking at the little girl). 'She comes to our school!'

So then Mother smiled at the little girl. And the old lady and Mother began to talk together as they looked at Miss Muggins' stuffs. And Milly-Molly-Mandy and the little girl began to talk too, as they waited.

Milly-Molly-Mandy found out that the little girl was called Bunchy, and the old lady was her grandmother, and they lived together in a little cottage quite a long way from the school and the crossroads, in the other direction from Milly-Molly-Mandy's.

Bunchy hadn't come to school before because she couldn't walk so far. But now she was bigger, and Granny walked with her half the way and she ran the rest by herself. She liked coming to school, but she had never played with other little girls and boys before, and it all felt very strange and rather frightening. So then Milly-Molly-Mandy said they should look out for each other at school next Monday, and play together during play-time. And she told her about little-friend-Susan, and Billy Blunt, and Miss Muggins' Jilly, and other friends at school.

Then Mother said to Miss Muggins, 'And this is all you have in the way of printed cottons? Well, now, I wonder, Milly-Molly-Mandy –'

And Bunchy's Grandmother said, 'Look here, Bunchy, my dear –'

So they both went up to the counter.

There was a light blue silky stuff which Mother and Bunchy's Grandmother said was 'not service-

able.' And a stuff with scarlet poppies and corn-
flowers all over it which they said was 'not suitable'.
And there was a green chintz stuff which they said
was too thick. And a yellow muslin which they said
was too thin. And there was a stuff with little
bunches of daisies and forget-me-nots on it. And a
big roll of pink-and-white striped cotton. And there
was nothing more (except flannelette or bolton-
sheeting and that sort of thing, which wouldn't do
at áll).

Milly-Molly-Mandy thought the one with daisies
and forget-me-nots was much the prettiest. So did
Bunchy. Milly-Molly-Mandy thought a dress of that
would be a very nice change.

But Miss Muggins said, 'I'm afraid I have only
this short length left, and I don't know when I shall
be having any more in.'

So Mother and Bunchy's Grandmother spread it
out, and there was really only just enough to make
one little frock. Bunchy's Grandmother turned to
look at the pink-and-white striped stuff.

Bunchy said, 'That's Milly-Molly-Mandy's stuff,
isn't it? It's just like the dress she has on.'

Milly-Molly-Mandy said, 'Do you always have
flowers on your dresses?'

'Yes,' said Bunchy, 'because of my name, you

know. I'm Violet Rosemary May, but Granny calls me Bunchy for short.'

Milly-Molly-Mandy said to Mother, 'She ought to have that stuff with the bunches of flowers on, oughtn't she? The striped one wouldn't really suit her so well as me, would it?'

Mother said, 'Well, Milly-Molly-Mandy, we do know this striped stuff suits you all right, and it washes and wears well. I'm afraid that blue silky stuff doesn't look as if it would wash, and the yellow muslin wouldn't wear. So perhaps you'd better have the same again. I'll take two yards of this striped, please, Miss Muggins.'

Milly-Molly-Mandy looked once more at the flowery stuff, and she said, 'It *is* pretty, isn't it!

But if Bunchy comes to school I can see it on her, can't I?'

Bunchy's Grandmother said, 'It would be very nice if you could come and see it on Bunchy at home too! If Mother would bring you to tea one Saturday, if you don't mind rather a walk, you could play in the garden with Bunchy, and I'm sure we should both be very pleased indeed, shouldn't we, Bunchy?'

Bunchy said, 'Yes! We should!'

Mother said, 'Thank you very much. We should like to come' – though she had not much time for going out to tea as a rule, but she was sure Aunty would get tea for them all at home for once.

So it was settled for them to go next Saturday, and the little girl called Bunchy was very pleased indeed about it, and so was Milly-Molly-Mandy.

Then Miss Muggins handed over the counter the two parcels, and Milly-Molly-Mandy and Bunchy each carried her own dress stuff home.

And when Milly-Molly-Mandy opened her parcel to show Father and Grandpa and Grandma and Uncle and Aunty what had been bought for her new dress after all, there was a beautiful shiny red ribbon there too, which Mother had bought to tie round Milly-Molly-Mandy's hair when she wore the new dress. So that would make quite a nice change, anyhow.

And as little-friend-Susan said, if Milly-Molly-Mandy didn't wear her pink-and-white stripes people might not know her at once.

And that would be a pity!

2. Milly-Molly-Mandy Finds a Train

Once upon a time Milly-Molly-Mandy was playing with Billy Blunt down by the little brook (which, you know, ran through the fields at the back of the nice white cottage with the thatched roof where Milly-Molly-Mandy lived).

They had got their shoes and socks off, and were paddling about in the water, and poking about among the stones and moss, and enjoying themselves very much. Only it was so interesting just about where their feet were that they might have missed seeing something else interesting, a little farther off, if a woodpecker hadn't suddenly started pecking in an old tree near by, and made Billy Blunt look up.

He didn't see the woodpecker, but he did see the something else.

'I say – what's that, there?' said Billy Blunt, standing up and staring.

'What's what, where?' said Milly-Molly-Mandy, standing up and staring too.

'There,' said Billy Blunt, pointing.

And Milly-Molly-Mandy looked there. And she saw, in the meadow on the farther side of the brook, what looked like a railway train. Only there was no railway near the meadow.

'It looks like a train,' said Milly-Molly-Mandy.

'Um-m,' said Billy Blunt.

'But how did it get there?' said Milly-Molly-Mandy.

'Must have been pulled there,' said Billy Blunt.

'But what for? Who put it there? When did it come?' said Milly-Molly-Mandy.

Billy Blunt didn't answer. He splashed back to get his boots and socks, and he splashed across the

They walked all round it, staring hard

brook with them, and sat on the grass on the other side, and began to dab his feet with his handkerchief. So Milly-Molly-Mandy splashed across with her shoes and began to put them on too. And with her toes scrunched up in the shoes (because they were still damp and wouldn't straighten out at first) she ran and hopped after Billy Blunt, up the little bank and across the grass to the train.

They walked all round it, staring hard. It hadn't got an engine, or a guard's van. It was just a railway carriage, and it stood with its big iron wheels in the grass, looking odd and out-of-place among the daisies and buttercups.

'It's like a funny sort of house,' said Milly-Molly-Mandy, climbing up to peep in the windows.

'I wish we could play in it. Look – that could be the kitchen, and that's the sitting-room, and that's the bedroom. I wish we could get in!'

It had several doors either side, each with a big 3 painted on. Billy Blunt tried the handles in turn. They all seemed to be locked. But the last one wasn't! It opened heavily, and they could get into one compartment.

'It's old,' said Billy Blunt, looking about. 'I expect they've thrown it away.'

'What a waste!' said Milly-Molly-Mandy. 'Well,

it's ours now. We found it. We can live in it, and go journeys!'

It was very exciting. They shut the door and they opened the windows. And then they sat down on the two wooden seats, and pretended they were going away for a holiday. When they stood up, or walked to the windows to look out, it was difficult to do it steadily, because the train rushed along so fast! Once it let out a great long whistle, so that Milly-Molly-Mandy jumped; and Billy Blunt grinned and did it again.

'We are just going through a station,' he explained.

The next moment Milly-Molly-Mandy nearly fell over and knocked Billy Blunt.

'We've stopped suddenly – the signal must be up,' she explained. So they each hung out of a window to look. 'Now it's down and we're going on again,' said Milly-Molly-Mandy.

'We're going into a tunnel now,' said Billy Blunt, pulling up his window by the strap. So Milly-Molly-Mandy pulled up hers – to keep the smoke out!

When the train stopped at last they got out, and everything looked quite different all round. They were by the sea, and the train was a house. One of the seats was a table, and they laid Billy Blunt's

damp handkerchief on it as a tablecloth, and put a
rusty tin filled with buttercups in the middle.

But after a while Billy Blunt began to feel hungry,
and then, of course, they knew it must be time to
think of going home. So at last they shut the door
of their wonderful train-house, and planned to meet
there again as early as possible the next day.

And then they jumped back over the brook, and
Billy Blunt went one way across the field, to his
home by the corn-shop; and Milly-Molly-Mandy
went the other way across the field, to the nice white
cottage with the thatched roof, where she found
Father and Mother and Grandpa and Grandma
and Uncle and Aunty just ready to sit down to table.

The next day Milly-Molly-Mandy hurried to get
all her jobs done – helping to wash up the breakfast
things, and make the beds, and do the dusting. And
as soon as she was free to play she ran straight out
and down to the brook.

Billy Blunt was just coming across the field from
the Village, so she waited for him, and together
they crossed over the brook, planning where they
would go for their travels today.

'There it is!' said Milly-Molly-Mandy, almost
as if she had expected the train to have run away in
the night.

And then she stopped. And Billy Blunt stopped too.

There was a man with a cap on, sitting on the roof of the train, fixing up a sort of chimney. And there was a woman with an apron on, sweeping

dust out of one of the doorways. And there was a baby in a shabby old pram near by, squealing. And there was a little dog, guarding a hand-cart piled with boxes and bundles, who barked when he saw Milly-Molly-Mandy and Billy Blunt.

397

'They've got our train!' said Milly-Molly-Mandy, staring.

''Spect it's their train, really,' said Billy Blunt.

Milly-Molly-Mandy edged a little nearer and spoke to the little dog, who got under the cart and barked again (but he wagged his tail at the same time). The woman in the apron looked up and saw them.

Milly-Molly-Mandy said, 'Good morning. Is this your train?'

'Yes, it is,' said the woman, knocking dust out of the broom.

'Are you going to live in it?' asked Milly-Molly-Mandy.

'Yes, we are,' said the woman. 'Bought and paid for it, we did, and got it towed here, and it's going to be our home now.'

'Is this your baby?' asked Billy Blunt, jiggling the pram gently. The baby stopped crying and stared up at him. 'What's it's name?'

The woman smiled then. 'His name is Thomas Thomas, like his father's,' she said, 'So it don't matter whether you call either of 'em by surname or given-name, it's all one.'

Just then the man on the roof dropped his hammer down into the grass, and called out. 'Here, mate, just chuck that up, will you?'

So Billy Blunt threw the hammer up, and the man caught it and went on fixing the chimney, while Billy Blunt watched and handed up other things as they were wanted. And the man told him that this end of the carriage was going to be the kitchen (just as Milly-Molly-Mandy had planned!), and the wall between it and the next compartment was to be taken away so as to make it bigger. The other end was the bedroom, with the long seats for beds.

Milly-Molly-Mandy stayed jiggling the pram to keep the baby quiet, and making friends with the little dog. And the woman told her she had got some stuff for window-curtains in the hand-cart there; and that they planned to make a bit of a garden round, to grow potatoes and cabbages in, so the house would soon look more proper. She said her husband was a tinker, and he hoped to get work mending pots and kettles in the villages near, instead of tramping about the country looking for it, as they had been doing.

She asked Milly-Molly-Mandy if she didn't think the baby would have quite a nice home, after a bit? And Milly-Molly-Mandy said she DID!

Presently the woman brought out from the hand-cart a frying-pan, and a newspaper parcel of sausages, and a kettle (which Milly-Molly-Mandy filled for her at the brook). So then Milly-Molly-Mandy and Billy Blunt knew it was time to be going.

They said good-bye to the man and woman, and stroked the little dog. (The baby was asleep.) And

as they were crossing back over the brook the man called after them:

'If you've got any pots, pans, and kettles to mend, you know where to come to find Thomas Tinker!'

So after that Milly-Molly-Mandy and Billy Blunt were always on the look-out for anyone who had a saucepan, frying-pan, or kettle which leaked or had a loose handle, and offered at once to take it to Thomas Tinker's to be mended. And people were very pleased, because Thomas Tinker mended small things quicker than Mr Rudge the Blacksmith did, not being so busy making horse-shoes and mending ploughs and big things. Thomas Tinker and his wife were very grateful to Milly-Molly-Mandy and Billy Blunt.

But as Milly-Molly-Mandy said, 'If we can get them plenty of work then they can go on living here. And if we can't have that train for ourselves I like next best for Mr Tinker and Mrs Tinker and Baby Tinker to have it – don't you, Billy?'

And Billy Blunt did.

3. Milly-Molly-Mandy and the Surprise Plant

Once upon a time Milly-Molly-Mandy was busy in her own little garden beside the nice white cottage with the thatched roof, planting radish seeds.

Milly-Molly-Mandy's father grew all sorts of vegetables in his big garden – potatoes and turnips and cabbages and peas, which Father and Mother and Grandpa and Grandma and Uncle and Aunty and Milly-Molly-Mandy ate every day for dinner. And he grew fruit too – gooseberries and raspberries and currants and apples, which Mother made into jams and puddings and pies for them all. But, somehow, nothing ever tasted *quite* so good as the things which grew in Milly-Molly-Mandy's own little garden!

There wasn't much room in it, of course, so she could grow only small things, like radishes, or spring-onions, or lettuces, and mostly there wasn't enough of them to give more than a tiny taste each to such a big family as Milly-Molly-Mandy's. But every one enjoyed those tiny tastes extra specially much, so that they always seemed to be a real feast!

Well this time Milly-Molly-Mandy was planting quite a number of seeds, because she thought it would be nice to have enough radishes to give at least two each to Father and Mother and Grandpa and Grandma and Uncle and Aunty and perhaps to little-friend-Susan and Billy Blunt, and, of course,

Milly-Molly-Mandy her own self. (How many's that?)

She was just crumbling earth finely with her fingers to cover up the seeds, when who should come along the road but Mr Rudge the Blacksmith, looking very clean and tidy. (He was going for a walk with the young lady who helped Mrs Hubble in the Baker's shop.)

'Hullo, Mr Rudge,' said Milly-Molly-Mandy, looking up at him over the hedge.

'Hullo, there!' said Mr Rudge, looking down at her over the hedge. 'What's this I see – some one digging the garden with her nose?'

'I don't dig with my nose!' said Milly-Molly-Mandy. 'I'm planting radish seeds, with my hands. But my nose tickled and – I rubbed it. Is it muddy?'

'That's all right,' said the Blacksmith. 'I always notice things grow best for people who get muddy noses. Well, what's it going to be this time?'

'Radishes,' said Milly-Molly-Mandy. 'A lot of them. For Father and Mother and Grandpa and Grandma and Uncle and Aunty. And some over – I hope.'

'Bless my boots!' said the Blacksmith. 'You've got a family to feed, no mistake. You ought to try growing something like – Now, wait a minute! I believe I've got an idea. Supposing I were to give you a plant; have you got any room for it?'

'What sort of a plant?' asked Milly-Molly-Mandy with interest.

'It's some I'm growing myself, and I've got one to spare. I don't believe your Dad's got any, so you'd have it all to yourself.'

'Is it something you can eat?' asked Milly-Molly-Mandy.

'Rather! – puddings, pies, what-not,' said the Blacksmith.

'Enough for Father and Mother and Grandpa and Grandma and Uncle and Aunty?' asked Milly-Molly-Mandy.

'Yes, and you too.'

'Could it go in there?' asked Milly-Molly-Mandy excitedly, pointing to a space beside the radish seeds. 'There's nothing in there yet. How big is the plant?'

'Oh, about *so* big,' said the Blacksmith, holding his hands five or six inches apart. 'It'll want a good rich soil. Got any rotten grass-cuttings?'

'Father has, I think,' said Milly-Molly-Mandy, 'he puts it in a heap over there to rot.'

'Well, you ask him to let you have some, quite a nice lot, and put it on the earth there, and I'll bring you along the plant tomorrow. It's a surprise plant – you stick it in and see what'll happen.'

'Thank you very much, Mr Rudge,' said Milly-Molly-Mandy, wondering whatever it could be.

Mr Rudge the Blacksmith went on down the road with the young lady (who had been patiently waiting all this time), and Milly-Molly-Mandy ran to ask Father if she could have some of the rotten grass-cuttings. He brought her some spadefuls (it was all brown and messy and didn't look the least bit like grass, but he said it was just how plants liked it), and she dug it into the space beside the radish seeds and hoped Mr Rudge wouldn't forget about the Surprise Plant.

And Mr Rudge didn't.

The very next evening, when he'd done banging horse-shoes on his anvil with a great big hammer, he took off his leather apron and shut up his forge; and presently Milly-Molly-Mandy, who was looking out for him, saw him coming along up the road.

He'd got the plant with its roots in a lump of earth wrapped in thick paper in his pocket.

Milly-Molly-Mandy helped him to take it out very carefully. And then he helped Milly-Molly-Mandy to plant it in the space beside the radish seeds.

And there it stood, looking rather important all by itself (because, of course, the radishes weren't up yet).

'It'll want a lot of water, mind,' said the Blacksmith, as he went out of the gate back to his supper, which he said was waiting for him. So Milly-Molly-Mandy said yes, good-bye, and thank you, and then she went and told Father about it.

Father came and looked at the plant very carefully (it had two rough scratchy leaves and two smooth seed-leaves). And Father said, 'A Surprise Plant, is it? Well, well!'

Then Mother came out and she looked at the plant, and she said. 'Isn't it a marrow?'

But Milly-Molly-Mandy was quite sure it wasn't a marrow because Mr Rudge had said that Father hadn't got any like this in his garden, and Father had lots of marrows.

Well, the Surprise Plant soon felt at home, and it began to GROW.

The radishes started to come up, but the Surprise Plant came faster. It spread out branches along the earth, with tendrils which curled round any stalk or twig they met and held fast. Soon it covered all the little radishes with its great green scratchy leaves, and filled up all Milly-Molly-Mandy's little garden.

Then it began to open big yellow flowers here and there, so that Milly-Molly-Mandy called out, 'Oh, come quick and look at my Surprise Flowers!' and Father and Mother and Grandpa and Grandma and Uncle and Aunty came to look.

Father said, 'Well, it seems to be getting on all right!'

And Mother said, 'Surely it's a marrow!'

And Grandpa said, 'No, 'tisn't a marrow.'

And Grandma said, 'It's got much the same sort of flower as a marrow.'

And Uncle said, 'You'll soon see what it is!'

And Aunty said, 'Whatever it is, it looks as if Milly-Molly-Mandy will be giving us a good big taste this time!'

But Milly-Molly-Mandy said, 'I don't see what there is to *eat* here – and there won't be any radishes now, because they're all hidden up in leaves.'

After a while Milly-Molly-Mandy noticed that one of the flowers had a sort of round yellow ball below the petals, just where the stalk joins on; and as the flower faded the ball began to grow bigger.

She brought Mother to look at it.

Mother said at once, 'Why! I know what it is now!'

Milly-Molly-Mandy said, '*What?*'

And Mother said, 'Of course! It's a pumpkin!'

'Oh-h-h!' said Milly-Molly-Mandy.

Fancy! – a real pumpkin, like what Cinderella went to the ball in drawn by mice, growing in Milly-Molly-Mandy's own little garden!

'Oh-h!' said Milly-Molly-Mandy again.

She didn't mind now if the radishes were spoiled – but anyhow enough came up to give one little red one each to Father and Mother and Grandpa and Grandma and Uncle and Aunty and a weeny one for Milly-Molly-Mandy herself (and how many's that?) – for just think! soon she would be able to go out into her very own little garden and cut a great big pumpkin for them!

Father and Mother and Grandpa and Grandma and Uncle and Aunty began to say, 'How's your coach getting on, Cinderella?' when they met her; and Uncle pretended he'd just seen a mouse running that way to gallop off with it to the ball!

It was a lovely hot summer, which was just what the pumpkin liked (as well as Milly-Molly-Mandy), and it grew and it grew. And do you know, other little pumpkin balls grew under other flowers too, and two of them grew so big that Father gave Milly-Molly-Mandy some straw to put on the ground underneath, for them to rest on. But the first pumpkin grew biggest.

When Mr Rudge the Blacksmith passed along that way he always stopped to look over the hedge, and he said her pumpkin was bigger than any of his own!

Well, September came, and corn was cut, and apples were picked, and the yearly Harvest Festival was to be held in the Village Church. Grown-ups sent in their gifts the day before, to decorate the Church, but children were to have a special Service in the afternoon, and bring their own offerings then.

Father sent in a big marrow and some of his best pears. Mother sent some pots of jam. Grandpa sent a large bunch of late roses. Grandma sent a little cream-cheese. Uncle sent a basket of nice brown eggs. Aunty sent some bunches of lavender.

And what do you suppose Milly-Molly-Mandy took to the Children's Service?

Well, first she looked at her pumpkins, the great big one and the second-best one. And then she said to Mother, 'Mother, what is a Harvest Festival for? – why do you send fruit and things to Church?'

Mother said, 'It's to say "thank you" to God for giving us such a lot of good things.'

'But what becomes of them, those apples, and the jam?' asked Milly-Molly-Mandy.

'Vicar sends them to the Cottage Hospital generally, so the people there can enjoy them.'

'Does God like that, when they're given to Him?' asked Milly-Molly-Mandy.

'Yes,' said Mother. 'He takes the *giving* part, the being thankful part, and the rest Vicar sends to people who need it most, so it's a double giving.'

'Well, I'm very thankful indeed for lots of things!'

On Sunday afternoon they all walked to Church

said Milly-Molly-Mandy. 'So hadn't I better give my pumpkin? We could eat the second-best one and the other little ones ourselves, couldn't we?'

So on the Sunday afternoon they all walked across the fields to Church, in their best clothes, Father and Mother and Grandpa and Grandma and Uncle and Aunty and Milly-Molly-Mandy – AND the pumpkin. She had cut through its stalk herself with a big knife (Father helping), and cleaned it carefully with a damp cloth (Mother helping), and it was so big and heavy that Father had to carry it for her till they came to the Church.

There was quite a number of children carrying things in: little-friend-Susan had a bunch of flowers from her garden, marigolds and Michaelmas-daisies, and nasturtiums, and Billy Blunt brought a basket of little yellow apples which grew by their back fence.

Milly-Molly-Mandy sat in a pew, next to Mother, looking over the big pumpkin in her lap till the time came to give it up.

And then all the children walked in a line to the front of the Church, and Vicar took their gifts one after another and laid them out on a table.

Milly-Molly-Mandy was so pleased to have such a beautiful pumpkin to give that when she had got rid of the burden she ran hoppity-skip back up the aisle, forgetting she was in Church till she saw Mother's face smiling but making a silent 'Ssh!' to her. And then she slid quietly into her seat, and sat admiring the things decorating the Church – the bunches of corn, and fancy loaves of bread (she guessed Mrs Hubble the Baker had sent those), the baskets of fruit and vegetables and flowers and eggs, and pots of preserves with the sun shining through them.

And the pumpkin lay, smooth and round and yellow, among the other things which the children had brought. (But somehow it didn't look quite so awfully big and important there in Church as it had done at home!)

When the Service was over everybody went home. And at tea-time Mother said, 'This week I ought to make some more jam. I was thinking how very nice it would be if we could have pumpkin-and-ginger jam this year, as a change from marrow-and-ginger!'

Then they all looked hopefully at Milly-Molly-Mandy.

And Milly-Molly-Mandy said at once, 'Yes! it would! Shall I go and cut my second-best pumpkin now? And the other little pumpkins?'

So that week Mother made lots of pots of pumpkin-and-ginger jam, Milly-Molly-Mandy helping. And on Saturday Mother let her ask little-friend-Susan and Billy Blunt to tea, and they all had pumpkin-and-ginger jam on their bread-and-butter (as well as chocolate cake and currant buns).

And Father and Mother and Grandpa and Grandma and Uncle and Aunty and little-friend-Susan and Billy Blunt and her own self all thought it was the very best jam they had ever tasted.

And the next time she saw Mr Rudge the Blacksmith, Milly-Molly-Mandy gave him a little pot of pumpkin jam all to himself, to say thank-you-for-giving-me-the-Surprise-Plant.

4. Milly-Molly-Mandy and the Blacksmith's Wedding

Once upon a time Milly-Molly-Mandy was going to a wedding.

It wasn't just the ordinary sort of wedding, where you stared through the churchyard railings, wondering at ladies walking outdoors in their party clothes and who the man in the tight collar was.

This was a very important wedding indeed.

Mr Rudge the Blacksmith was marrying the young lady who helped in Mrs Hubble the Baker's shop. AND (which Milly-Molly-Mandy thought the most important part) there were to be two bridesmaids. And the bridesmaids were Milly-Molly-Mandy and little-friend-Susan.

Milly-Molly-Mandy was sorry that Billy Blunt couldn't be a bridesmaid too, but Billy Blunt said he didn't care because *he* thought the most important part came later.

In the Village, in olden days, when the blacksmith or any of his family got married, he used to 'fire the anvil' outside his forge, with real gun-powder, to celebrate! That's what Mr Rudge the Blacksmith said. He said his father had been married that way, and his uncle, and both his aunts, and his grandpa, and his great-grandpa a long time back. And that was how he meant to be married too, quite properly.

Billy Blunt didn't think many blacksmiths could be properly married, for he had never seen a black-smith's wedding before, nor even *heard* one, and neither had Milly-Molly-Mandy, nor little-friend-Susan.

Anyhow, though he wasn't a bridesmaid, Billy Blunt had a proper invitation to the wedding, like Mr and Mrs Blunt (Billy Blunt's father and mother), and Mr and Mrs Moggs (little-friend-Susan's father and mother), and Milly-Molly-Mandy's Father and Mother and Grandpa and Grandma and Uncle and Aunty, and some other important friends. (For, of course, only important friends get proper invitations to weddings; the other sort have to peep through the railings or hang round by the lane.)

Well, it was only a few days to the wedding now, and Milly-Molly-Mandy and little-friend-Susan and Billy Blunt were coming home from afternoon school. And when they came to the corn-shop (where Billy Blunt lived) they could hear *clink-clang* noises coming from the Forge near by; so they all went round by the lane to have a look in. (For nobody can pass near a forge when things are going on without wanting to look in.)

Mr Rudge the Blacksmith was mending a plough, which wasn't quite so interesting to watch as shoeing a horse, but there was a nice piece of red-hot metal being hammered and bent to the right shape. The great iron hammer bounced off each time, as if it knew just how hot the metal was and didn't want to stay there long, and the iron anvil

418

rang so loudly at every bang and bounce that the Blacksmith couldn't hear anyone speak. But presently he turned and buried the metal in his fire to heat it again, and the Blacksmith's Boy began working the handle of the bellows up and down till the flames roared and sparks flew.

It was just quiet enough then for Milly-Molly-Mandy to call out:

'Hullo, Mr Rudge.'

And Mr Rudge said, 'Hullo, there! Been turned out of school again, have you? Go on, Reginald, push her up.'

So the boy pushed harder at the handle, and the fire roared and the sparks flew.

'Is that really his name?' asked Milly-Molly-Mandy.

'My name's Tom,' said the boy, pumping away.

'Can't have two Toms here,' said the Blacksmith. 'That's my name. He'll have to be content with Reginald. Now then, out of the way, there!'

They all scattered in a hurry as the Blacksmith brought the piece of metal glowing hot out of the fire with his long-handled tongs, and laid it on the anvil again, and began to drill screw-holes in it. The drill seemed to go through the red-hot iron as easily as if it were cheese. As it cooled off and turned grey and hard again, the Blacksmith put it back into the fire. So then they could talk some more.

'Where do you put the gunpowder when you fire the anvil?' asked Billy Blunt.

'In that hole there,' said the Blacksmith, pointing at his anvil.

So Billy Blunt and Milly-Molly-Mandy and little-friend-Susan bent over to see. And, sure enough, there was a small square hole in the top of the anvil. (You look at an anvil if you get the chance, and see.)

'That won't hold very much,' said little-friend-Susan, quite disappointed.

'It'll hold a famous big bang – you just wait,' said the Blacksmith. 'You don't want me to blow up all the lot of you, do you?'

'Have you got the gunpowder ready?' asked Milly-Molly-Mandy.

'I have,' said Mr Rudge.

'Where do you keep it?' asked little-friend-Susan, looking about.

'Not just around here, I can tell you that much.' said Mr Rudge.

'Where do you get the gunpowder?' asked Billy Blunt.

But the Blacksmith said he wasn't giving away any secrets like that. And he brought the piece of

metal out of the fire and started hammering again.

When he had put it back into the fire Milly-Molly-Mandy said:

'Aunty has nearly finished making our bridesmaids' dresses, Mr Rudge.'

'I should hope so!' said the Blacksmith. 'How do you suppose I'm to be married next Saturday if you bridesmaids aren't ready? Go on, Reginald, get a move on.'

'They're long dresses, almost down to our feet.' said little-friend-Susan. 'But we're to have a lot of tucks put in them afterwards, so that we can wear them for Sunday-best. And when we grow the tucks can be let out.'

'That's an idea,' said the Blacksmith. 'I'll ask for tucks to be put in my wedding suit, so that I can wear it for Sunday-best afterwards.'

Whereupon the Blacksmith's Boy burst out laughing so loudly, as he worked the bellows, that he made more noise than the other three all put together.

The Blacksmith fished the red-hot metal from the fire, and plunged it for a second into a tank of water near by, and there was a great hissing and steaming, and a lot of queer smell.

'What do you do that for?' asked Billy Blunt.

'Tempers the iron,' said the Blacksmith, trying it against the plough to see if it fitted properly; 'brisks it up, like when you have a cold bath on a hot day.'

He laid it on the anvil, and took up a smaller hammer and began tapping away. So Milly-Molly-Mandy and little-friend-Susan and Billy Blunt thought perhaps it was time to go now, so they said good-bye and went off home to their teas.

And Milly-Molly-Mandy and little-friend-Susan had another trying-on of their bridesmaids' dresses after tea. And Aunty stitched and stitched away, so that they should be ready in time for the wedding.

Well, the great day came. And Milly-Molly-Mandy and little-friend-Susan, dressed alike in long pink dresses with bunches of roses in their hands, followed the young lady who helped Mrs

Hubble the Baker up the aisle of the Church, to where Mr Rudge the Blacksmith was waiting.

Mr Rudge looked so clean in his new navy blue suit with shiny white collar and cuffs and a big white button-hole, that Milly-Molly-Mandy hardly knew him (though she had seen him clean before, when he played cricket on the playing-field, or walked out with the young lady who helped Mrs Hubble the Baker).

Then, when the marrying was done, Milly-Molly-Mandy and little-friend-Susan followed the Bride and Bridegroom down the aisle to the door, while everybody in the pews smiled and smiled, and Miss Bloss, who played the harmonium behind a red curtain, played so loudly and cheerfully, and Reginald the Blacksmith's Boy who pumped the bellows for her (so he did a lot of pumping one way and another) pushed the handle up and down so vigorously, it's a wonder they didn't burst the harmonium between them. (But they didn't often have a wedding to play for.)

Then the two Bridesmaids, with the Bride and Bridegroom, of course, stood outside on the Church step to be photographed.

Then everybody walked in a procession down the lane, past the Blacksmith's house and past the Forge (which was closed), and up the road to the Inn, where a room had been hired for the wedding-breakfast (though it was early afternoon).

And then everybody stood around eating and drinking and making jokes and laughing and making speeches and clapping and laughing a lot more.

And Milly-Molly-Mandy and little-friend-Susan and Billy Blunt ate and laughed and clapped as much as anyone (though I'm not sure if Billy Blunt laughed as much as the others, as he was so busy 'sampling' things).

They had two ice-creams each (as Grandma and one or two others didn't want theirs), and they had a big slice of wedding cake each, as well as helpings of nearly everything else, because Mr Rudge insisted on their having it, though their mothers said they'd had quite enough. (He was a very nice man!)

And THEN came the great moment when everybody came out of the Inn and went to the Forge to fire the anvil.

Mr Rudge unlocked the big doors and fastened them back. And then he and Father and Uncle and Mr Blunt and Mr Smale the Grocer between them pulled and pushed the heavy anvil outside into the

They stood on the Church step to be photographed

lane. (The anvil had been cleaned up specially, so it didn't make their hands as dirty as you might think.)

And then Mr Rudge put some black powder into the little square hole in the anvil (Billy Blunt didn't see where he got it from). And the men-folk arranged a long piece of cord (which they called the fuse) from the hole down on to the ground. And then Mr Rudge took a box of matches from his pocket, and struck one, and set the end of the fuse alight.

And then everybody ran back and made a big half-circle round the front of the Forge and waited.

Mother and Mrs Moggs and Mrs Blunt wanted Milly-Molly-Mandy and little-friend-Susan and Billy Blunt to keep near them, and Mr Rudge kept by the young lady who used to help Mrs Hubble the Baker (but she wasn't going to any more, as she was Mrs Rudge now, and Mr Rudge said she'd have her work cut out looking after him). She seemed very frightened and held her hands over her ears, so he kept his arm round her.

Milly-Molly-Mandy and little-friend-Susan put their hands half over their ears and hopped up and down excitedly. But Billy Blunt put his hands in his pockets and stood quite still. He said he didn't want to waste any of the bang.

The little flame crept along the fuse, nearer and nearer. And it began to creep up the anvil. And they all waited, breathless, for the big bang. They waited. And they waited.

And they waited.

'What's the matter with the thing?' said Mr Rudge, taking his arm away from the young lady who was Mrs Rudge now. 'Has the fuse gone out? Keep back, everybody, it isn't safe yet.'

So they waited some more. But still nothing happened.

At last Mr Rudge walked over to the anvil, and so did the other men (though the women didn't want them to).

'Ha!' said Mr Rudge. 'Fuse went out just as it

427

reached the edge of the anvil. Now what'll we do? It's too short to re-light.'

'I've got some string,' said Billy Blunt, and he rummaged in his breeches pocket.

'Bring it here, and let's have a look at it,' said Mr Rudge.

So Billy Blunt went close and gave it to him (and took a good look into the hole at the same time).

'Will that carry the flame, d'you think?' said Father.

'Might do, if you give it a rub with a bit of candle-wax,' said Mr Smale the Grocer.

'I think I've got a bit of wax,' said Billy Blunt, rummaging in his pocket again.

'Hand it over,' said Mr Rudge. 'What else have you got in there – a general store?'

'It's bees-wax, not candle-wax, though,' said Billy Blunt.

'Never mind, so long as it's wax,' said Mr Blunt.

'It's got a bit stuck,' said Billy Blunt, still rummaging.

'You boys – whatever will you put in your pockets next?' said Mrs Blunt.

'Better turn it inside out,' said Uncle.

So Billy Blunt pulled his whole pocket outside. And there *was* a lot of things in it – marbles, and horse-chestnuts, and putty, and a pocket-knife, and a pencil-holder, and a broken key, and a ha'penny, and several bus tickets, and some other things. And stuck half into the lining at the seam was a lump of bees-wax, which they dug off with the pocket-knife.

'You have your uses, William,' said Mr Rudge. And he waxed the string, and arranged it to hang from the anvil along the ground. And he struck a match and lit the end. And everybody ran back again in a hurry, and made a big half-circle round the anvil, and waited as before.

And the little flame crept along, and it paused and looked as if it were going out, and it crept on again, and it reached the anvil, and it began to creep up, and everybody waited, and Milly-Molly-Mandy and little-friend-Susan put their hands over their ears and smiled at each other, and Billy Blunt put his hands deep in his pockets and frowned straight ahead.

And the little flame crept up the string to the top of the anvil, and everybody held their breath, and Milly-Molly-Mandy pressed her hands hard over her ears, and then she was afraid she might not hear enough so she lifted them off – and, just at that very moment, there came a great big enormous
BANG!

And Milly-Molly-Mandy and little-friend-Susan jumped and gave a shriek because they were so splendidly startled (even though they were expecting it). And Billy Blunt grinned and looked pleased. And everybody began to talk and exclaim together as they went forward to look at the anvil (which

wasn't hurt at all, only a bit dirty-looking round the hole).

Then everybody shook hands with the Blacksmith and his Bride, and told them they certainly had been properly married, and wished them well. And the Blacksmith thanked them all heartily.

And when it came time for Milly-Molly-Mandy

and little-friend-Susan and Billy Blunt to shake hands and say thank-you-for-a-nice-wedding-party, Mr Rudge said:

'Well, now, what sort of a wedding it would have been without you bridesmaids, and Billy Blunt to provide all our requirements out of his ample pockets, I just cannot conceive!'

And everybody laughed, and Mr Rudge smacked Billy Blunt on the shoulder so that he nearly fell over (but it didn't hurt him).

So then Milly-Molly-Mandy and little-friend-Susan and Billy Blunt each knew that they had been very important indeed in helping to give Mr Rudge a really proper Blacksmith's Wedding!

5. Milly-Molly-Mandy and Dum-dum

Once upon a time Milly-Molly-Mandy was wandering past the Big House down by the cross-roads, where the little girl Jessamine, and her mother, Mrs Green, lived (only they were away just now).

There was always a lot of flowers in the garden of the Big House, so it was nice to peep through the gate when you passed. Besides, Mr Moggs, little-friend-Susan's father, worked there (he was the gardener), and Milly-Molly-Mandy could see him now, weeding with a long-handled hoe.

'Hello, Mr Moggs,' Milly-Molly-Mandy called through the gate (softly, because you don't like to shout in other people's gardens, even when you know the people are away). 'Could I come in, do you think?')

Mr Moggs looked up and said, 'Well, now, I shouldn't wonder but what you could!'

So Milly-Molly-Mandy pushed open the big iron gate and slipped through.

'Isn't it pretty here!' she said, looking about her.

'What do you weed it for, when there's nobody to see?'

'Ah,' said Mr Moggs, 'you learn it doesn't do to let things go, in a garden, or anywhere else. Weeds and all suchlike, they get to thinking they own the place if you let 'em alone awhile.'

He went on scratching out weeds, so Milly-Molly-Mandy gathered them into his big wheelbarrow for him.

Presently Mr Moggs scratched out a worm along with a tuft of dandelion, and Milly-Molly-Mandy squeaked because she nearly took hold of it without noticing (only she just didn't).

'Don't you like worms?' asked Mr Moggs.

'No,' said Milly-Molly-Mandy; 'I don't!'

'Ah,' said Mr Moggs. 'I know some one who does, though.'

'Who?' asked Milly-Molly-Mandy, sitting back on her heels.

'Old Dum-dum's very partial to a nice fat worm,' said Mr Moggs. 'Haven't you met old Dum-dum?'

'No,' said Milly-Molly-Mandy. 'Who's old Dum-dum?'

'You come and see,' said Mr Moggs. 'I've got to feed him before I go off home.'

He trundled the barrow to the back garden and emptied it on the rubbish heap, and Milly-Molly-Mandy followed, carrying the worm on a trowel.

Mr Moggs got a little tin full of grain from the tool-shed, and pulled a lettuce from the vegetable bed, and then he went to the end of the garden, Milly-Molly-Mandy following.

There was a little square of grass fenced off with wire-netting in which was a little wooden gate. And in the middle of the square of grass was a little round pond. And standing at the edge of the little round pond, looking very solemn, hunched up in his feathers, was Dum-dum.

'Oh!' said Milly-Molly-Mandy. 'Dum-dum is a duck!'

434

'Well, he's a drake, really,' said Mr Moggs; 'see the little curly feathers on his tail? That shows he's a gentleman. Lady ducks don't have curls on their tails.' He leaned over the netting and emptied the grain into a feeding-pan lying on the grass. 'Come on, quack-quack!' said Mr Moggs. 'Here's your supper.'

Dum-dum looked round at him, and at Milly-Molly-Mandy. Then he waddled slowly over on his yellow webbed feet, and shuffled his beak in the

pan for a moment. Then he waddled slowly back to his pond, dipped down and took a sip, and stood as before, looking very solemn, hunched up in his feathers, with a drop of water hanging from his flat yellow beak.

'He doesn't want any supper!' said Milly-Molly-Mandy. 'Why doesn't he?'

'Feels lonely, that's what. Misses the folk up at the Big House. They used to come and talk to him sometimes and give him bits. He's the little girl Jessamine's pet.'

'Poor Dum-dum!' said Milly-Molly-Mandy. 'He does look miserable. Would you like a worm, Dum-dum?'

He came waddling over again, and stretched up his beak. And down went the worm, *snip-snap.*

'Doesn't he make a funny husky noise? Has he lost his quack?' asked Milly-Molly-Mandy.

'No,' said Mr Moggs, 'gentlemen ducks never talk so loud as lady ducks.'

'*Huh! huh! huh!*' quacked Dum-dum, asking for more worms as loudly as he could.

So Milly-Molly-Mandy dug with the trowel and found another, a little one, and threw it over the netting.

'Do you suppose worms mind very much?' she asked, watching Dum-dum gobbling.

'Well, I don't suppose they think a great deal about it, one way or t'other,' said Mr Moggs.

He dug over a bit of ground with his spade, and Milly-Molly-Mandy found eight more worms. So Dum-dum made quite a good supper after all.

Then Milly-Molly-Mandy leaned over the wire-netting and tried stroking the shiny green feathers on Dum-dum's head and neck. And though he edged away a bit at first, after a few tries he stood quite still, holding his head down while she stroked as if he rather liked it.

And then suddenly he turned and pushed his beak into Milly-Molly-Mandy's warm hand and left it there, so that she was holding his beak as if she were shaking hands with it! It startled her at first, it felt so funny and cold.

'Ah, he likes you,' said Mr Moggs, wiping his spade with a bunch of grass. 'He's a funny old bird; some he likes and some he doesn't. Well, we must be going.'

'Mr Moggs,' begged Milly-Molly-Mandy, still holding Dum-dum's beak gently in her hand, 'don't you think I might come in sometimes to cheer him up, while his people are away? He's so lonely!'

'Well,' said Mr Moggs, 'I don't see why not – if you don't go bringing your little playmates running around in here too. Look, if I'm not about you can get in by the side gate there.' And he showed her how to unfasten it and lock it up again. 'But mind, I'm trusting you,' said Mr Moggs.

So Milly-Molly-Mandy promised to be very careful indeed.

After that she went into the Big House garden
every day after school, to cheer up poor Dum-dum.
And he got so cheerful he would run to his fence to
meet her, saying, '*Huh! huh! huh!*' directly he heard
her coming. She used to go into his enclosure to

play with him, and pour water on to the earth for
him to make mud with. (He loved mud!)

One day Milly-Molly-Mandy thought it would
be nice if Dum-dum could have a change from that
narrow run, so she asked Mr Moggs if she might let

him out for a little walk. And Mr Moggs said she might try it, if she watched that he didn't eat the flowers and vegetables or get out into the road. So Milly-Molly-Mandy opened his little wooden gate, and Dum-dum stepped out on his yellow feet, looking at everything with great interest.

He was so good and obedient, he followed her along the garden paths and came where she called, like a little dog. So she often let him out after that. She turned over stones and things for him to hunt slugs and woodlice underneath. Sometimes she took him in the front garden too, and showed him to Billy Blunt through the gate.

One morning Milly-Molly-Mandy was very early for school, because the clock at home was fast. At first, when she found no one round the school gate, she thought it was late; but when she found it wasn't she knew why little-friend-Susan hadn't been ready when she passed the Moggs' cottage!

So, as there was plenty of time, she thought she'd go and visit Dum-dum before school today. So she slipped in by the side gate, and found him busily tidying his feathers in the morning sunshine. He looked surprised and very pleased to see her, and they had a run round the garden and found one slug and five woodlice (which Dum-dum thought

439

very tasty for breakfast!). Then she shut him back
in his enclosure, and latched his little gate, and shut
the side gate and fastened it as Mr Moggs had
showed her, and went off to school (And she only
just wasn't late, this time!)

Well, they'd sung the hymn, and Miss Edwards
had called their names, and everybody was there
except Billy Blunt and the new little girl called
Bunchy. And they had just settled down for an
arithmetic lesson when the little girl Bunchy hurried
in, looking rather frightened. And she told Miss
Edwards there was a great big goose outside, and
she dared not come in before because she thought
it might bite her!

'A goose!' said Miss Edwards. 'Nonsense! There
are no geese round here.'

And Milly-Molly-Mandy looked up from her
exercise book quickly. But she knew she had shut
Dum-dum up carefully, so she went on again
dividing by seven (which wasn't easy).

And then the door opened again, and Billy Blunt
came in with a wide grin on his face and a note in
his hand. (It was from his mother to ask Miss
Edwards to excuse his being late, because he'd had
to run an errand for his father, who had no one else
to send.)

And who DO you think came in with him, pushing between Billy Blunt's legs through the doorway, right into the schoolroom?

It was Dum-dum!

'Billy Blunt!' said Miss Edwards. 'What is this?'

'I couldn't help it, ma'am,' said Billy Blunt. 'He would come in. I tried to shoo him off.' (But I don't really think he had tried awfully hard!)

'You mustn't let it come in here,' said Miss Edwards. 'Turn it out. Sit down, children, and be quiet.' (Because they were all out of their places, watching and laughing at the duck that came to school.)

'Oh, please, Teacher –' said Milly-Molly-Mandy, putting up her hand.

'Sit down, Milly-Molly-Mandy,' said Miss Edwards. 'Take that duck outside, Billy Blunt. Quickly, now.'

But when Billy Blunt tried again to shoo him out Dum-dum slipped away from him, farther in, under the nearest desk. And Miss Muggins' Jilly squealed loudly, and pulled her legs up on to her seat.

'Please, Teacher –' said Milly-Molly-Mandy again. 'Oh, please, Teacher – he's my duck – I mean, he's a friend of mine –'

441

Who DO you think came in with him?

'What is all this?' said Miss Edwards. 'Be quiet, all of you! Now, Milly-Molly-Mandy – explain.'

So Milly-Molly-Mandy explained who Dum-dum was, and where he lived, and that she thought he had come to look for her – though how he had got out and found his way here she couldn't think. 'Please, Teacher, can I take him back home?' she asked.

'I can't let you go in the middle of school,' said Miss Edwards. 'You can shut him out in the yard now, and take him back after school.'

So Milly-Molly-Mandy walked to the door, saying, 'Come, Dum-dum!'

And Dum-dum ran waddling on his flapping yellow feet after her, all across the floor, saying '*Huh! huh! huh!*' as he went.

How the children did laugh!

Billy Blunt said, 'I'll just see that the gate's shut.' And he hurried outside too (lest Miss Edwards should say he needn't!)

He tried to stroke Dum-dum as Milly-Molly-Mandy did, but Dum-dum didn't know Billy Blunt well enough. He opened his beak wide and said, '*Huhhh!*' at him. So Billy Blunt left off trying and went and shut the gate.

'He must have some water,' said Milly-Molly-

443

Mandy (because she knew ducks are never happy if they haven't).

So they looked about for something to hold water, other than the drinking-mug. And Billy Blunt brought the lid of the dustbox, and they filled it at

the drinking-tap and set it on the ground. And Dum-dum at once began taking sip after sip, as if he had never tasted such nice water before.

So Milly-Molly-Mandy and Billy Blunt left him there, and hurried back to their lessons.

Directly school was over the children rushed out to see Milly-Molly-Mandy lead the duck (drake, I mean) along the road back to his home. (It wasn't easy with so many people helping!) Mr Moggs was just coming away from the Big House, but he went back with her to find out how Dum-dum had escaped, for his gate was shut as Milly-Molly-Mandy had left it. And they found Dum-dum had

made a little hole in his wire-netting and pushed through that way and under the front gate. So Mr Moggs fastened up the hole.

And while he was doing it Milly-Molly-Mandy noticed that the windows were open in the Big House, and the curtains were drawn back.

'Oh!' said Milly-Molly-Mandy. 'Have the people come back?'

'They're coming tomorrow,' said Mr Moggs. 'Mrs Moggs is just airing the place for them.'

'Then I shan't be able to come and see Dum-dum any more!' said Milly-Molly-Mandy.

And she felt quite sad for some days after that, to think that Dum-dum wouldn't want her any more, though she was glad he wasn't lonely.

Then one day (what DO you think?) Milly-Molly-Mandy met the little girl Jessamine and her mother in the post-office, and the little girl Jessamine's mother said, 'Mr Moggs tells me you used to come and cheer up our old duck while we were away!'

Milly-Molly-Mandy wondered if Mrs Green was cross about it. But she wasn't a bit. She said, 'Jessamine is going to boarding school soon – did you know? – and she was wondering what to do about Dum-dum. Would you like to have him for keeps, when she has gone?'

And the little girl Jessamine said, 'We want him to go to someone who'll be kind to him.'

Milly-Molly-Mandy *was* pleased!

She ran home to give Father the stamps she had been sent to buy, and to ask the family if she might have Dum-dum for keeps.

And Mother said, 'How kind of the Greens!'

And Father said, 'He can live out in the meadow.'

And Grandma said, 'It will be very lonely for him.'

And Grandpa said, 'We must find him a companion.'

And Aunty said, 'You'll have to save up and buy another one.'

And Uncle said, 'I've been thinking of keeping a few ducks myself, down by the brook. Your Dum-dum can live along with them, if you like, Milly-Molly-Mandy.'

Milly-Molly-Mandy was very pleased indeed.

The next day she hurried down to the Big House to tell the little girl Jessamine and her mother. And they let her take Dum-dum home with her at once.

So she led him slowly by the short cut across the fields to the nice white cottage with the thatched roof. And he followed her beautifully all the way. In fact, he walked right over the step and into the kitchen with her!

When Uncle saw him following her about he said:

> 'Milly-Molly had a duck.
> It's little head was green.
> And everywhere that Milly went
> That duck was to be seen!'

447

'Yes, and he did follow me to school one day, like Mary's little lamb!' said Milly-Molly-Mandy.

And do you know, old Dum-dum didn't want to live down by the brook with the other ducks; it was too far from Milly-Molly-Mandy. He chose to live in the barn-yard with the cows and Twinkle-toes the pony, and drink out of Toby the dog's drinking-bowl. And whenever the garden gate was undone Dum-dum would waddle straight through and make for the back door and knock on it with his beak, till Milly-Molly-Mandy came out to play with him!

6. Milly-Molly-Mandy and the Gang

Once upon a time Milly-Molly-Mandy was in Mr Smale the Grocer's shop, to get some things for Mother. There was someone else just being served, so while she waited she looked from the doorway at Billy Blunt, who was spinning a wooden top on the pavement opposite, outside his father's corn-shop.

Presently some boys came along the road. As they passed Billy Blunt one of the boys kicked his top into the gutter, and another pulled his cap off and threw it on the ground; and then they went on down the road, laughing and shouting to one another.

Billy Blunt looked annoyed. But he only picked up his cap and dusted it and put it on again, and picked up his top and wiped it and went on spinning.

And just then Mr Smale the Grocer said, 'Well, young lady, and what can I do for you this morning?' So Milly-Molly-Mandy had to come away from the door and be served.

Milly-Molly-Mandy had seen the boys before.

They didn't belong to the Village, but had come to stay near by, and they were always about, and always seemed to be making a lot of noise.

Well, Milly-Molly-Mandy got the things Mother wanted – a tin of cocoa, and a tin of mustard, and some root-ginger (for making rhubarb-and-ginger jam). And then she left the shop, to go across and speak to Billy Blunt.

But as she stepped over the step the boys were

coming back again, up her side of the road this time, and they bumped into her so that the basket of groceries was knocked out of her hand. The tins came clattering out, and the paper of root-ginger burst all over the pavement.

And instead of saying 'Sorry!' the boys only grinned broadly and went on their way, turning back to look at her now and then.

Billy Blunt came across the road to help.

'Billy!' said Milly-Molly-Mandy, 'I believe they meant to do that! They bumped into me on purpose!'

Billy Blunt said, 'Lot of donkeys.' And began picking up bits of ginger.

'What did they want to do it for?' said Milly-Molly-Mandy. 'And pull your cap off too!'

Billy Blunt only grunted, and picked up more bits of ginger.

Mr Smale the Grocer came to his door to see what was going on, and said, 'Them stupid young things knocked your basket, did they? Tell your mother to give that ginger a rinse in cold water and it'll be all right. Out to make nuisances of themselves, they are. They've got something to learn, stupid young things!'

Miss Muggin's niece, Jilly, came running over. She had been watching from Miss Muggins' Draper's shop opposite.

'They're a gang, they are,' she told Milly-Molly-Mandy and Billy Blunt. 'They try to knock people's hats off and make them drop things all the time. They've got a leader, and they're a gang!'

'They're donkeys,' said Billy Blunt. And he went back to his own side of the pavement, winding up his top as he went.

Milly-Molly-Mandy said, 'Thank you!' to him, and started off home with her basket. And Miss Muggins' Jilly went with her a little way, talking about 'the gang' and the naughty things they did.

'They're silly,' said Milly-Molly-Mandy. 'I shouldn't take any notice of them.'

'Oh, I don't,' said Miss Muggins' Jilly. And she went right on talking about them till they came to the duck-pond. There they parted, and Milly-Molly-Mandy went on up the road to the nice white cottage with the thatched roof, where Mother was waiting for her groceries. (She washed the ginger, and it was all right.)

The next morning little-friend-Susan came round to see if Milly-Molly-Mandy was coming out to play.

Milly-Molly-Mandy was just helping Mother to clean the big preserving-pan that the rhubarb-and-ginger jam had been cooked in. So Mother gave little-friend-Susan a spoon so that she could help to clean it too! And when the pan was as clean as they could make it with their two spoons they washed their sticky hands and faces, and then Mother gave them a big slice of bread-and-jam each to take out into the fields to eat.

So they went over the road and climbed the stile and strolled along the field-path, eating and talking and enjoying themselves very much.

And they were just turning down the lane leading to the Forge (which is always a nice way to go if you're not going anywhere special) when little-friend-Susan said, 'Look at those boys; what are they doing?'

Milly-Molly-Mandy looked, licking jam off her fingers, and she saw they were the boys whom Miss Muggins' Jilly called 'the gang'. They were peeping round the hedge by the next stile.

453

'They're waiting to knock our hats off, only we haven't got any on!' said Milly-Molly-Mandy.

'Hadn't we better go back?' said little-friend-Susan.

'No!' said Milly-Molly-Mandy. 'They're just silly, that's what they are. I'm going on.'

So they went on, and climbed over the stile, Milly-Molly-Mandy first, and then little-friend-Susan.

And just as she had got over one of the boys jumped out of the hedge and knocked the piece of bread-and-jam (only a very small piece now) out of little-friend-Susan's hand into the dirt, and ran behind the hedge again.

Little-friend-Susan didn't like having her last piece of bread-and-jam spoiled. But Milly-Molly-Mandy even more didn't like seeing who the boy was who did it.

'It's Timmy Biggs,' she said – 'you know, that boy who won the race at the Fête, and Billy Blunt used to practise with. Why did he want to do that?'

Little-friend-Susan was looking at her bread-and-jam. 'I can't eat this now,' she said. 'I'll take it to the ducks.' (Because, of course, you never waste bread.)

So Milly-Molly-Mandy just called out, 'You're silly, Timmy Biggs!' at the hedge, and they went on past the Forge and down to the duck-pond. (The Blacksmith wasn't hammering or doing anything interesting, so they didn't stop to watch.)

Billy Blunt was in his garden by the corn-shop, busy with the lock of the old cycle-shed which stood in one corner. He saw them coming down the back lane, and as they didn't pass the garden fence he knew they must have turned the other way. So presently he wandered out and found them by the duck-pond.

There were five ducks quacking and paddling in the water, and little-friend-Susan was tearing her bread into as many bits as she could, but it didn't go very far!

'Hullo, Billy,' said Milly-Molly-Mandy, as soon as he came near. 'What do you think – Timmy Biggs has gone and joined that gang. He knocked Susan's bread-and-jam into the dirt.'

'I saw him with them,' said Billy Blunt.

'We ought to do something,' said Milly-Molly-Mandy.

'Umm,' said Billy Blunt.

'Knock their caps off and see how they like it!' said little-friend-Susan.

'I don't see why we have to be silly just because they are,' said Milly-Molly-Mandy. 'I don't want to be in their sort of gang.'

'Might start a gang of our own,' said Billy Blunt.

'Oh, *yes*!' said Milly-Molly-Mandy and little-friend-Susan exactly together. (So then they had to hold each other's little finger and think of a poet's name before they did anything else. 'Robert Burns!' said Milly-Molly-Mandy. 'Shakespeare!' said little-friend-Susan.)

Then they set to work to think what they could do in their gang.

'It must be quite different from that other one,' said Milly-Molly-Mandy. 'They knock things down, so we pick things up.'

'And they leave field-gates open, so we close them,' said little-friend-Susan.

'And we could have private meetings in our old cycle-shed,' said Billy Blunt. 'It's got a lock and key.'

That was a splendid idea, and the new gang got busy right away, clearing dust and spiders out of the cycle-shed. (There were no bicycles kept there now.)

And while they were in the middle of it – sweeping the floor with the garden broom, scraping the corners out with the garden trowel, and rubbing the tiny window with handfuls of grass – suddenly they heard shouting and footsteps running. And through the fence they saw boys tearing down the road from Mrs Jakes the Postman's wife's gate.

'Come on,' said Billy Blunt to his gang.

And they all ran out to see what had happened.

Mrs Jakes was in her yard, flapping her hands with annoyance, her clean washing lying all along the ground.

'Oh-h-h!' she cried, 'those boys! They untied the end of my clothes-line. And now look at it!'

Billy Blunt picked up the end of the rope, and they all tried to lift the clothes-line to tie it up again, but it was too heavy with all the washing on it. So Mrs Jakes told them to un-peg the clothes and take them carefully off the ground, so as not to dirty them any more. The grass was clean and the things were nearly dry, so they weren't much hurt – only one or two tea-cloths needed to be rinsed where they had touched against the fence.

The new gang collected the pegs into a basket,

They all ran out to see what had happened

and helped Mrs Jakes to carry the washing into her kitchen, and she was very grateful for their help.

'It's not near so bad as I thought when I first saw that line come down,' she said. 'Do you three like gooseberries?'

She gave them a handful each, and they went back to the cycle-shed and held a private meeting at once.

The next day Miss Muggins' Jilly found out about

the new gang, and asked if she could join. She wanted to so much that they let her. And they made up some rules, such as not telling secrets of their private meetings, or where the key of the cycle-shed was hidden, and about being always on the look-out to pick things up, and mend things, and shut gates, and about being faithful to the rules of the gang, and that sort of thing.

Well, they were kept quite busy in one way and another. They helped Mrs Critch the Thatcher's wife to collect her chickens when they were all let loose into the road. And they kept an eye on the field-gates, that cows and sheep didn't get a chance of straying. And they rescued hats and caps and things belonging to other children when they were knocked off unexpectedly. And whenever there was anything important to discuss or if any of their gang had anything given to them, such as apples, they would go along to the cycle-shed and call a private meeting.

They liked those meetings!

One day, when they had been having a meeting, they saw Timmy Biggs hanging about by the Blunt's fence, alone. And when Billy Blunt purposely wandered over that way Timmy Biggs said to him, 'I say – I suppose you wouldn't let me join your

461

gang? I don't like that other one – I'd rather join yours. Could I?'

Billy Blunt told him he'd have to think about it and ask the others.

So he did, and they agreed to let Timmy Biggs join, if he promised to keep the rules. So he joined, and they started a rounders team on the waste ground near the school.

Then two of the other boys took to hanging round watching, as if they wanted to join in. And presently they spoke to Billy Blunt.

'We don't like our gang much; we're tired of it,' they said. 'It was his idea.' And they pointed at the third boy, who was sauntering by himself down the lane. He had been their gang leader.

With seven of them now they could play rounders splendidly, with Billy Blunt's bat, and Milly-Molly-Mandy and Miss Muggins' Jilly taking turns to lend their balls. The cycle-shed was too small now to hold their meetings, so they used it as a place to put the gang belongings in or to write important notices.

Not long after, just as the whole gang was going to begin a game, Milly-Molly-Mandy and Billy Blunt and little-friend-Susan began whispering together, and glancing at where the once-leader of the other gang was sitting under a tree, watching them (but pretending not to), because he had nothing much else to do.

When they had finished whispering Billy Blunt walked over to the tree.

'If you want to join in, come on,' he said.

'Well, I don't mind,' said the boy. And he got up quite quickly.

They had a grand game with so many players, and they worked up a very fine team indeed.

And do you know, when, a few weeks later, the time came for those three visiting boys to leave the Village and go back home, nobody felt so very pleased to see them go.

And Milly-Molly-Mandy and Billy Blunt and little-friend-Susan and Miss Muggins' Jilly and Timmy Biggs would have been quite sorry, only that now they could just manage to squeeze into the cycle-shed to have their private meetings again!

7. Milly-Molly-Mandy goes Sledging

Once upon a time, one cold grey wintry day, Milly-Molly-Mandy and the others were coming home from school.

It was such a cold wintry day that everybody turned up their coat-collars and put their hands in their pockets, and such a grey wintry day that it seemed almost dark already, though it was only four o'clock.

'Oooh! isn't it a cold grey wintry day!' said Milly-Molly-Mandy.

'Perhaps it's going to snow,' said little-friend-Susan.

'Hope it does,' said Billy Blunt. 'I'm going to make a sledge.'

Whereupon Milly-Molly-Mandy and little-friend-Susan said both together: 'Ooh! will you give us a ride on it?'

'Haven't made it yet,' said Billy Blunt. 'But I've got an old wooden box I can make it of.'

Then he said good-bye and went in at the side

gate by the corn-shop where he lived. And Milly-Molly-Mandy and little-friend-Susan ran together along the road to the Moggs' cottage, where little-friend-Susan lived. And then Milly-Molly-Mandy went on alone to the nice white cottage with the thatched roof, where Toby the dog came capering out to welcome her home.

It felt so nice and warm in the kitchen, and it smelled so nice and warm too, that Milly-Molly-Mandy was quite glad to be in.

'Here she comes!' said Grandma, putting the well-filled toast-rack on the table.

'There you are!' said Aunty, breaking open hot scones and buttering them on a plate.

465

'Just in time, Milly-Molly-Mandy!' said Mother, pouring boiling water into the teapot. 'Call the men-folk in to tea, but don't keep the door open long.'

So Milly-Molly-Mandy called, and Father and Grandpa and Uncle soon came in, rubbing their hands, very pleased to get back into the warm again.

'Ah! Nicer indoors than out,' said Grandpa.

'There's a feel of snow in the air,' said Uncle.

'Shouldn't wonder if we had a fall before morning,' said Father.

'Billy Blunt's going to make a sledge, and he *might* let Susan and me have a ride, if it snows,' said Milly-Molly-Mandy. And she wished very much that it would.

That set Father and Uncle talking during tea of the fun they used to have in their young days sledging down Crocker's Hill.

Milly-Molly-Mandy did wish it would snow soon.

The next day was Saturday, and there was no school, which always made it feel different when you woke up in the morning. But all the same Milly-Molly-Mandy thought something about her little bedroom looked different somehow, when she opened her eyes.

Everything outside was white as white could be

'Milly-Molly-Mandy!' called Mother up the stairs, as she did every morning.

'Yoo-oo!' called Milly-Molly-Mandy, to show she was awake.

'Have you looked out of your window yet?' called Mother.

'No, Mother,' called Milly-Molly-Mandy, sitting up in bed. 'Why?'

'You look,' said Mother. 'And hurry up with your dressing.' And she went downstairs to the kitchen to get the breakfast.

So Milly-Molly-Mandy jumped out of bed and looked.

'Oh!' she said, staring. 'Oh-h!'

For everything outside her little low window was white as white could be, except the sky, which was dark, dirty grey and criss-crossed all over with snow-flakes flying down.

'Oh-h-h!' said Milly-Molly-Mandy again.

And then she set to work washing and dressing in a great hurry (and wasn't it cold!) and she rushed downstairs.

She wanted to go out and play at once, almost before she had done breakfast, but Mother said there was plenty of time to clear up all her porridge, for she mustn't go out until the snow stopped falling.

Milly-Molly-Mandy hoped it would be quick and stop. She wanted to see little-friend-Susan, and to find out if Billy Blunt had begun making his sledge.

But Father said, the deeper the snow the better for sledging. So then Milly-Molly-Mandy didn't know whether she most wished it to snow or to stop snowing!

'Well,' said Mother, 'it looks as if it means to go on snowing for some while yet, so I should wish for that if I were you! Suppose you be Jemima-Jane and help me to make the cakes this morning, as you can't go out.'

So Milly-Molly-Mandy tied on an apron and became Jemima-Jane. And she washed up the breakfast things and put them away, and fetched whatever Mother wanted for cake-making from the larder and the cupboard, and picked over the sultanas (which was a nice job, as Jemima-Jane was allowed to eat as many sultanas as she had fingers on both hands, but not one more), and she beat the eggs in a basin, and stirred the cake-mixture in the bowl. And after Mother had filled the cake tins Jemima-Jane was allowed to put the scrapings into her own little patty-pan and bake it for her own self in the oven (and that sort of cake always tastes nicer than any other sort, only there's never enough of it!)

469

Well, it snowed and it snowed all day. Milly-
Molly-Mandy kept running to the windows to look,
but it didn't stop once. When Father and Grandpa
and Uncle had to go out (to see after the cows and
the pony and the chickens) they came back looking
like snowmen.

'Is it good for sledging yet, Father?' asked Milly-
Molly-Mandy.

'Getting better every minute, Milly-Molly-
Mandy, that's certain,' answered Father, stamping
snow off his boots on the door-mat.

'I wonder what Susan thinks of it, and if Billy

470

has nearly made his sledge yet,' said Milly-Molly-Mandy.

But it didn't stop snowing before dark, so she couldn't find out that day.

The next day, Sunday, the snow had stopped falling, and it looked beautiful, spread out all over everything. Father and Mother and Grandpa and Uncle and Aunty and Milly-Molly-Mandy put on their Wellington boots, or goloshes (Milly-Molly-Mandy had boots), and walked to Church. (Grandma didn't like walking in the snow, so she stayed at home to look after the fire and put the potatoes on.)

Billy Blunt was there with his father and mother, so afterwards in the lane Milly-Molly-Mandy asked him, 'Have you made your sledge yet?'

And Billy Blunt said, ''Tisn't finished. Dad's going to help me with it this afternoon. I'll be trying it out before school tomorrow, probably.'

Milly-Molly-Mandy was sorry it wasn't done yet. But anyhow she and little-friend-Susan had a grand time all that afternoon, making a snowman in the Moggs' front garden.

On Monday Milly-Molly-Mandy was in a great hurry to finish her breakfast and be off very early to school.

She didn't have long to wait for little-friend-Susan

either, and together they trudged along through the snow. It was quite hard going, for sometimes it was almost over the tops of their boots. (But they didn't always keep to the road!)

When they came to the Village there, just outside the corn-shop, was Billy Blunt's new sledge. And while they were looking at it Billy Blunt came out at the side gate.

'Hullo,' he said. 'Thought you weren't coming.'

'Hullo, Billy. Isn't that a beauty! Have you been on it yet? Can we have a ride?'

'You'll have to hurry, then,' said Billy Blunt, picking up the string. 'I've been up on the hill by Crocker's Farm, past the cross-roads.'

'I know,' said Milly-Molly-Mandy; 'near where that little girl Bunchy and her grandmother live. Can we go there now?'

'Hurry up, then,' said Billy Blunt.

So they all hurried up, through the Village, past the cross-roads and the school, along the road to Crocker's Hill, shuffling through the snow, dragging the sledge behind them.

'Isn't it deep here!' panted Milly-Molly-Mandy. 'This is the way Bunchy comes to school every day. I wonder how she'll manage today. She isn't very big.'

'We've come uphill a long way,' panted little-friend-Susan. 'Can't we sit on the sledge and go down now?'

'Oh, let's get to the top of the hill first,' panted Milly-Molly-Mandy.

'There's a steep bit there. You get a good run,' said Billy Blunt. 'I've done it six times. I went up before breakfast.'

'I wish I'd come too!' said Milly-Molly-Mandy.

'Sledge only holds one,' said Billy Blunt.

'Oh!' said Milly-Molly-Mandy.

'Oh!' said little-friend-Susan.

They hadn't thought of that.

'Which of us has first go?' said little-friend-Susan.

'Don't suppose there'll be time for more than one of you, anyhow,' said Billy Blunt. 'We've got to get back.'

'You have first go,' said Milly-Molly-Mandy to little-friend-Susan.

'No, you have first go,' said little-friend-Susan to Milly-Molly-Mandy.

'Better hurry,' said Billy Blunt. 'You'll be late for school.'

They struggled on up the last steep bit of the hill. And there were the little girl Bunchy and her

grandmother, hand-in-hand, struggling up it through the snow from the other side. The little cottage where they lived could be seen down below, with their two sets of footprints leading up from it.

'Hullo, Bunchy,' said Milly-Molly-Mandy.

'Oh! Hullo, Milly-Molly-Mandy,' said Bunchy.

And Bunchy and her grandmother both looked

very pleased to see them all. Grandmother had just been thinking she would have to take Bunchy all the way to school today.

But Milly-Molly-Mandy said, 'I'll take care of her.' And she took hold of Bunchy's little cold hand with her warm one (it was very warm indeed with pulling the sledge up the hill). 'You go down in the sledge, Susan, and I'll look after Bunchy.'

'No,' said little-friend-Susan. 'You wanted it just as much.'

'Sit *her* on it,' said Billy Blunt, pointing to Bunchy. 'We can run her to school in no time. Come on.'

So Bunchy had the ride, with Billy Blunt to guide the sledge and Milly-Molly-Mandy and little-friend-Susan to keep her safe on it. And Grandmother stood and watched them all go shouting down the steep bit. And then, as Bunchy was quite light and the road was a bit downhill most of the way, they pulled her along easily, right up to the school gate, in good time for school.

And Bunchy *did* enjoy her ride. She thought it was the excitingest thing that had ever happened!

And then after afternoon school (Bunchy had her dinner at school because it was too far for her to go home for it) Billy Blunt told her to get on his sledge again. And he and Milly-Molly-Mandy and little-friend-Susan pulled her all the way home (except up the steepest bit). And Grandmother was so grateful to them that she gave them each a warm currant bun.

And then Milly-Molly-Mandy and little-friend-Susan took turns riding down the hill on Billy Blunt's sledge. It went like the wind, so that you had to shriek like anything, and your cap blew off, and you felt you could go on for ever! And then, *Whoosh!* you landed sprawling in the snow just where the road turned near the bottom.

Milly-Molly-Mandy and little-friend-Susan each got tipped out there. But when Billy Blunt had gone to the top of the hill with the sledge for his turn he came sailing down and rounded the bend like a bird, and went on and on and was almost at the cross-roads when the others caught him up. (But then, he'd had plenty of practice, and nobody had seen him spill out at his first try!)

It seemed a long walk home to the nice white cottage with the thatched roof after all that, and Milly-Molly-Mandy was quite late for tea. But Father and Mother and Grandpa and Grandma and

477

Uncle and Aunty weren't a bit cross, because they guessed what she had been up to, and of course, you can't go sledging every day!

In fact, it rained that very night, and next day the snow was nearly all gone. So wasn't it a good thing that Billy Blunt had got his sledge made in time?

READ MORE IN PUFFIN

For children of all ages, Puffin represents quality and variety – the very best in publishing today around the world.

For complete information about books available from Puffin – and Penguin – and how to order them, contact us at the appropriate address below. Please note that for copyright reasons the selection of books varies from country to country.

On the worldwide web: www.puffin.co.uk

In the United Kingdom: Please write to *Dept. EP, Penguin Books Ltd, Bath Road, Harmondsworth, West Drayton, Middlesex UB7 0DA*

In the United States: Please write to *Consumer Sales, Penguin USA, P.O. Box 999, Dept. 17109, Bergenfield, New Jersey 07621-0120.* VISA and MasterCard holders call 1-800-253-6476 to order Penguin titles

In Canada: Please write to *Penguin Books Canada Ltd, 10 Alcorn Avenue, Suite 300, Toronto, Ontario M4V 3B2*

In Australia: Please write to *Penguin Books Australia Ltd, P.O. Box 257, Ringwood, Victoria 3134*

In New Zealand: Please write to *Penguin Books (NZ) Ltd, Private Bag 102902, North Shore Mail Centre, Auckland 10*

In India: Please write to *Penguin Books India Pvt Ltd, 706 Eros Apartments, 56 Nehru Place, New Delhi 110 019*

In the Netherlands: Please write to *Penguin Books Netherlands bv, Postbus 3507, NL-1001 AH Amsterdam*

In Germany: Please write to *Penguin Books Deutschland GmbH, Metzlerstrasse 26, 60594 Frankfurt am Main*

In Spain: Please write to *Penguin Books S. A., Bravo Murillo 19, 1° B, 28015 Madrid*

In Italy: Please write to *Penguin Italia s.r.l., Via Felice Casati 20, I 20124 Milano*

In France: Please write to *Penguin France S. A., 17 rue Lejeune, F-31000 Toulouse*

In Japan: Please write to *Penguin Books Japan, Ishikiribashi Building, 2-5-4, Suido, Bunkyo-ku, Tokyo 112*

In South Africa: Please write to *Longman Penguin Southern Africa (Pty) Ltd, Private Bag X08, Bertsham 2013*